Advance Praise for *Silent Words*

"Feminist sleuth Tyler Jones is more human and courageous than ever. *Silent Words* is a thoughtful, evocative book about how discovering the truths of our families often gives us the energy to move on in the world."

—Mary Logue, *Still Explosion*

"Drury is a very good stylist and a wonderful story teller. What more could anyone want?"

—Sandra Scoppetone, *My Sweet Untraceable You*

"Who wouldn't want to shake their family tree and dig up secrets from the past? Leisurely paced and more engaging than ever, *Silent Words* is Joan Drury's second in what I hope will be a long series to come."

—Randye Lordon, *Sister's Keeper*

"I think that *Silent Words* is a beautifully written, highly skilled novel, with lovely characters and atmosphere."

—Kathy Gale, The Women's Press, London

Praise for *The Other Side of Silence*

". . . a traditional whodunit that is also a provocative look at abuse of women." —*The San Francisco Chronicle*

"Joan Drury's at once sobering, entertaining, and witty adult story is one of the most courageous books to come along in quite some time. The reader has to step out of their own comfort zone to digest this novel, but it is well worth the effort. Tyler Jones is witty, vulnerable, and has the inner soul of human decency and compassion."
—*The Midwest Book Review*

"Drury writes extremely well and is one of the few lesbian mystery writers who can handle first-person narration without sounding like a Chatty Cathy doll. Her characters are realistic; the plot is inventive and believable. . . . *The Other Side of Silence* is a cut above the rest both in style and substance, and will leave feminist lesbian mystery readers hungry for more."
—Kathleen DeBold, *Lambda Book Report*

"I love feminist mysteries, and this is a particularly fine example . . . *The Other Side of Silence* has been nominated for the 1994 Minnesota Book Awards, and yet is packed with uncompromising radical feminism. Very exciting."
—Angela Johnson, *off our backs*

"Drury has penned a nifty mystery with intriguing characters you'll want to meet again and again."
—Dennis Armstrong, *The Blotter*

SILENT WORDS

JOAN M. DRURY

SILENT WORDS

JOAN M. DRURY

SPINSTERS INK
DULUTH

First edition
10-9-8-7-6-5-4-3-2

Spinsters Ink
32 E. First St., #330
Duluth, MN 55802-2002

Cover art by Pamela Davis

Production: Charlene Brown   Jami Snyder
Helen Dooley   Jean Sramek
Emily Gould   Amy Strasheim
Kelly Kager   Liz Tufte
Claire Kirch   Nancy Walker

Library of Congress Cataloging-in-Publication Data

Drury, Joan M., 1945–
   Silent words / by Joan M. Drury — 1st ed.
      p.   cm.
   ISBN 1-883523-13-3 (pbk: alk. paper)
   I. Title.
PS3554.R827S5   1996
813'.54—dc20
                                                         96–24756
                                                              CIP

Printed in the U.S.A. on recycled paper with soy-based ink

I write for those who cannot speak,
voices unrehearsed.
Grandmothers who came before me whisper silent words—

Pauline Brunette Danforth
"For My Grandmothers"

Acknowledgments

A good deal of this book was written at Norcroft: A Writing Retreat for Women (located not far from the mythical Stony River). I need to acknowledge the importance of this place in my writing life. It's especially imperative that I pay my indebtedness to the women who were residents with me (three different times)—Elliot, Anastasia Faunce, Bonnie Fournier, Susan Gaustad, Cherry Hartman, Cheryl Nyland-Littig, Maya Sharma, Pam Turner, Kay Jordan Whitham. And also to the women who keep (or have kept) Norcroft going—Marilyn Crawford, Kelly Kager, Jean Sramek, Pamela Mittlefehldt, Willie Williamson, LeeAnn Villella, Patty Delaney, Liz Tufte, Susie Colehour, and Arlinda Keeley as well as countless other people who have been a part of this miracle. My writing shed was not quite big enough for all the voices who crowded in there with advice, opinions, suggestions, and general reinforcement.

My fabulous coworkers at Spinsters Ink and Harmony Women's Fund (listed above) have made it all possible: my writing, my feminist activism, my editing, my organizing, everything. And I have special appreciation for Spinsters because they did such a stellar job producing this book—Zad Walker, Jami Snyder, Liz Tufte, and Claire Kirch plus a steady stream of valuable volunteers, interns, and freelancers. My editor (also my daughter), Kelly Kager, couldn't be better. Her clear thinking, kind prodding, and incisive insights resulted in a better book. Charlene Brown, my copyeditor, was precise and helpful and thorough, in just the way that copyeditors should be.

My immediate family—sons Scooter and Kevin, daughters Kelly and Karie, granddaughter Mirranda—all inspire me and surround me with love and support. I am blessed by their presence and especially their ability to be that which they are uniquely positioned to be: themselves.

I am grateful to my parents, Barbara and Edward Drury, for so many reasons that I won't even attempt to enumerate. I am equally grateful to the people of Cook County, Minnesota—more than I will name, mostly because their warm, open hearts have always made me feel at home. I especially need to mention Kelly Stattelman at the Cook County Court House and the librarians at the Grand Marais Public Library for all the help they gave me. I would be remiss if I didn't specifically mention Irving Hansen and his coworkers who have made possible my presence, and my mother's presence before me, these past fify-plus years in the County. And then there are the many women who've been the mainstays of the "summer people," who've fired my imagination and filled my childhood and adulthood with endless stories.

My first readers, Pamela Mittlefehldt and Paula Barish, were incredibly helpful in shaping this book, as always. My friends, stretching around the world, are always with me—instructing me, laughing with me, challenging me, correcting me, encouraging me, believing in me. What a blessing! One special friend, Marilyn Crawford, has been constant in friendship and work that has supported me continuously and gracefully for more than twenty years now. Words cannot do justice to the overflowing gladness I feel for having this beloved woman in my life.

I appreciate Pauline Brunette Danforth's contribution: her fine poem, "All My Grandmothers," gave this book its title. I hope we shall meet someday.

And I'm also thankful to all the feminists I've known, read, heard, encountered over the years: the women who are working so hard, so tirelessly, with such determination and dedication and faith to change the world. May my words move other women as much as their words have moved me!

To my mother
Barbara Houghtaling Drury
who gave me the North Shore
and
to the "old maid" schoolteachers
those early "spinsters" in my life
who settled the Shore and spun their stories
teaching me
entertaining me
informing me
inspiring me

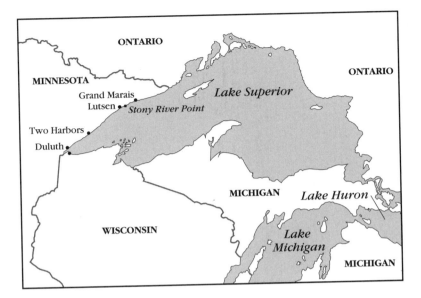

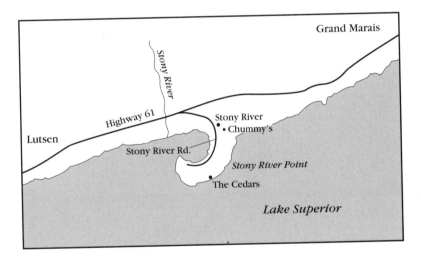

SILENT WORDS

JOAN M. DRURY

WOMENSWORDS

Tyler Jones

Few deaths have the impact that losing a parent does. Oh, I'm reasonably certain—as reasonably certain as anyone without children can be—that having a child die is probably more traumatic than having a parent die. After all, we expect our parents to die, and we also expect our children to outlive us. Expectations notwithstanding, the truth is: we're never prepared for or ready for anyone we love to die. And, I suspect, that losing a mother—for most of us—is harder than losing a father. For a variety of reasons, not the least of which is in our sexist family systems, mothers tend to have much greater impact on their children than fathers—either positive or negative or, as I suppose is usually the case, a mixture of the two.

There are parents who have long, drawn-out, difficult deaths—ordeals with a great deal of suffering and pain and diminishment of any kind of quality in their lives. And while we feel relief that they are no longer suffering from excruciating pain, we are always taken by surprise at our own anguish at their demise. And sometimes a parent is healthy and robust and talks to us one night on the phone and is dead by morning. And sometimes we believe that's worse than the long, drawn-out kind of dying, because we weren't prepared, weren't ready. No matter what: it hurts, it hurts a lot—regardless of how it happens.

Because the pain of death is not about the dead person. It's about us, those of us still breathing. As long as we continue to breathe in and out, we continue to have the capacity to feel pain. And a loss, no matter how big or small, creates pain. A loss, no matter if death seemed the best option or death didn't even seem imminent, creates pain. A loss, as Gertrude Stein might have said, is a loss is a loss is a loss is a loss.

I have friends who say to me, confidently, "I'm ready for her to die. She's a mere shadow of her old self, she's almost always in pain, and feels confused and scared. It will be better—for her, for me, for everyone—when she dies." I nod on the outside, shake my head on the inside. There's no way to tell someone that we are never "ready" for death. No matter how awful a life is, it has no bearing on that moment when any individual actually stops that oh-so-taken-for-granted breathing—in and out, in and out.

Death transforms the individual who just died, surely, but also transforms our lives, the still-living, in ways we can't imagine beforehand. And death itself, I believe, is unimaginable. A person

WOMENSWORDS

is here one minute, the next: GONE. It's true, I don't believe in life after death. It's not that I don't believe it doesn't exist; it's just that I don't believe we can *know* what exists or doesn't. Some friends think that my reaction to death would be different if I believed in the hereafter.

I think they're missing the point. It's not that I need to be comforted by the concept of ongoing life. What do I care if my mother's happy in some new existence? What do I care if she is resting in the glory of god or busily taking up residence in a new body or teaching soul life to novice souls? I want her *here* with *me,* right now. I want *my* relationship with her—the good, the bad, the impossible—intact. Couldn't we at least have phone conversations? Letters?

And then, there are the friends who are convinced that their mother's or father's death is not going to affect them at all because their mother or father was nasty, abu-

> When we mourn our parents, we mourn the parents we had as well as the ones we never had. With death, all bets are off: the last chance at reconciliation or change or hope is gone.

sive, absent. I think these friends are, also, in for a surprise. Loss is loss—not based on the quality of a relationship but on the absence of it. In fact, sometimes I think that the pain from a disappointing parent is even worse because we now have to come face to face with the reality that the relationship is never going to improve or change. No matter how much we convince ourselves that this relationship is no good and never going to be any good, the human spirit contains an unquenchable hope for the best.

When we mourn our parents, we mourn the parents we had as well as the ones we never had. With death, all bets are off: the last chance at reconciliation or change or hope is gone. Whatever relationship we had with our parents, that's it. No more chances for something else.

And then, there's the final realization: when our parents die, death moves just a little closer to us.

PROLOGUE

"Tyler?" I leaned over my mother. I put my ear right next to her mouth, in order to hear her. Her breath was hot against my skin and had the stale smell of medicine, decay, death. A smell that was to stay with me for weeks after she died.

"It's okay, Mom, everything's okay," I falsely assured her. Or maybe not so falsely. After all, who's to say what's "okay"? Death was probably more okay than the excruciating grasp she had on life at that moment.

Her hand, quivering and bent, fluttered for a second before grasping my shirt with surprising strength as she pulled me closer. "Tyler?"

"I'm here, Mom." I tried to soothe her. "I'm here."

Her voice was a raspy whisper. I didn't want to encourage her to talk. It exhausted her. She persisted. "Go home, Tyler."

Go home? She wanted me to leave her and go home? Was she losing it altogether? "What?" I asked, trying to pull back so I could look at her.

She tightened her hold on my shirt. "Tyler. Listen to me." She spaced her words pedantically, breathlessly. "Go home. To Minnesota. Shake . . ." she hesitated, hacking a little.

"Mom . . ." I tried, again, to calm her.

She ignored me. ". . . Shake the skeletons in the closet." Having said that, she exhaled deeply as she let go of my shirt. Her eyes, her sparkling blue eyes that always glowed with enthusiasm, were dull and flat. Her pale, almost translucent lids lowered over them as her body relaxed, exhausted from the effort of giving me this message.

My own eyes were damp while the lump that seemed to be constantly in my throat grew even larger. I smoothed the sheet and blanket over her ravaged body, ran my fingertips lightly over her forehead—pushing her damp hair backward. There were few places where I could touch her anymore, few places that weren't so racked with pain that even feathery contact didn't cause more discomfort. Someone once said, "Dying is easy. It's living that's hard." I wished that whoever that was, was there at that moment. I wished that dying was as easy as he—it must've been a man, I thought, someone who never actually took care of the sick and dying—thought it was.

Her eyelids flew open, and again, she forced herself to focus on me. "Tyler? Did you hear me?"

"Mom," I tried to reassure her with my voice. "Mom, just rest. I heard you. I'll do it. I promise." Although, really, I had no idea what it was I was promising.

She started to slide away again but murmured, "You can find it all out, Tyler. It's time for the truth."

"Okay, Mom, okay. Don't worry. I'll do it." What the hell was she talking about?

She smiled, a shadow of a smile, and calmly opened her eyes—gazing right at me. "I love you, Tyler."

"Mom," my voice broke. "I love you, too."

1

Two months later, I was in my car with Agatha Christie— better known as Aggie—my golden retriever, heading east from San Francisco toward Minnesota. East across the Sierras, the Great Salt Lake Desert, the Rockies, the seemingly endless prairie of the Great Plains. A trip I was familiar with in ways I'd long ago forgotten. Every summer of my childhood, from before I could remember to the summer I was fourteen and my grandmother died, my mother and sister and I made this trip halfway across the continent, heading to my mother's childhood home in northern Minnesota.

I was the grown-up now, and my mother and sister weren't with me. My mother was dead. My sister was angry, so angry she might never talk to me again. And I'd lost my father. Once more. In a new way, a deeper way.

I was driving a 1992 "jasmine yellow" Cabriolet convertible. With the promise of additional cash when my mother's estate would be settled, I now had enough money to feel comfortable about buying a new car for the first time in my life. My old Volkswagen bug would never have made it to Minnesota and back anyway. It had been a faithful servant for twelve of its seventeen years and deserved its well-earned retirement. I felt a pang, though, thinking about her, my Lady Bug. She was one more loss for me right now. But this new car was slightly larger, making more room and comfort for my considerable size, rode smoother, and gave me a sense of devilishness. It was June, and I had the top down, feeling a little like I was maybe Thelma or Louise.

"An ordinary woman starts out on an ordinary journey with no sense of foreboding. The wind whips her hair around her face [that's a lie: my dark hair, getting lighter all the time with the constant additions of grey hairs, is too closely cropped to my head to be 'whipped'], and her dog, part-wolf and part-domestic, howls to the moon." I laughed aloud at myself. Always the writer, always the drama. And I realized, with a stab of pain, that this was the first time I'd laughed since Mother died.

Every mile, every familiar landmark brought fond memories and sharp pain. Everyone said, "Thank god she's released from all that suffering," because it was bad for her the last months of her life. And, of course, they were right: it was a blessing that she'd died. That didn't make it any easier for me. She was gone. Forever. The woman who'd been there—and as often as not, not been there—all my growing-up years. The woman who scolded and cajoled me, pushed me and blossomed with pride for me—always expecting more from me. The woman who was often too caught up in her own life to remember that I might need something from her. The woman with whom I'd made peace many years ago; the woman for whom I had enormous respect as well as love.

2

My mother had tilted at windmills, creating an incredible role model for me that neither she nor I totally realized most of her life. She'd started, as the young wife of an up-and-coming banking executive, with safe and acceptable causes: March of Dimes, American Cancer Society, Girl Scouts, the symphony, that sort of thing. Later, as she got more politicized and cared less about my father's need for "image," she moved on to organizations like WAR (Women Against Rape) and Green Peace and Amnesty International and projects like homelessness and AIDS. Her last years had mostly been dedicated to fighting American imperialism, especially in Central American countries through the organization she had helped to found, SALSA (Strong Alliances with Latinas and Sud Americanas).

And now she was gone. At thirty-nine, I was motherless. Bereft.

My sister, Magdalene, also seemed lost to me. It was a peculiar kind of loss because we'd barely talked to one another for years. When Magdalene gave birth to her second child, she and her stuffy, conservative husband decided that it was best their children not be exposed to their perverted (read "queer") aunt and so requested, formally and directly, that I drop out of their lives. It was no particular loss to me, so I agreed. After all, they were right-wing Republicans and a tad too religious for my taste. I'm not saying it didn't feel bad, didn't hurt, even if I didn't much care about them. Rejection, I guess, always feels bad. It's just that it didn't seem to be an enormous loss. Mostly, in fact, it was a relief.

When my parents divorced, my father moved to San Diego and, more or less, divorced me, too. I was in my mid-twenties by then and had become a rather vocal and public radical feminist lesbian. He found me distasteful, to put it mildly. Magdalene and her husband followed Dad to the land of sunshine and conservatives in southern California, and Mom and I stayed in the weirdo-politico's hangout of the Bay area. San

Francisco Bay area, that is. My mother grew up in the Midwest and always hated it that people on the West Coast acted as if the San Francisco Bay area could be called "the Bay area" with impunity.

"After all," she used to say, "it could be the Green Bay area. It could be the Thunder Bay area or the Bengal Bay area." I smiled and felt that familiar ice-pick kind of stab somewhere in the vicinity of my heart that seemed to accompany any memory that stirred me these days.

"Oh, Aggie, when's it going to hurt less?" I lamented, knowing this would bring her up to nuzzle against my shoulder. I needed the healing of touch. When she stuck her head between the front seats, as I knew she would, I wrapped one arm around her neck and rubbed my cheek against her fur, keeping my eyes on the road. "Oh, Aggie," I repeated, blinking back the tears.

Magdalene and Mom and I used to sing songs, every song we could think of or remember the words for, on this trip across the country.

"She'll be coming around the mountain, when she comes, when she comes . . ."

"O' Susannah, oh don't you cry for me . . ."

"I-'v-e been working on the r-a-i-l-road . . ."

I raised my voice, belting out all the songs I could remember, knowing the wind snatched the sounds and carried them far out over the surrounding land, all the way back to the ocean where my mother's ashes had been sprinkled, making it some kind of memorial to her.

Even in those days, Magda and I didn't much like each other. She was four years older than me and displayed haughty signs of disdain for almost everyone but Father. She was a puzzlement to Mother, but I just thought she was a snot.

Still. On this trip, stuck together in the car for four to five days, we sang and played games and talked and took turns sitting in the front seat with Mom and . . . I don't know, called a truce, I guess. Although she quickly reverted to her old drippy self the minute we reached our cousin's house in a suburb of Minneapolis, Magda let her dislike of Mom and me disappear—at least for the length of the car trip.

"Row, row, row your boat, gently down the stream . . ."

"Make new friends but keep the old . . ."

"Home, home on the range, where the deer and the antelope play . . ."

Mother had a house in Berkeley, a big old three-story affair that students and refugees and others who needed sanctuary lived in. She left this house to SALSA. I expected this. What I didn't expect was that she had two other houses in Berkeley, pieces of her divorce settlement from my father, and she left these to me. She also owned a house in Minnesota— my grandparents' house, actually, that I had assumed was long gone. She left this to me also. This was about the extent of her estate. SALSA was the beneficiary of her life insurance. And there was some personal property she said Magdalene and I had first dibs on, the rest to go to SALSA. Two houses in Berkeley and one in Minnesota would net a tidy sum of money once they were sold.

Magdalene was coldly furious. In front of Mother's lawyer, Enid Ames, she said to me, icily, "You did this. You convinced Mother to leave me and my children out of her will. You're evil, and she was influenced by you."

I shook my head, feeling the heavy bewilderment and thickness that settles over one in the early days of bereavement. "Magda," I said. "It wasn't like that. Mom and I never talked about her will. I didn't even know she owned these houses in Berkeley. Or Grandpa's house in Minnesota."

Enid cleared her throat and said, "Ms. Champion . . ."

"*Mrs.* Champion," Magdalene snapped at her.

"Uh, yes, sorry. Mrs. Champion, you've read the letter Weezie left for you. You know why she's done what she's done. Ms. Jones had nothing to do with it."

"Well," Magdalene snapped, "you would say that, wouldn't you?" There was special emphasis on the "you." Enid and I looked at each other and sighed. It did not take a Miss Marple to figure out that Magdalene had decided Enid was a lesbian so, naturally, aligned with me. And she was partially right. Enid was a lesbian. But she'd been Mom's attorney, and I barely knew her. It didn't matter, though; Magda had clearly made up her mind.

"Ms.—Mrs. Champion . . ." Enid began again, but Magdalene cut her off.

"I don't need to hear anymore from the likes of you." She was gathering her things together. "I assure you, however, this is not the end of it. You will be hearing from my attorney." And she swept regally out of the room.

I stared stupidly at the door as she exited, feeling mostly confusion. I shook my head slowly and said, "I'm sorry, Enid. Maybe this is the only way she's able to grieve."

Enid waved a hand in the air. "Don't apologize, Tyler. I specialize in probate. Nothing surprises me."

I nodded, still feeling fuzzy-brained. "Enid, can you tell me what was in that letter to Magdalene?"

She shook her head, "No. Only Mrs. Champion can tell you that. I can tell you, though, because Weezie told me I could, why she's done what she's done." I nodded encouragement. Enid took a big breath, hesitated for a moment, and then said, "Your father's will leaves his entire estate to Magdalene and her children."

I felt the hot sting of her words somewhere behind my eyes, behind my brain even, in some desert land that was trying hard to swallow her words and bury them in the sand. It's not that it was a surprise . . . No, that's not true. It was a surprise or I wouldn't have been reacting that way. It's just

6

that . . . I'd never really thought about my father's will. If I had, I probably would've expected this. But still, it seemed such a vicious slap in my face. I bent my head when I realized my eyes were filling up with tears. And I certainly had a better understanding of what Magda must have been feeling.

Enid remained quiet during these thoughts, probably giving me room to absorb this news. Finally she leaned across her desk and said, "I'm really sorry, Tyler. There was just no way I could soften that blow. When your mother knew she was going to die, she contacted your father and asked him about his will. She suspected he'd do something like this, but she had to be certain. When he corroborated her worst fears, she made the decision to leave to you what didn't go to SALSA. I'm sure she explained all this to Mrs. Champion, but it's hard to make sense of things when you're in the first throes of loss. And she, Mrs. Champion, would feel rejected, even if she weren't reeling from her mother's death. Do you understand?"

I nodded and thought, the way I feel rejected by Dad, even though it shouldn't be a surprise. "This talk of her lawyer, could this be awfully messy? Maybe it would be easier if I just gave one of the houses to her."

Enid firmly shook her head. "No. Your mother's will is very simple and explicit. Any lawyer who reads it will know there's no case. Mrs. Champion will probably understand, in time, her mother's thinking. After all, as I understand it, she will be getting a great deal more from her father's estate than you are from your mother's."

When I got tired of singing or couldn't remember any more songs we'd sung together or found the lump in my throat too large to sing around, I'd push in some of my CD's on the car player. I brought my favorite "comfort" albums along, almost all piano: Fatha Hines, Glenn Gould, Amina

Claudine Myers, Vladimir Horowitz, Art Tatum, Johanna Harris.

After Mother's death, I spent the next couple of months sleepwalking through my life. I put my mother's houses—my houses, I guess—up for sale, disposed of my mother's ashes in the Pacific out at Point Reyes, transferred the three-story house to SALSA, attended to all the other death details I could manage, bought my new car, arranged for Mary Sharon—my dear friend who lived in the lower-level studio of my little house—to move upstairs into my area while she sublet her flat to someone else, and got a leave of absence from the *Chronicle,* where I wrote a weekly column. I was alone now on the open road. No mother or sister with me. No father waiting back in San Francisco for our return. No mother or sister or father for me anywhere.

"I could've danced all night, I could've danced all night..."

"Somewhere over the rainbow . . ."

"Show me the way to go home . . ."

2

Ostensibly, I was going to Minnesota to sell the house there. My grandfather's house. No, actually my grandmother's house. This was the first mystery. I hadn't figured out yet what was going on about this house. My grandmother had died twenty-five years ago. Later, I went to college in Minnesota, but we never went there together as a family after Grandma's funeral.

Because I was fourteen and probably wanted to stay in California with my friends, I never questioned this, never wondered why we didn't continue going to visit my grandfather. After all, it was the "Summer of Love" in San Francisco, and most of my energies were directed toward finding ways of escaping vigilant parents, who were worried about drugs, to go hang out in Haight-Ashbury or the Panhandle. Much more important than grandparents in Minnesota were opportunities to see Grace Slick with Jefferson Airplane or Country Joe and The Fish or Janis Joplin.

Then Grandpa died, the summer before I went to Minnesota to go to college, and we didn't go to his funeral. Now it seems odd that I never questioned any of this, but at the time, I guess my small world commanded all my attention.

And I never thought to ask about the house; I just assumed that it had been sold or something. I always intended, during my four years at the University of Minnesota and the three years I lived there afterward, to go spend some time on the North Shore of Lake Superior where my mother had grown up and I had spent my childhood summers. But somehow, time slipped quickly by and only once, in those seven years, did I manage to get up there with a group of friends. It was in the winter. We rented a cottage, went skiing, and drank way too much—or at least I did.

We were only a few miles from the old family homestead, so I drove over there late one afternoon. The driveway was not plowed, and the house didn't appear to be occupied. I tramped in through the deep snow to find all the outside shutters closed, giving the place an eerie sense of emptiness. I walked a little beyond the house toward the edge of the cliff, overlooking the forbidding but breathtaking beauty of a partially frozen sea. I stopped abruptly when I realized I wasn't certain where the edge of the cliff was and didn't want to topple over it. I had never been there in the winter and found the snow disorienting. Dark came early in the north country, so I left soon.

In my mother's papers, I discovered that the house had never belonged to my grandfather. My grandmother's parents had built it in the early part of the century. She inherited it when they died and deeded it to my mother at her death. Apparently my mother had allowed my grandfather to go on living there.

The oddest piece of all this, though, was that the house seemed to be owned solely by my mother—and now me. This confused me because it seemed strange that my mother's sister, my Aunt Thalia, would be cut entirely out of this inheritance. I tried to remember any dissension between Grandma and Aunt Thalia. This was impossible, because Grandma was singularly sweet-natured. At least, that's how I remembered her. Then I tried to remember any problems between my mother and her father, any stories I'd overheard or scenes I'd witnessed. They never seemed particularly close; in fact, sometimes I thought my grandfather didn't much like my mother. But . . . that was it, that was all I could bring to mind. And yet—we never went to see him again after Grandma died. And Mother didn't go to his funeral. What did it all mean?

But I was wrong. This wasn't the first mystery; it was the second one. The first mystery was my mother, on her deathbed, telling me to "go home and shake all the skeletons." What was it she said? "You can find it. It's important. It's time for the truth." Something like that.

This was my real reason for going back to Minnesota. To keep my promise to my mother. To find out—what? I didn't know what. But something. Some secret. Some silence that needed to be broken.

3

Aunt Thalia had not attended the memorial service we had for Mother. She sent flowers and a note explaining her arthritis was so bad that travel was out of the question. I had not seen her for years. When I lived in Minnesota, at first, I spent holidays with her. But soon I found excuses to avoid even that much contact. My cousins, Sondra and Corky, were gone by then and rarely came home for holidays. That left Aunt Thalia, a hearty woman who complained a great deal, and Uncle Cyrus, a man whose silence was larger than he was, and me, a budding feminist/dyke. We had little in common.

Sondra was three years older than me and great chums with Magda. The two of them spent their summers on the North Shore poring over *Vogue* and *Seventeen* and *Cosmopolitan*, dyeing their hair various colors that invariably ended up resembling some washed-out version of green seaweed, and hanging out at Chummy's Store, where Old Man Chummy's hunky teenaged grandson was working.

Corky and I found more adventurous activities. Corky—Corcoran really but never called that except by his mother—was a year older than me and a very satisfactory companion. We built forts in the woods and rafts that fell apart when the first wave hit them and went swimming in the pond at the foot of the falls on Stony River and built dams and trails and sometimes got in a bit of trouble. On rainy days (when Magda and Sondra did the same things that they did on sunny days), Corky and I read books—sometimes to one another, sometimes to ourselves. Usually Nancy Drew or the Hardy Boys. And sometimes we made up our own books, each of us outdoing the other in bizarre and hair-raising plot twists. It was a fine way to spend one's summers.

The last I'd heard of them was in the '70s when I was living in Minnesota. Sondra was going to some fancy school out East and making her mother very unhappy by participating in those "outlandish student rebellions." I didn't know exactly what that meant and couldn't imagine the Sondra of my youth doing any such thing, so I believed that Aunt Thalia was just exaggerating. As for Corky, he was just bumming around, going to school sporadically, just as often being expelled. Because I was so accustomed to Thalia's litany of complaints, I never paid much attention to the details.

When I arrived in Minneapolis, I checked Aggie and me into a motel, after first getting lost: towns change as freeways multiply. After calling Aunt Thalia, I took Aggie to a park by Lake of the Isles and let her stretch her legs. I threw a stick for her until my arm gave out, and then I just strolled around while she made wild chase for any number of squirrels. I think she thought she'd arrived in doggie heaven. Squirrels and trees are far more common in Minnesota than in California. When I decided her exercise needs had been at least

14

partially met, I bundled Aggie back into the car and headed for Brooklyn Center, where my Aunt Thalia lived.

It was early evening, sunny and just short of hot. I had little trouble finding Thalia's house—it was the same one she'd had since I was a little girl. Leaving Aggie in the car, I pushed the front-door buzzer. I could hear a very loud TV blaring from inside and was wondering if anyone could hear the doorbell when Thalia suddenly loomed on the other side of the screen door.

"My goodness, Tyler," she exclaimed, "look at what a big girl you are! Of course, that's just so silly of me," she added as she opened the door. "Your grandma was nearly six feet, wasn't she? I always forget. Me being so petite and all." She simpered, and I cringed inwardly. She was small—a wiry shape stretching over a body no more than 5'2" or 3" tall. My mother, like Thalia, was on the slight side but not as short. I, on the other hand, am less than an inch shy of 6 feet. My first lover told me, many years ago, that it was a law: if a woman was 6 feet tall, she *had* to be a lesbian. I smiled at the memory but decided not to share it with Thalia.

I stepped into the living room and the full blare of the TV. The shades were pulled, and my eyes needed time to adjust to the dimness after being outside. I made out Uncle Cy, sitting in a chair in the corner of the living room, his body leaning slightly toward the sound. I raised my hand in greeting but realized his eyes didn't move from the screen. Thalia waved me toward the back of the house, toward what I knew was the kitchen: her domain.

"The old coot can't hardly hear a thing," she shook her head as she reached for the coffeepot, "but he won't admit it, so that TV is loud enough for everyone in the neighborhood to hear." She got me a cup and poured without asking me if I wanted any and set it down on the table while she refilled her own cup. She didn't ask me if I wanted any cream or sugar, either. The members of this family, I remembered, drank their coffee black and strong. "'Course I don't much care if the noise disturbs anyone in this neighborhood anymore. All colored, you know. Oh, Black, I guess. Sondra's always correcting me about something like that." I cringed again as she lit up a cigarette, depositing the match in an overflowing ashtray. "Can't afford to move out; our house is paid off, you know. Otherwise we sure as hell wouldn't stay here any longer. 'Course Cy, he's just glued to that damn TV anyway, so he don't mind what kinda drug deals are going down all around us. It's a sad world we're livin' in, Tyler, a sad world. Don't feel safe anywhere anymore."

I tried to change the subject by saying, "Does Sondra live here again? In the Cities, I mean?"

Thalia nodded, "Yeah, she's gotta house with all those kids—all colors, you know. She's always tellin' me I should be doin' somethin' about my racism, what with my having grandchildren who are colored and all." She snorted. "Mmm-hph. Might be her kids, might not. I don't think I count them as grandkids."

I was thoroughly confused. "Where does she live, Aunt Thalia?"

"Oh, a crappy neighborhood in Minneapolis. She's so uppity—remember how uppity she always was?" I didn't nod, not certain of what I was being asked to agree to, even though I did, of course, remember how "uppity" she was. "Well, she still is. Knows everything about everything. You know what I mean? So, she has to live in a *mixed* neighborhood, good for her kids. It's just a crappy neighborhood, that's all."

I was beginning to think that I might like the woman my "uppity" cousin had grown into. "So, she's married and has . . . how many kids?"

"She's not married!" Thalia spit out. "Never been. Kids. I don't know. I guess she has five, maybe six. I don't pay much attention."

I thought that either I was a lot more tolerant when I was younger or Thalia had gotten a lot more unbearable as she aged. "How about Corky?" I asked. "What's he doing? Does he live around here?"

"Oh, that one," she snorted again. "Who knows what he does? A little of this, a little of that. If you ask me," which of course I was, "he just does as little as possible. I don't know where he lives now. If he's still shrimping, he's probably down in New Orleans. Or if he's doing that oil stuff, somewhere in Texas. I don't know. He doesn't have much time for his folks."

An uncomfortable silence followed this, and I thought I'd best come to the point and get out of there. "Aunt Thalia, I want to ask you some questions. I'm a little confused about some things I found out after Mom died."

"Oh yeah, your mom. That was a sad thing, wasn't it?" She was shaking her head slowly. "I so wanted to get out for the funeral, but—you know—this arthritis just gets me down, it does. The doctor says I should get out of the climate here in Minnesota. Too humid. Go somewhere like Arizona. But how'd I do that? It isn't as if Cyrus's pension amounts to anything. We just get by, we do. No, we can't go anywhere else. And my arthritis, it just keeps getting worse and worse."

"Yes, well . . . I'm so sorry, Aunt Thalia." I didn't know what to say in the face of her strong current of words. "About Mom. I didn't know that she still owned Grandma's house up in Stony River. And I was really surprised to find out that she owned it all by herself. Was there some reason it wasn't left to both of you?"

Thalia's face set in a rigid mask of anger as she stumped over to the coffeepot for refills. I put my hand over my cup, not wanting any more of her bitter, stale coffee. "She never told you?" she asked as she resettled herself across the table from me. When I shook my head, she said, "Well. It all came

17

out after Mama died. Or Alma, I mean. She wasn't my mom, actually, you know."

I shook my head slowly. "No, I didn't know."

"Well, that house belonged to Alma's parents—they built it up there on that high cliff back in the early part of the century, before the road from Duluth was even made. They used mostly local materials, getting some things—like all them windows—shipped up on the *America*—that boat that took supplies and mail and passengers to all the little towns around the lake, before the roads were built. So Alma pretty much grew up in that house. When she married my daddy, that would be in 1927, I was already three years old. Daddy'd been married before her—I think he just married her to take care of me, you know—but my mama, my real mama had died having me."

She paused, and I asked, "And you never knew this, when you were growing up? Never knew that Grandma wasn't your . . . birth mother?"

"No," her brows furrowed in anger. "No, they never told me, and I never woulda thought such a thing."

"So, the house . . ."

"Oh yeah, that. Well, Alma's parents were killed together in that boating accident a year or two after she married my daddy. So, the house was always in her name, I guess. Somethin' about you get to keep property separate if you inherit it from your own family. I don't know those kinda details. So when Mama . . . Alma died, she left letters for both Weez and me, explaining all this and leaving the house just to Weez." Her face was like granite.

I was stunned. I remembered Grandma as this gentle, loving soul—always humming a little, smelling like something good out of the kitchen, dispensing tender touches to one's cheek. How could she do something that seemed so cruel? There must be more to the story. I was also startled by the similarity of these two stories, Grandma's death and Mom's death: both leaving letters—or letter in Mom's case—explaining things, and both leaving a house—houses in Mom's case—to one daughter only. I briefly wondered if Magda wasn't really my sister but was pretty sure that wasn't part of the similarity.

"So you see," Thalia said, "it's not so surprising that Weezie and I didn't much resemble one another. All we had in common was a daddy. And Alma, you know, she was a great big fat woman," she paused, eyeing me in such a way that I thought I could hear the echo of her thought—"just like you"—but she didn't actually say it out loud, "and apparently my real mama was a wee thing."

"So you know who your mother was?"

"No," she answered. "Well, yes, Daddy told me what her name was when I asked him about it after Alma's death. But I don't remember. I mean, she died when I was born, so it doesn't much matter to me now."

"Aunt Thalia, did you ask Grandpa why Grandma left the house like that to my mom and not you? Even if you weren't her own flesh and blood, she'd raised you as such all those years. It seems a strange thing to do at the end."

"Yeah, well, she was stranger than people thought. Everyone always thought she was so good. I did ask Daddy. It was devastatin', as you can imagine, for me. He didn't want to talk about it. Just told me that Alma wasn't as nice as everyone always thought. I guess not." She emphasized this with a sniff.

I thought about this for a couple of minutes, trying to reconcile what she was telling me with what I remembered. It wasn't easy to do. "Grandma was an only child, wasn't she?"

Thalia hesitated. "Yes," she answered abruptly. "Yes, she was the only one."

"Thalia," I pushed a little because her answer sounded false. "Are you sure?"

"Of course, I'm sure, " she snapped, then relented. "Well, there was a sister, I think. But she died young or something. I never knew nothin' about her."

"How young?" I asked, intrigued about this great-aunt I'd never heard of.

"I just told you," she snapped again, "I never knew nothin' about her."

I let it go, feeling a little tickle of excitement inside of me. A lead, I thought, to my mother's mystery, to her "skeletons in the closet"? I knew it wouldn't be hard to find out at least birth and death statistics to this unknown great-aunt.

4

Before I left for Lake Superior the next morning, I dialed the number Thalia'd given me for Sondra. "She's always home," Thalia had assured me. "Doesn't do much." Sondra sounded delighted to hear from me and gave me her address, insisting I had to stop before I went north.

"If you can stand total chaos," she warned me.

The "crappy" neighborhood she lived in was an area I remembered from my University days called the Wedge, so-called because it was pie-shaped and wedged in between three main streets. It was not crappy. *Counterculture* was the term we used in the '70s. It looked much the same now: single-dwelling homes interspersed with duplexes, triplexes, and apartment buildings that ran the gamut from neat-and-tidy to shabbily disheveled.

Sondra's house, a two-story Victorian, definitely leaned toward the latter category. The exterior was covered with what I believe is called Depression brick—a kind of tarpaper siding that vaguely resembles brick. Although the grass was sparse to nonexistent, gaily-colored flowers adorned each step leading to the front door.

I picked my way through an array of tricycles, bicycles, pogo sticks, a badminton racket—no, two badminton rackets, a wagon, assorted bats and balls, and additional paraphernalia that loudly heralded the presence of children. Before I could knock, the front door burst open—nearly knocking me off the steps.

"Oops! Sorry," a Native American girl in her early teens apologized. "I'm in a hurry," she unnecessarily explained, then yelled back into the house, "Mom! Someone's here for you! Ghia! Come on! We'll be late!" She gamboled down the steps and picked a bike up. "Ghia!" she shouted again, and I stepped out of the way as the door flew open once more.

This time a younger girl, probably South Asian, maybe Indian, came hurrying out. "Hi!" she said, as she flew by. "Patsy, hold your horses! I'm coming!"

And just as suddenly, Sondra was there. "Patsy! Ghia!" She turned toward me with an apologetic expression. "Just a sec, Tyler. You need lunch money, Girls."

"Oh yeah," the older girl responded, dropping the bike and loping back to Sondra.

"Come here a minute, Ghia," Sondra instructed the younger girl. "I want you to meet my cousin."

"Mom! We're going to be late!"

Sondra tsk-ed with her tongue and handed some money over to the older girl. "This will only take a minute. Patsy, Ghia, this is Tyler."

"Hi," they peremptorily greeted me, and my own "hi" was lost as they kissed and hugged Sondra and mounted their bikes, calling, "Bye, Mom, see you tonight."

"Have a good time," Sondra called, turning to me. "I'm sorry, Tyler, they're off for the day on a park board field trip. Look at you! You grew up to be a majestic Amazon, didn't you?" It was a nice response to my decidedly hefty six-foot stature. She enveloped me, as much as she could considering her own diminutive size, in a firm hug. "I'm so glad you called! Come on in. Wait. Don't you have a dog with you?" She looked around.

Her mother must have told her about Aggie. "She's in the car."

"Does she get along with other dogs?"

"Usually," I responded.

"Bring her in then," she insisted. "She won't want to sit out in the car by herself." When I looked doubtful, she added, "Believe me, Tyler, she couldn't possibly do any damage to this place."

I laughed and got Aggie, who was very pleased to be let out of the car. Following Sondra into the house, I said, "I must say, Sondra, you certainly did not turn out in any way like I might have imagined."

Her laughter could have filled a cathedral with its rich, warm tones. "Sonny, Tyler. Everyone calls me Sonny. Except my mother, of course. I'm still Sondra and Corky is still Corcoran." We both laughed. Her living room was furnished with what appeared to be Goodwill castoffs, the walls festooned with children's paintings and drawings. Passing through the dining room, which was dominated by a huge table completely covered with papers and books and an ancient typewriter as well as a not-so-ancient computer, Sonny turned to me, saying, "Tyler, I'm so sorry about your mother. You must be just devastated."

I nodded, speechless as I find myself to be in the face of sincere sympathy. Again she hugged me, and tears splashed out of my eyelids. She continued on to the kitchen and indicated a place at the table, "I always liked your mom. She had a good heart, didn't she?" I nodded again, not yet ready to talk. Sonny busied herself with coffee, and I looked around the room. The cheerful yellow walls were papered with more children's artwork, the appliances were relics, the table I sat at was rickety and scarred but not without charm. The backyard was tiny, grassless, fenced, and filled with more children's playthings. One young, White girl with glasses, about eight or ten I'd guess, was stretched out on a chaise lounge with a book while two younger, Black girls were playing in a sandbox—which looked pretty much the same as the rest of the backyard except that pieces of wood were demarcating its boundaries. Two medium-sized dogs were drinking out of a child's wading pool.

"Funky, isn't it?" Sonny asked as she placed coffee in front of me. "Sugar, cream?"

"Cream would be nice," I agreed. "My god, Sonny, it looks to me like we'll need years to catch up!" She laughed, putting a container of half-and-half on the table. "Tell me about these kids."

Aggie, who'd been politely sitting by my side, stood up somewhat stiffly but with her tail moving back and forth slowly, as an enormous tabby strolled through the room. Sonny laughed again, "I forgot about Jazz. Will . . . what's her name?"

"Aggie," I supplied.

"Will Aggie mind?"

"I don't think so. She believes all living things are here for her to play with."

Sonny laughed again. "I don't think Jazz will see it quite that way. She's kind of old, you know, rules the roost." Indeed, as Aggie approached her, bending down in a playful manner, Jazz reached over and, with great economy, punched Aggie in the nose with a resounding thwack. Sonny and I both chuckled, and Aggie jumped back, then began to circle the cat warily.

"The kids," Sonny said, coming back to our conversation. Unlike her mother, Sonny made a good cup of coffee. "Well, that's a story. Patsy, the oldest one you met out front? She's fourteen and my own daughter. As well as the one with the book out back. That's Maya. She's eleven. Different fathers. I wasn't married to either of them. Then Ghia, you met her out front too, she's thirteen years old. She's been with us since she was two; at first a foster kid, then I adopted her. The others are all foster children. The two in the sandbox are sisters, six and seven years old. Lily and Rose. And there's one more upstairs napping. Annabelle. She's thirteen months old and was born with AIDS."

I was counting. "Six? You've got six kids?"

"Well, yeah," she agreed. "Sort of. As I said, three of them are my own, and the other three are foster children. Maybe they'll stay, maybe not. It all depends. Except for Annabelle, of course. If we're lucky, she'll live another year."

"Sonny, I'm amazed! Whatever happened to that snotty Sondra who looked down her nose at Corky and me, painted her fingernails and toenails to match her lipstick . . ." I noticed she had neither nail polish nor lipstick on her body now. "And spent her summers practicing walking like an Eileen Ford model?"

She laughed her booming laugh again. "I just grew up. And got bored with all that stuff. You know, the civil rights movement, the anti-war movement, feminism—I got educated, my consciousness raised, my horizons broadened. Magda isn't still like that, is she? Want to go out, Aggie?" she asked. Aggie looked interested, having finally given up on making friends with Jazz.

Sonny called out the back door, "This is Aggie, kids."

Maya glanced up only momentarily from her book while both the littler girls abandoned their elaborate city and went to pat Aggie, who thought that was just swell. The two dogs approached Aggie carefully.

"Reuben and Alfie," Sonny told me, and my eyebrows raised. She laughed and said, "The kids named them."

Aggie, knowing her doggie etiquette, dropped to the ground and let out a welcoming yip as she rolled on her back, exposing her jugular and tender tummy. The little girls immediately shrieked with delight as they rolled on the ground with Aggie, thinking she was doing this for their benefit. In moments, the three dogs and two girls were tumbling around one another.

"What kind of dogs are Reuben and Alfie?"

She shrugged again, "Brown dogs."

After a moment of watching the kids and dogs, I said slowly, "Magda turned out just as one might've predicted. She is married to an investment banker who wears three-piece suits, has two children—a boy and a girl, lives in a pristine suburb between L.A. and San Diego, has her hair and nails done weekly, goes to church, and votes Republican."

"You're kidding, right?" Sonny exclaimed. "No? Oh my god, I can't imagine! Whatever do you talk about when you get together?"

I shrugged. "No problem. We don't get together." I told her about my sister's decision regarding her children vis-à-vis their lesbian auntie. Then I asked her about Corky.

"Oh, that one," she said, echoing her mother and yet contradicting her also with a voice filled with affection. "He's out for adventure is all. He's done a little of everything. Logging, working on the fishing boats out of Seattle, shrimping boats out of New Orleans, crewing on sailing charters in the Caribbean, troubleshooting for oil companies—now he's on cargo ships, working in the South Seas."

"A life of romance!" I exclaimed.

"Yes, that's it exactly. Ma rumbles a lot about how he's never gonna settle down and, you know, she's right. By her standards. He's not going to come back to the Midwest and buy a house and get a wife and kids and a dog. He is settled, though, in his own way. He's happy, and that's all that counts. He only comes around about once every five years, but he writes. Not to Ma and Pop much because she just writes back full of reprimands and aspersions. He sends my kids—all of them—postcards from every place he goes and exotic presents and stories, oh the stories he brings back to them! He thinks it's great the way I live, and I think it's great the way he lives. We both get vicarious pleasure from each other's choices."

"How do you manage?" I asked. "I mean financially but also emotionally. I should think six kids would be a terrible drain. Do you do it alone?"

"Oh no, not entirely," she answered. "I get help from the women I do political work with. You see, I became a foster mother, initially, because they'd pay me to stay home. I figured I could take a couple of kids in with my own—and have the leisure to do the political work I do and augment what little pay I get. Well, I discovered that I've got a talent for parenting, so the foster thing kind of took over." She gestured to her dining room table. "But, you see, I still do the other work."

"So what do you do, mostly?"

"I write articles for newspapers, magazines—both mainstream and not-so-mainstream. A bunch of us put out a monthly dealing with feminist issues, anti-oppression work, racism, ageism, classism, ableism, heterosexism, that stuff. Then I just do consulting, especially in regard to personnel issues, to women's organizations and businesses. I make a little money. Not much. A little of this, a little of that. And you, Tyler, I know quite a lot about what you do."

"You do?" I asked as we went upstairs because the baby had started crying.

27

"Sure. How many Tyler Joneses do you think exist in feminist circles? I know you write 'Womenswords'—our paper carries it. Very good, by the way. I've always meant to write you but . . ." She was changing Annabelle's diaper, who was sucking her fist and staring suspiciously at me. "Hi, Snookums, how're you? This is my cousin, Tyler. She's okay, really." She turned her attention back to me. "And I know you wrote that wonderful book *The Undeclared War: Violence against Women.*"

"You thought it was wonderful? Really?" It didn't matter how many times I heard that; I still wanted to hear it again.

She smiled at me. "Yes, Tyler, it was wonderful. Heartbreaking, infuriating, enlightening, essential. I have a copy downstairs waiting for you to sign it."

I smiled back at her. The upstairs rooms seemed filled with beds and books, books and beds. They were untidy, but didn't appear to be dirty. Just as Sonny hoisted the baby onto her shoulder, where Annabelle promptly buried her face in Sonny's neck, someone yelled from downstairs. "Sonny? I'm here."

"Oh, good," Sonny started down the stairs with me following, the baby peeping shyly at me. "The babysitter's here. We can go to lunch."

5

We left Aggie with Sonny's kids and walked a couple of blocks to a vegetarian cafe on Lyndale. I didn't tell Sonny I'd probably prefer McDonald's. We talked enthusiastically about our childhood memories—what a pain Corky and I thought she and Magda were; and what a pain Magda and she thought Corky and I were; of our shared politics—finding that we even knew some people in common; of her folks—particularly their racism and chosen isolation in a mixed neighborhood and her mother's endless complaints (both things resulting in Sonny spending very little time with them); of my folks—my mother's political activism and her death, my father's conservatism and eschewal of my existence; of her school and back-to-Minnesota history, my school and coming-out and back-to-California history; of our heartbreaks; of our shared passion

29

with writing and feminism—twenty-some years of catching up.

When most of the food, surprisingly good, was finished, I asked, "So. No special relationship in your life?"

She grinned. "Lots of special relationships, Tyler. Most of them under fifteen. And others who are friends, not lovers."

I nodded. "Good answer."

"I get tired of that question, sometimes. You know, like the only 'special' relationships are between lovers. Maybe I'd feel differently if I didn't have the kids. I don't know. But my good women friends—no relationship with a man has ever approximated those relationships. Actually, I don't seem able to live with lovers, only with kids whom I love. And with work that I love. But Tyler, seeing as how you brought this up, how about you?"

I shrugged. "I like your answer. I have a lot of special relationships, with women who are dear friends and women I work with. And Aggie. No kids, though. Although some friends have kids now—it's the big thing in lesbian circles these days, you know—and I'm pretty fond of a couple of them. Lovers?" I clucked my tongue, looking out the window momentarily. "I don't think that's my forte. I'm not very good at letting people get close to me—unless they're in that non-threatening category of 'friends.' I've been hurt, and I guess I've done my share of hurting. Less pain—coming or going—when you're on your own." I shrugged again. "I think I'm a love agnostic—not sure, one way or another, if it really exists. And, for about ten years, I managed to really keep people at arm's length in a trite manner: by crawling into a bottle." She nodded, and I asked, "You knew that?"

"Sure. You wrote about it in your column."

"Oh yeah. I always forget how much people know about me from my columns. Anyway, I just feel out of practice now. The other thing is I really like living alone. I guess that's lucky, under the circumstances."

She nodded agreement, saying, "I know what you mean. I like having things my own way, too. More and more as I get older."

When we started to wind down—knowing we weren't through but also knowing we'd see each other again—I asked her, "Sonny. What do you remember of Grandma and Grandpa?"

She shrugged. "Grandpa was sort of distant, not unpleasant but not really present. Wouldn't you say?" I nodded. "And Grandma was a love. Full of warmth and uncritical appreciation, not to speak of endless good things to eat. God! Remember her sticky buns?"

"To die for!" I agreed.

"What are you wanting to know, Tyler?"

I smiled, shaking my head a little. "I don't know exactly." I told her about Mother's deathbed demand and her mom's revelations. "I think Aunt Thalia knows something she's not telling me. Were you around when Grandpa died?"

"Not really. I was at school, but I came home for the funeral. You want me to tell you what I remember?" I nodded. "In some ways, Tyler, I won't be real accurate because Mom was so upset, and I was so immune to her complaints by then that I only half-listened to them. Still, I do remember some of it. She was furious that your mother didn't come to the funeral. That had to do with Grandma's funeral. Remember that?" I nodded.

"I was older than you—seventeen, when Grandma died—so I heard a lot of things, I suppose. Like she told you, that's when she found out she wasn't Grandma's daughter. This devastated her. I mean, her whole orderly world was tilted. She'd been lied to, deceived into believing in a mother that didn't exist. She didn't know what to do, how to handle it. I told her then—and have reiterated this since, uselessly—that she ought to find out more about her birth mother. That it might help. She prefers to just be furious with everybody—Grandma and

31

Grandpa and your mom. In some ways, she blamed your mom the most. Because it was easier, of course, to blame someone who was still alive and not one of her parents. But also because Grandma left Aunt Weezie the house. That seemed to be the cruelest blow. Of course, everything Grandpa had went to Mom, but it wasn't about who got what. It was about her awful feelings of rejection."

"I know." I filled her in on what had happened with Mom's will, my father's will, and Magda's reaction to it all. "Isn't it odd that Mom did the same thing with Magda and me that Grandma did with her and Thalia?"

"Very odd," Sonny agreed.

"And Magda must have felt the same way your mom felt. She's going to get a lot of money from Dad, but she felt it was an insult that Mother left everything to me. And took it out on me. Probably for the same reasons—because I'm alive and Mom isn't."

"Makes sense."

"But, Sonny, doesn't this thing with Grandma's house seem strange to you? I mean, I know it hurt Magda that Mom left everything to me—everything that didn't go to SALSA, that is—but at least it makes some sense. What with Dad's *very* considerable estate going to Magda. But Grandma's house— that doesn't make so much sense. Even if Thalia wasn't her own child, she raised her as if she were—never even told her she wasn't. Why would she cut her out of her life at death?"

"I don't know. It's always puzzled me, too."

"It just doesn't seem like Grandma. At least not as I remember her, anyway. I feel like there's more to this story."

"I'm sure there is," Sonny agreed. "Once, after Mom had been up visiting Grandma, she came home and I remember her being very worked up. I didn't really pursue it. I was a teenager, and mostly, you know, I just found these adult crises to be so 'boring.'" We smiled at one another. "But it was something about Grandma's sister . . ."

I sat up straighter, "And?"

"I don't really know anything about it. I'm sorry, Tyler. That teenaged stuff again. When Grandma died and all this other stuff came out, I remember Mom saying something about 'that sister, this is about that sister.' At the time, I thought she was talking about Aunt Weezie actually, but later I came to a different conclusion."

"Why?"

"Because after Grandpa died and Weezie didn't come and Mom was railing on and on, she said something again about 'that sister, Louisa.' I said, 'You mean Louise, don't you?' and she snapped at me, 'No! Not her, Alma's' (she'd taken to calling her mom Alma by then) 'sister.' When I pressed her, she just clammed up and told me to 'leave her alone, didn't she have enough problems?'"

"Louisa?" I said softly. "You think Grandma had a sister named Louisa?"

Sonny shrugged. "I don't know for sure; it's all a jumble now and, actually, was all a jumble then. But that was the impression I got."

"Louisa." I repeated. "So maybe Mom was named after Grandma's sister."

"Makes sense."

"But I wonder what a long-dead sister would have to do with Grandma and Mom and your mom and the odd disposition of that house. You know, until Mom died, I didn't even know she still owned that house."

"It is a mystery, isn't it? I wonder what it's all about?"

"Well, I intend to find out. This has got to be what Mom wanted me to unravel."

6

Leaving Minneapolis we drove north through the flattish farmlands of central Minnesota, land full of green-growing things: corn, hay, sod, a tree farm or two. Land where only the farmhouses enjoyed the protection of trees, the rest being tilled and sown or grazed by slow-moving cows. Land in which everything was varying shades of startling green to this California girl, who was accustomed to the brittle yellow of summer at home. Land that was, nonetheless, familiar and soothing to me. Further north, the slight roll of the farmland sharpened to larger rises and deeper dips, the fields giving way to forests of mixed pine and deciduous trees, rocky out-croppings shouldering the freeway, and an abundance of rivers and lakes.

Coming over the hill above Duluth, where the partial expanse of Lake Superior spread out beyond vision below, I caught my breath in timeless wonder at the sight of this gorgeous inland sea. I stopped to pick up some McDonald's and traveled up the road a little before pulling over. While I sat on the rocks fulfilling my cholesterol needs, Aggie raced the shore, jumping in and out of the water, chasing seagulls. Before starting out again, I put the top of my little car up. Just coming down the hill into Duluth, I felt the temperature plummet. I remembered that June was more like spring than summer along the edge of this incredible body of water.

Memories that had been teasing me during the drive cross-country now flooded through my mind, like the rivers pouring down from the hills in a frenzy of whitewater, cascades, and falls to deposit themselves in the lake. Every place-name caught my eye, jogged my memory: we used to stop for smoked fish at Knife River; my mother's childhood friend, Georgia Abbott, lived at Castle Danger; we had picnics at Baptism River; we went swimming at Temperance River.

I was startled by masses of wildflowers—the bright orange of Indian paintbrush, purple and pink lupine, and something blue I couldn't identify—lining the ditches on either side of the highway. They were lovely, but I didn't remember them from my childhood. Daisies were the only wildflowers I remembered. Daisies.

Northeast of Lutsen was the turnoff for Stony River, a small settlement between the highway and a point that extended like a giant crooked finger into the lake. When I was a kid, this "town" consisted of Chummy's Store and gas station, the adjoining post office, a one-room schoolhouse, and a garage for fixing cars and just about anything else. The local residents' homes were scattered in the woods on either side of the highway and around the small cluster of buildings that constituted "town."

On the point extending out from the town, only two houses belonged to "locals"—The Cedars, my grandparents' place, and White Rock Cove, the showplace owned by the local lumber barons, the Johannsens. Every other place was inhabited by "summer folk"—those people who lived elsewhere the rest of the year and spent their summers or part of their summers on Lake Superior. I wondered, as I pulled off the highway, if this was still true.

The schoolhouse appeared to be someone's house now, but Chummy's was still there—although the adjoining post office was boarded over. A large faded-blue sign with faded-yellow lettering proclaiming "Chummy's" spread across the second floor of the store, where Old Man Chummy used to live alone, his wife having run off years before with the bakery goods man. As I got out of the car and stretched my legs, warning Aggie to stay put, I wondered how old Old Man Chummy would be. Let's say in 1965, when I would've been 12, he was . . . what? At least 60, wasn't he? He couldn't still be running this place, could he? I speculated, as I filled my tank with gas, about whether or not the place had been sold. Maybe the new owners just kept the name.

I went in to pay for my gas and get some groceries. A grizzled old man, black-and-gray stubble covering his head and face, was leaning on the counter, talking to a younger man on the other side. Grizzly turned to stare at me while the man by the cash register greeted me affably. I, in turn, stared back at the younger man.

He grinned, lifted his eyebrows, and said, "Can I help you with something?"

"Charley?" I asked. "Charley Chummy? Is that you?"

An even more familiar grin spread across his face as he said, "It sure is me, but you have me at a distinct disadvantage, ma'am. I don't seem to recollect you . . ." He let the sentence trail off as he carefully scrutinized me.

"Well," I smiled, too. "It's been a long time." This was the Chummy grandson who had inspired such interest in Magda and Sondra. I stretched out my hand. "I'm Tyler Jones. I used to spend my summers at my grandparents' place. You know, Alma and Holger Schmidt."

"Oh yeah!" he agreed, shaking my hand firmly. "I remember. Didn't you have an older sister? Oh yes, the gorgeous Maggie."

I laughed. "I have to tell you, Charley, no one but you, in Magdalene's forty-three years, has ever called her Maggie."

He joined me in laughter and said laconically, "Well now, I guess that's because no one was quite as special as me."

I smiled widely, knowing with this easy banter that I had—in some way—come home. "You bet, Charley. You were special, that's so."

He turned toward the older man and said, "This here's Lyle. Lyle Johannsen. Don't know if you ever knew him, probably knew his brother, Burt, who owns the place at the end of the point."

I nodded, shaking hands with Lyle, and he said, "Knew your grandparents. Good people. And your mom, I guess, too. Which one is she?"

"Weezie," I said, the familiar lump dropping into my throat again.

"Oh yeah. Weezie. She's been gone a long time now."

"Yes," I nodded, smiling. "A long time." After a pause, I added, "She just died actually." I could barely say the words out loud.

"No!" Lyle protested. "Surely she's too young for dying."

Aren't we always? "Cancer," I answered succinctly.

He shook his head, rubbing a gnarly hand across the stubble on his chin. "Aw, I'm so sorry, Miss. It's hard to lose someone like that."

I made an attempt at a smile, then said, "I've got to get some groceries."

Lyle grunted and said, "Nice meeting you. Welcome back to Stony River."

I smiled my appreciation and ducked down one of the aisles, surreptitiously wiping my eyes. I didn't want to cry in front of people I didn't even know. Actually, I didn't want to cry at all.

When I brought my first armload of groceries to the counter—Cheerios, milk, cream, eggs, 7-up, bread—Lyle was gone, and Charley said, "Maggie's forty-three?" At my nod, he continued. "It's hard to believe. 'Course it shouldn't be, because I'm forty-five, but then—you know, I've been here all along with me as I got older. There were a couple of other siblings, weren't there? No, wait, not siblings. Cousins. Let me see. Sandy and what's-his-name? Skinny little kid with a big mouth. Funny nickname—Bottlecap? Coffee?"

"Corky," I corrected, laughing. Charley had always pretended not to remember Corky's name. "And *Sondra*."

"Oh yeah. Couldn't get away with calling her Sandy, no way. Frosty little . . ."

"She goes by Sonny these days, and believe me, she's thawed."

"Yeah?"

"Oh yeah. She has six kids."

"Six? Wow! She's been busy, hasn't she? How about Maggie?"

"Two kids. She lives south of L.A., but Sonny lives in the Cities. You'll probably see her this summer. I think I've got her convinced to come visit me."

"So you're here for the summer?" He rang up my gas. When I nodded, he added, "Place is a wreck, you know. Been empty too many years. Kids partying in there and such."

"I imagine. You're still here, huh? Take the old place over from your grandpa?"

He looked a little sheepish. "Yeah. After high school, I went in the Navy. Ended up in 'Nam. After that . . ." he busied himself, suddenly rearranging items on a shelf for a minute, ". . . I just wanted to come back to this quiet little backwater.

You know?" He looked at me expectantly. I nodded. "So. I did what everyone does 'round here. Went to work for Johannsen. Worked part-time for Gramps. 'Bout five years ago—he was 88—he decided to retire and offered the store to me. So. Here I am."

"Is he still alive?"

He shook his head, sadness washing across his face. "Tough old bird. He died last year. Boy, that guy was full of stories. Just full of 'em."

I'll have to hear some of those stories someday, I thought. "I'm sorry, Charley. I know how hard it is to lose someone you care so much about." We looked at one another, helplessly, both knowing there wasn't a thing we could say that would make any difference.

Charley's thick, long lashes were clearly wet. "I did, you know, I did care a lot about that old geezer. You know, my dad just took off, before I was ever born. Gramps was always there. He taught me how to be a man. I cared about my mom, but Gramps—he was the only dad I ever had."

I nodded solemnly as he wiped down the windows on the freezer. After a few minutes, I said, "So, Charley, aren't you married?"

"Naw," he said, looking relieved, probably because I'd changed the subject. "Was, but that didn't work out. Got a coupla kids though. Even got a grandkid!"

"No kidding? They all live around here?" I think I was starting to talk in the same clipped cadence he used.

"My daughter with the baby, she and her husband live in Grand Marais. Not my son. He lives out by Seattle. How about you?"

"Nope," I said. "No marriage. No kids." I decided I wouldn't blurt out, just yet, that there wasn't going to be any marriage or kids. "I still live in San Francisco where I grew up. Although I came here for college."

"That so? Where'd you go?"

"The University. In the Cities. So, Charley, maybe you can help me."

"Be glad to, if I can."

"Used to be a guy who did a lot of work for the summer folk out on the point, sometimes worked for my grandparents if it was something Grandpa couldn't do himself. Jerome Something-Or-Other was his name. Is he still around? Still doing handiwork like that?"

"Sure," Charley grinned. "That would be Jerome MacRae. He worked for his dad all those years and just kept doing it after his dad died. Sort of a caretaker, handyman, jack-of-all-trades Jerome is. In his sixties now. Still strong as a horse, quiet as a rabbit, smart as a fox. Can fix anything, can Jerome."

"Great. I suspect I'm going to need a lot of help, fixing the old place up. Maybe I can get a phone number?"

"Sure," he agreed and rattled off a number.

"Wait! I've got to get paper," I fished in my bag, pulling out a piece of paper and a pen.

"His wife—Gertie?" Charley said, after giving me the number again. "She does a lot of cleaning around here. Probably could use her help, too."

"Great." I wrote her name down on the paper as well.

"So, Tyler. You gonna live here? Fix that place up and stay or what?"

"I don't know, Charley," I dodged. "My mom left me the place and. . ." I stopped, not quite certain where I was going.

"I'm truly sorry," he interrupted, and I bobbed my head in acknowledgment of his sympathy, feeling annoyance at the tears rising in my eyes, again. Focus on that fly, the one walking on the edge of the counter, I said to myself.

"Anyway, I don't know exactly what I'm going to do. Get it fixed up enough to stay this summer and then . . ." I shrugged. "Maybe I'll sell it. Unless it's been destroyed by the years of vacancy, I remember it as a grand old house."

41

"Oh, that it is," Charley agreed. "I doubt it's wrecked beyond help. It's such an oddity up here, you know. Not a cabin or lodge or cottage even, never felt much like the North Shore. More like a city house. You know what I mean?"

I smiled, nodding and remembering. "My grandma once told me that her dad wanted a house like the great summer homes of the rich and famous out on Long Island, and that's why he built this great big house up here in Minnesota's north woods." I was getting excited, now, to go see it. "I've got to go, Charley. I want to see it before it gets dark. Know of anyplace around here that allows dogs? I've got to have someplace to stay until I can move in there."

"Oooh," Charley puckered his mouth. "That's kind of tough, Tyler. It's always so crowded up here in the summer, you know. Shoulda made reservations ahead of time. Let me call around. See what I can find."

"Thanks, Charley."

While Charley made calls, I piled more groceries on the counter—coffee, butter, peanut butter, orange juice, onions, potatoes, bananas, and cookies. A man came, glanced curiously at me, grabbed a package of cigarettes, and said, "Put it on my account, Charley." Charley nodded as he continued to talk on the phone. I wandered around the store, making sure there was nothing else I might need. I picked up a copy of the *Cook County News* and paged through it. Yes, there was a listing of AA meetings; I put the paper on top of my groceries.

Eventually, Charley got off the phone. "Bad news, Tyler. Every place is full or doesn't take dogs. I've got an idea, though." I looked encouraging, hoping he wasn't going to suggest we shack up together. Although, if Magda was his type, I probably wasn't. "I've got Gramps's fishing shack up on Deer Yard Lake. Remember that lake?"

"Sort of," I agreed. "North in the hills, right? Kinda near Pike Lake?"

"Right. You know, I live upstairs here and mostly never have time to get up there in the summer. It's not much, Tyler. Got an outhouse, but there is electricity and a pump inside. Little fridge. I reckon you'll be in your own place within a couple of days and . . . Well, maybe it's too shabby for you."

"No!" I disagreed. "It sounds perfect! What a nice thing to do, Charley. You want me to pay you now or later?"

"Aw no, you don't gotta pay me anything. Christ, it's gonna be a little dirty, Tyler. I haven't been up there for a bit. But it's pretty up there, and your dog—what kinda dog?"

"Golden retriever. Her name's Aggie. Agatha Christie, actually."

"—she can run loose up there. It's not too bad. Not fancy but—hey—beggars can't be choosers."

"Right," I agreed. "Charley, you'll have to let me take you out to dinner or something to repay your kindness."

He grinned and said, "Oh, well, we'll work something out." He rang the groceries up and put them in a box. Then he drew a map how to get there. "It's only about ten minutes from here. This road?" he pointed to the map. "Just before you get to the cabin? Looks as if it's an unused logging road, but don't worry. People who live down there don't like people poking around, so they don't do much with that road. You'll find it okay. I hope it ain't too dirty."

"Thanks a million, Charley. What about a key?"

Charley snorted. "No key, Tyler. Just push the door open. You can latch it from the inside though, if you're a little skittish."

I smiled. No key. "Great. Thanks again. I'll probably see you tomorrow. Oh, has it got a phone?"

Charley laughed, "Tyler, this place is pretty primitive. There's no phone. You wanta use my phone before you go?"

"Yeah, I want to call Jerome. See how soon he can get out to my place. Hey, what happened to the post office, Charley?"

"Oh, back in '70 we got annexed. Kinda like school consolidation, you know. Regional P.O. said we were too close to Grand Marais to warrant having a separate office, so . . ." He snapped his fingers, "No more post office." He waved in the direction of where the post office used to be. "See? You can get in there from the store now. I keep the videos in there."

No keys in Stony River, Minnesota, but they've got videos. I called the MacRaes, and Jerome agreed that he'd come by the next morning to look things over with me. Telling Charley that I wanted to pick his brain about local history and stuff, I took my leave—heading out toward my grandma's place on the point.

7

It was nearly 9 p.m. when Aggie and I arrived at Grandma's house. But in high summer, nine at night still leaves almost an hour of light in this north country. The point extended first south, then west into the lake. The dirt road that led to the end of the point, where the big Johannsen place was, hugged the inside of the finger, running alongside the Stony River Bay. All the houses were, consequently, built on the open lakeside of the point. My grandparents' place was built on high cliffs just at the crook of the finger, so it had fantastic views in three directions: up lake toward Grand Marais; straight out over the endless roll of water that stretched toward the distant but unseen Michigan coast; and down lake toward Duluth, where one point after another jutted into the lake, creating a scenic vista of wild waves colliding with dark forest. Rising far above these points were the serrated silhouettes of the Sawtooth Mountain Range, dancing back toward Duluth. The oldest mountain range in the States, Charley's grandfather used to tell us, so old that years of erosion and glaciers had worn the peaks down to big hills.

Just offshore was a little rock pile of an island where the seagulls nested, and we could watch the lake's constantly restless energy throw itself against this rocky impediment. Rare hot summers when the lake warmed up to barely tolerable, Corky and I swam out to this little island. Most summers, however, the lake was far too icy for us to be able to stay in it that long. Then we canoed out—always being careful to do this after the baby seagulls were out of their nests.

Somewhere on the other side of the hills and dense forest behind us was a sunset. All we got here on the lake were the reflected colors powdering the distant horizon in mostly pastel hues. It was enough. Layers of lavender and rose and blue and deep purple piled high on one another. I pulled in the short driveway. You could almost always tell the locals from the summer folk by how close their houses were to the road. Summer folk didn't need to think about shoveling out long driveways all winter.

The large, two-story frame house of now-faded brown shingles with pale yellow trim and shutters loomed between me and the lake and filled me with such a quickly moving array of emotions that I couldn't properly identify them: excitement, sadness, nostalgia, confusion, happiness, depression—not necessarily in that order. I sat in the car staring at it until Aggie let out an impatient yelp.

"Sorry, Girl," I reached back and petted her. "You've had enough of cars for a while, haven't you?" She was delighted to be let out and immediately began exploring. On the road, the signpost was still standing, but no sign accompanied it. "The Cedars," it had always read—the majority of trees being enormous cedars. The yard resembled a meadow—tall, unmown grass interspersed with the bright hues of Indian paintbrush

46

and buttercups and daisies. "Aggie," I called. "Be careful of that cliff out there." I wondered if I should do something more concrete to warn her. She wasn't a dumb dog, but dogs don't have excellent depth perception.

I walked out toward the cliff, being careful myself not to let the tall grass deceive me into getting too close to the edge. There was a low hedge of junipers that had been planted along the brink of the cliff some eighty years ago, to discourage anyone from stumbling over the side. To my knowledge, no one had ever fallen. Not far from the rim was an old stone patio, also built years ago. I wondered if the wooden swing that used to sit there was still around.

I carefully walked closer to the cliff's edge to see if there were any remnants of the lift that used to take us back and forth to the rocky promontory below. The wooden deck for approaching the lift looked rotten and unsafe, but the metal box that hauled us up and down the steeply descending (or ascending, if you were at the bottom) track looked intact. I couldn't see much of the track, which hugged the face of the cliff as it descended in a diagonal toward the shore below, without stepping on this rickety-looking deck, so I backed away.

I turned around, and my breath caught jaggedly in my throat. The house that contained so much of my childhood, shabby and a little dilapidated now, stood staring majestically and sightlessly out to sea. The immense porch that wrapped around three sides of the first floor had all of its wooden shutters closed, but the windows on the second floor danced a little with the colors from the horizon. I suddenly slumped to the ground and put my head back and wailed. Howled. Cried and shrieked as I had not done once since my mother died. Aggie came to me immediately, nudging me and whining slightly. I buried my face in her neck and sobbed until only hiccoughs were left.

When my grief seemed to be spent, at least temporarily, I realized the light was fading quickly. "We'll have to go through the inside tomorrow, Aggie," I said, soothing her worried demeanor. "It's getting too late, and we'll never find Charley's shack in the dark. We better go, sweet pal."

Charley had given us a good map, so I had no problem getting to the place before the deep darkness of the northern woods settled over us. I was glad we made it in time because the path to the structure would have been hard to negotiate without some light. Once inside, I turned the lights on and found outside floodlights for both the lake side and the road side. I quickly brought in the groceries and one small traveling suitcase.

Then, before it was completely dark, Aggie and I walked down to the small lake's edge. Just this five or so miles up into the hills and away from Lake Superior resulted in a noticeable rise in the temperature. There was a cacophonous buzz and screech of a million night bugs and critters: cicadas and green frogs and crickets and owls, other things I couldn't identify. I'd forgotten about night noise in Minnesota. It was familiar and oddly pleasant. I jumped and Aggie barked a warning when the darkness was rent by unearthly laughter. I laughed at myself, thinking how long it had been since I had heard a loon.

The inland lakes, without the majesty of the big lake, have their own charm. The sound of little waves lapping at the shore, the beauty of an enormous hillside of trees reaching straight up on the opposite shore, the moon now rising behind that hill. Aggie and I stumbled back up to the cabin.

It was dirty, as Charley had warned, but with just a film of dust—not years of accumulated filth. It was one room. There was a wide window on the lake side with a table and two chairs in front of it, a glass full of silverware the centerpiece. One wall held a miniature stove, refrigerator, and sink, with a pump instead of faucets, and a couple of open shelves with two cups, two plates, two bowls, one pot, one frying pan. On the other wall was an oversized bunk bed piled high with inviting-looking, heavy quilts. On the back wall were some hooks, apparently the closet.

I unloaded the groceries first, putting away the refrigerator stuff and arranging the rest on top of the fridge. Then I took things out of my suitcase, hanging them on the hooks and putting toiletries on a little shelf by the sink.

"Come on, Aggie," I said. "I'm not going out to that outhouse by myself. You have to protect me from the bears." She agreed cheerfully. I found a flashlight, and we followed a little path through the woods. I only tripped once over a tree root. I was glad for the darkness, not wanting to see too much of the outhouse on this first trip. Sitting on the stool with the door open, I realized I'd also forgotten about the state bird: the mosquito. By the time I pulled my pants up, I was already swatting at the swarming biters.

Back in the cabin, I opened the front window. There was a constant plunking noise as moths batted the screen, trying to reach the light in the shack. I didn't even bother to wash my face or brush my teeth. I just turned the light off, stripped my clothes off, and crawled under that pile of quilts on the bottom bunk. Aggie settled at my feet, and I fell into an exhausted, dreamless sleep.

8

In the morning light, the cabin looked a little shabbier than it had the night before, but it was homey, I decided. After another trip to the outhouse, I walked again to the lake's edge and looked around. There were other cabins nearby, I knew, because I'd passed some on my way here the night before, but I could not see anyone else—and assumed no one could see me. So I shed my clothes and took a bath in the lake. Aggie went wild, decided we were playing some wacky water game together, and almost made it impossible for me to wash myself. The water was cold but not icy like it would be in Superior. I got out, feeling clean and shimmering with energy.

After pulling on sweatpants and a sweatshirt and discovering there was no toaster, I made toast the old-fashioned way: in the oven. I took my peanut-butter toast and orange juice to the little bench by the water's edge and ate while the sun rose above the hill across the lake. Aggie's long years of insisting I get up early to walk her had finally succeeded (almost) in making me a morning person. Birds were twittering, and a loon's soft tremolo came pirouetting across the lake—followed a few minutes later by a mother loon with one baby on her back and another trailing behind her. Even Aggie was so relaxed that she only raised her ears at such a sight, rather than plunging in after the intruders. Just as I finished my breakfast, a boat puttered out into the lake—early fishers— and I was glad my bath was over.

I was anxious to get down to The Cedars, so I decided to clean up the little cabin later. I stopped at Chummy's, hoping there might be coffee. This time Aggie got out of the car but waited outside for me. Charley came out to meet her.

"Hi Girl," he said easily, scratching Aggie's ears vigorously. She immediately leaned against his legs with abandon. It was clear that Aggie was in love; she was such a slut. "Morning, Tyler. The place okay?"

"Oh Charley! It's wonderful! I can't begin to thank you enough. I slept like a log and had a nice bath in the lake this morning. This is a real treasure."

"Good. I got to worrying later. I mean, it's not like a big city or anything here."

"Charley . . ." I remonstrated.

"And I don't know what you're used to. I hope it's not too dirty."

"Naw," I responded. "I wanted to get down to The Cedars early. Can I use your phone again? I've got to get a phone installed."

"Sure," he agreed. "Help yourself. Want some coffee?"

"Is the Pope Catholic?" I responded enthusiastically. After I'd made arrangements with the phone company, Charley and I sat out in front of the store drinking our coffee and swatting bugs. Another bench, I thought, this one overlooking the road and Stony River Bay.

"Weren't the mosquitoes and blackflies eating you alive when you went swimming this morning?" he asked.

"I guess not," I replied. "I think I'd notice if they were. Maybe it was too early for them."

"Yeah. Maybe. Bad year for blackflies this year." After a slight pause, he continued, "'Course, seems to me we say that every year." He said this so seriously, I laughed. "No really. You know, like every year we can hardly wait for summer to come, then right away we start complaining 'bout the bugs and how they're worse than ever. 'Course it's June. They do get better by August. Not too many bugs in California, is there?"

I thought this was the oddest conversation, and yet it was typical Minnesota small talk. I could imagine, if I closed my eyes and thought about it, having this exact conversation with Mary Sharon, my closest friend back in California but a true Minnesotan. I answered Charley, "Nope. Not too many bugs out there. We don't even have screens on our windows."

"Really? Can't imagine that. Nope. Just can't imagine it."

An old truck—really old, maybe from the early '50s—pulled up to the pumps. Lyle, whom I'd met the night before, got out and said, "Morning, Charley," and nodded in my direction.

Charley got up, disturbing Aggie, who'd gone comalike under the ministrations of his hands, and stretched. "Hey, Lyle, how ya doin'? I'll get you a cup." He went inside and returned a moment later with another cup of coffee.

Lyle was putting gas in his ancient truck. "Thanks," he said, immediately taking a swig from the cup even though steam was rising out of it.

"So where you off to, Lyle?" Charley asked.

"What makes you think I'm off to anywhere?" Lyle responded gruffly. Charley huffed a little and said, "Come on, Lyle. You walk up here most mornings for your coffee. You got the truck, you're goin' somewhere."

"Humphh," Lyle snorted. "Think you know everything. Maybe I'm just getting my truck gassed up for later."

"Mmm-hmm." Charley sipped his own coffee. "Going to visit your mom, Lyle?"

"Maybe. Maybe," Lyle agreed.

"Tyler's interested in the old stories, Lyle. Bet your mom could tell her a thing or two."

Lyle peered at me for a few seconds, like he wasn't sure he knew who I was, then said abruptly, "Yeah, that she could, I reckon. Thanks for the coffee, Charley. Put the gas on my account."

Charley brought me some fresh coffee when he came back from writing down Lyle's gas on his account. Lyle waved and drove off. After scalding my tongue trying to sip the coffee too quickly, I said, "I'm impressed that vehicle is still running. It must be about forty years old."

"I think," Charley said, "it's a 1951, actually. That would make it 41. Oh yeah, Lyle takes good care of that truck. It's his baby."

I squinted after the departing truck and said, "I have this memory of the Johannsens being kind of fancy. Living in that Lundie place and, I don't know, putting on airs, I guess." Lundie was a Minnesotan architect who'd designed and built many North Shore lodges. These buildings, mighty resorts to small cabins, all had a distinctive mix of Scandinavian carving, massive beam work, and the rusticity of the American wilderness. Most of the houses he did on Superior were designed and built during the '40s and '50s. Even when I was a little girl, people coveted these unique places.

"That's the brother you're remembering," Charley responded. "Burt. He is fancy. Off in Washington now, being a senator and all."

"Really?"

Charley nodded. "Yeah. Lyle never lived down here when we were kids. Lived up in the woods on the Gunflint Trail.

Kind of a hermit type. Except, of course, he was the plant foreman at the lumber company."

"And he lives at the Johannsen place on the end of the point now?"

"Sort of. Remember that place?" I nodded. The land was the largest on the point, the road dead-ending into it, creating a lot with views on all three sides, rivaling my grandparents' vista. "That Lundie fella? He's gotten kind of famous in more recent years. Anyway, they've got a guest cabin as big as some of the cabins along here, and Lyle lives there now. Sort of taking care of the place for Burt and his wife, who're mostly in Washington."

"So, is Lyle married, or does he just live there alone?"

"Alone. Never did get married." Charley answered, leaning over to rough up Aggie's belly. She was putty in his hands.

"And Burt's a senator?"

"Yep. He was governor for two terms. Now senator. Lots of talk about him running for prez in 2000."

"Really?" The name was vaguely familiar, now that I thought about it. Someone who made his mark—if I remembered correctly—during the Anita Hill hearings. I wrinkled my nose in distaste, hoping I was wrong. "How old is he now?"

"Burt? Mmm," Charley thought a moment, sipping some of his coffee. "Probably about 63, maybe 64."

Something about his tone made me think he wasn't so fond of Senator Johannsen. "Is he any good? You know, a good senator?"

Charley's eyebrows raised as he looked at me quizzically. "He's a politician, Tyler." I smiled, he shrugged. "I don't know. Some folk think he's good. He's been in office for twelve years. Something like that. He's not my man."

"Why not?"

"Lots of reasons. The short answer—he's too conservative for me. My mother's family? They were Finns." That was answer enough. The Finns in northern Minnesota were known for their leftist politics, or at the very least—liberal. "Boy, I miss having a dog. My lab—had it since I got back from 'Nam?—died a couple of months ago. I should get another one. So what do you do, Tyler? You a teacher or somethin' that you can take off for the whole summer?"

"I write. I write a column for a newspaper. It's syndicated."

"What's it about? Your column, I mean. Like that Erma Bombeck or something?"

I smiled. "No. It's more like investigative and opinion pieces. Mostly I write about the realities of being female in this society."

"That feminist stuff, huh? That's good. Things should change some, shouldn't they?"

"Yup," I agreed, feeling no need to elaborate.

"So, you're like a journalist, huh?"

"Yup," I agreed again. "I write other things, too. I've written a book, and I'm working on another one now."

"That's pretty impressive. Are you famous?"

"I don't think so. You never heard of me, did you?"

"Well no, but I don't read a whole lot. Only author I can think of is that Ross Macdonald. Don't suppose you write books like his, do you?"

I smiled. "No. My first book was nonfiction. It's about violence against women. The book I'm trying to write now is a novel, but not a mystery like Macdonald writes."

"Well, it's kinda neat that you write books. I know an author now."

"Yup," I agreed. "You do."

A couple had been walking toward the store from the point and were now close enough to wave and say, "Good morning." They were probably in their fifties. The woman was wearing a turquoise polyester pantsuit, had tight curls on her head—colored a suspiciously even brown, and had a definite lilt to her stride. She walked right up to me and stuck her hand out. "Hi. You must be that Schmidt granddaughter. We're neighbors. I'm Nancy and this is my better half—I should just say 'other' half, I'm certainly not convinced he's better—Piggy. McDermott," she added. "We live just beyond your place."

Small town, I thought; they already know who I am. I stood up and shook Nancy's hand. "Hi. I'm Tyler Jones." Then I shook Piggy's hand and said, hesitantly, "Piggy?"

"Oh yeah, well, the name's Percival. Can you imagine? I mean, even Percy. Just a tad too sissyish for me. And I was always a mite pudgy," he patted his ample midsection and continued, "so it became Piggy pretty early on. Now, I guess everyone's just used to it. Only sounds odd to newcomers."

"Well. It's very nice to meet both of you."

"We're just delighted to hear you're fixing that place up. It's fantastic but kinda run down, now. Be better for the whole point to get it fixed up, won't it, Piggy?"

"Oh yeah. Thinkin' about selling it, Tyler?"

"Maybe," I answered and shrugged. "I don't know yet."

Piggy was handing me his card. "Keep me in mind if you decide to sell it. I've been selling houses in this area for about ten years now. I'm pretty good at it, aren't I, Charley?"

"He's a whiz," Charley concurred.

"Of course, houses like your grandparents'—that's no work at all for me. All those city folk are wanting to get up here and buy, buy, buy. Just let me know if you want any advice."

"Thanks, Piggy, I will."

Without the softening effect of the twilight sky, The Cedars did, indeed, look pretty run down. Before going inside, Aggie and I walked the property. The separate garage was leaning and looked none too safe. One door hung askew while the other had fallen off altogether. I entered it cautiously. There wasn't much inside—some piles of wood, a rusty scythe, some empty or near-empty paint cans. I suppose if there'd been any equipment left, it would've been "borrowed" years before. I was pleased to find the old wooden swing pushed back in one corner. It seemed to be firm and stable. Maybe Jerome and I could carry it out to the patio.

I approached the house with excitement and trepidation. I couldn't get in the screen door to the porch, which meant that it was locked from the inside. I made my way around to the kitchen door, unlocking it with the old-fashioned key Mom had left me. The kitchen, never particularly modern even in my youth, was not auspicious. The refrigerator, something out of the forties, had no door, undoubtedly removed for safety reasons. The stove was missing altogether. The sink, looking unbelievably low to my six-foot self, was one of those sinks that were open underneath. Tatters of a long-disintegrated curtain hung around the space below the sink in shreds. The linoleum was vintage 1930s, cracked and curling. I stood in the middle of the room, slowly swiveling my head and blowing out my breath in discouragement.

"This'll have to be gutted completely. I wonder how much that will cost?" I turned the faucet on. Nothing. But it might just be turned off somewhere, I thought. Or prayed—I'm not sure which.

I moved through the swinging door into the front room, which ran the width of the house and served as both dining room and living room. It was a mess, but would only require cleaning. And painting. The floors were wide planked and pegged—scratched up plenty. Most of the furniture had been removed. I wondered if Aunt Thalia had removed it or if intruders had helped themselves.

There were a couple of ratty chairs, looking as if some critters had been helping themselves to nesting materials for years, and a large, square dining table. I was surprised no one had taken this, but my guess was that it was too big to move through any of the doors. Only two of the four benches, which used to sit one on each side, were present. There were a couple of cigarette burns on the tabletop and some carving: "Debbie loves Kenny"—that sort of thing. Nothing that couldn't be sanded off. I ran my hand over the tabletop, remembering all the times I'd eaten at this table, played parcheesi at this table, written letters to my dad at this table. I was grateful it was still here.

The rest of the room was cluttered with paper and beer bottles and unidentifiable pieces of junk. The enormous two-story, rock fireplace on the far end of the room was intact. I looked up at the balcony that overlooked this room, the upstairs bedrooms being situated over the road side of the house. A few of the balusters were broken or missing, but overall, the balustrade looked fairly sturdy.

I opened the French doors leading out to the porch, unlocked the outside door, and let Aggie in—who was beginning to worry about my disappearance. It was gloomy on the porch with all the shutters closed. The eyelets on the ceiling appeared to be substantial. I pulled the shutters up, one by one, attaching them to these eyelets, and light filled the porch. I was delighted to see that the metal cots were still there. There were two on the sunrise side of the porch, where Corky and I slept, and two on the sunset side of the porch, where Magda and Sondra sometimes slept. Mostly they slept inside, where "civilized people always sleep."

I stood looking at those cots with great affection. They were dark green. The summer I was eleven and Corky was twelve, we painted them. The wide front porch narrowed to mere strips wrapping around the sides of the house. In these strips were the cots, with just enough room for us to walk alongside them. Corky and I had placed ours head to head so that we could talk easily to one another.

Often we didn't care so much about talking as we did about listening to the grown-ups, who always sat on the front part of the porch, talking freely as if they thought we went to sleep the minute we got in bed. Well, sometimes we did. But mostly we lay there and whispered to one another, and just as our limbs began to melt into the mattresses, one or the other of the adults might start telling an interesting story that we were never meant to hear and then the two of us were wide awake.

This is how we first heard about the rum running that had occurred along this shore during Prohibition—how many locals had made a tidy sum of money smuggling booze from Canada into this country illegally, and how many thought the Johannsens got their start with this easy money. This was one of our favorite stories. We made up many stories of our own to go with it and never tired of looking—on our grandparents' land but also all over on the point—for the secret smugglers' caves. We would try to get Grandpa to tell us more stories, but he never would.

"You never heard me talking any such nonsense! No sir, warn't me, you heard." He was right, when we thought about it. Other visitors, neighbors who came to sit on the porch with my mother and grandparents, always brought those rum-running stories up. In fact, Grandpa pooh-poohed them or even left the porch.

"But Grandpa," Corky would insist, "you must've been around when that stuff was happening. You must know some-thing about it!"

"Nothin' to know," he'd insist. "Just a lot of fantasy, that's all. Folk wantin' to make things more interestin' than they were."

When we asked Grandma, she'd just laugh and say, "Oh yeah, I reckon there was some activity back in them days. Less'n folks like to remember, I 'spect, but some nonetheless." When we'd press her to tell us some stories, she'd get a little vague and wave a flour-encrusted wooden spoon at us, saying, "I'm busy, kids, you gotta run along. I don't know that stuff anyway. It was men's doings. You ask your grandpa."

But we already knew that would get us nothing. So we'd go and ask the other old-timers. Some would tell us stories, others would put us off. But always—there would be some version of the cave we never found.

We heard other stories, too. About the railroad tracks that'd been laid late one fall, on almost frozen ground, and the locomotive that had been abandoned at the end of those unfinished tracks because of an early blizzard. In the spring, when they went back to retrieve the engine, it was gone! Just disappeared! They figured those tracks had been laid on frozen ground that was really a bog, and when the ground thawed, that engine just sank into the bog! Oh how we loved that story! How much we liked to think about that locomotive sitting at the bottom of a swamp somewhere!

Other stories were less interesting to us but seemed to have endless interest to the grown-ups: whose wife was messing with what delivery person; so-and-so's daughter being sent away to school to her aunt's out East—"As if that fools anyone"—it fooled us, and we never quite dared to ask what that was about, although Corky speculated that it had to do with her getting some dread disease or other, but I insisted that it was something about her "period." A lot of men "couldn't seem to keep their flies closed"—this one really confused us because it seemed so trivial, but we decided that Corky better pay special attention to his fly. I laughed aloud, thinking about this, and somehow doubted that Corky was paying all that much attention to his fly anymore.

Another story we never tired of hearing was the one about Grace Kelly's mom having grown up in the hills above the lake. There was a lake named after her: Lake Christine. She got sent to high school in Pennsylvania—probably with an aunt but hopefully not for the above-mentioned reasons—

where she eventually got married and had a baby girl she named Grace. It had not been so many years before we heard these stories that Grace had had her own storybook wedding with the Prince of Monaco. We thought it was pretty cool to know people who knew Christine, Grace Kelly's mom, when she was a little girl.

I pulled myself out of my reverie and reached over and shook each of the cots, then walked to the other end of the porch and shook the cots there, too. All were sturdy and the springs appeared to be fine, but they needed mattresses. In addition to the cots, I was pleased to see that one of the benches from the dining table was there. Then I shuffled back through the living room to the two bedrooms and bath on the back of the house. Whenever I moved my feet, a cloud of dirt rose around me. Both Aggie and I were coughing.

The smaller bedroom had been Grandma's sewing room and Grandpa's office. Grandpa's enormous desk, too big to get through any of the doors, was still in the office. I wondered how it had gotten in there in the first place and finally decided they must've ordered it from someplace like Sears, and it had come in pieces, to be assembled. I opened drawers and was surprised to find some papers still in them. I looked out the back window, which overlooked Stony River Bay and the woods on the other side of the bay. If I move Grandpa's desk under this window, I thought, it'd be a fine place to set up my laptop and work.

The fourth bench for the dining room table was in the larger bedroom, which had been Grandma and Grandpa's. Nothing else but stacks of newspapers, old cloths, and more beer cans was in this room. I dragged the bench out to the table. I'd forgotten how heavy these large, solid-wood benches were. The other one on the porch I left there, so I'd have something to sit on.

The bathroom had been updated in the '50s—I remember how "modern" we thought it was—and it looked serviceable still, once cleaned.

The railing going up the stairs and across the balcony was not as substantial as I had thought. It clearly needed to be replaced, for safety's sake. There were three bedrooms and another bathroom upstairs. Here my mother and Aunt Thalia had each had a room; those two rooms were empty now, except for more trash. And the third one—a long, narrow room—still had its original two sets of bunk beds in it, minus mattresses. These had been intended for us kids, but only Sondra and Magda ever slept in them. And sometimes snooty friends of theirs. No matter what the weather, Corky and I always slept on the porch.

I had just gone to my car to get paper and pencil so I could start making lists when another old truck, not as old as Lyle's, drove in. This must be Jerome, I thought.

9

The next weeks were filled with a physical busyness that sent me to bed early and exhausted every night. It felt wonderful to be that bone tired. I think it was the best antidote to grief that I could have chosen. Jerome and I managed, that first day, to lug the large swing out to the stone patio by the cliff's edge. It was not only heavy but awkward, and it made a satisfying thwonk! when Jerome and I nearly dropped it on the patio, we were so relieved to get it out of our hands.

We were scrubbing and scouring and tearing out. A lot of it I did alone because Jerome and his wife, Gertie, could only work on my house when they didn't have other work lined up. Jerome and I decided to gut the kitchen ourselves; it would cut down on the costs. He found me a plumber and assured me that he could do most of the other work. We decided on pre-made birch cabinets that we'd paint white and Formica counters. I also ordered a modest stove and refrigerator, neither of which had a modest price, and a kitchen sink. When we started to rip up the old linoleum, we discovered a narrow-slatted, tongue-and-groove wood floor underneath.

I was ecstatic. "This is great, Jerome! We'll just finish this instead of putting any other flooring down."

He looked doubtful. "You want a wood floor in your kitchen?"

"Oh yeah! It's gorgeous," I was brushing my hand across the floor, feeling a bubble of excitement for how beautiful this kitchen was going to be.

"This here linoleum," Jerome was saying in his naturally dour style, "was glued down, Tyler. It's going to be a mighty headache getting it all off the floor."

"Well," I responded cheerfully, "we'd have to sand that off anyway, to make it smooth for a new floor. We'll just sand, then seal it with polyurethane or some such thing that'll make it easier to clean. It'll be gorgeous, Jerome."

He was still looking doubtful. "I guess," was the most enthusiasm I could get out of him.

I cleaned the little office first and moved the desk, with Jerome's help, under the window. I would have to get a chair, but in the meantime, Jerome and I carried one of the benches into that room. I set my laptop on the desk and decided it was going to be a splendid place to work. Most of my energy was being consumed by the house, but—sooner or later—I'd be ready to write again.

In the meantime, I put out my portable calculator and worked over my finances. How much could I swing now, and how soon might my mother's houses in Berkeley sell? Both houses had minimal mortgages left on them, so I was going to realize quite a lot of cash. Probably more than half a million. Spending my savings didn't feel too dangerous, but I didn't want to be stupid and spend all of it on a house I was just going to sell. I *was* going to sell this place, wasn't I? How much did I actually want to sink into it? Then, I asked myself, why are you fixing this place up at all? You aren't going to move here. You could just sell it as is. But it didn't matter that I didn't have an answer for that question. In fact, it was clear to me that I resented the question. My compulsion to fix the place up had taken on a life of its own, and—for inscrutable reasons—it seemed essential to honor this impulse of mine.

As soon as I had a phone installed, I called Mary Sharon in California. "Passed the Bar yet?" I started the conversation with no preamble. Mary Sharon had just finished law school and was spending her summer studying for the Bar.

"Hah, hah," she responded. "I'll probably never pass, Tyler. This is too hard, and my brain is fried after three years of this grind."

Mary Sharon always undercut her abilities. "Mary Sharon, you're going to pass. I know it."

"You don't know it, Tyler. You can't know that. Lots of people don't pass on their first try. Or second or third, even."

"Yeah, but you're not lots of people, Mary Sharon. Some people—they're just destined for success. You know what I mean? And you're one of them."

"You're crazy, you know that? How are you?"

"I'm fine. Absolutely and thoroughly exhausted, but fine. I'm tearing apart an old house and scrubbing and scouring every inch of it. It consumes my waking hours and knocks me out at night. It's terrific!"

After a pause, Mary Sharon—thinking she knows me oh-so-well—said, "Tyler. Is this how you're avoiding your feelings? What do you think?"

"I know what you mean, Mary Sharon, but I don't think so. I think it's how I'm *living* my feelings. I don't know if I can explain this . . . But I feel closer to Mom here than any-where, and somehow, reclaiming this house is some kind of tribute to her. Does this make any sense at all?"

"Maybe," she acceded.

"Anyway, I don't think I'm avoiding my feelings. I think—in a very odd way—I'm wallowing in them. And—speaking of feelings—I'm in love."

"Sure," Mary Sharon casually responded. "I'll bet."

"Cynic."

"No, Tyler, I'm not a cynic. I just know you. Remember me? I'm the one who believes in love. Now you . . ." she stopped and changed direction. "Who's the lucky woman?"

"My cousin, Sonny. She's nothing like she was as a kid. She's great! A radical feminist doing activist work. Funny. Smart."

"Lesbian?"

"Well, no. Not exactly."

"Not exactly? Is that like being a little pregnant?"

"Well, not at all, I guess."

"Hmpph. That's it then, isn't it? Easy to be in love with a straight woman. Safe."

"Yup," I cheerfully agreed. "Especially when she's got six kids."

"Six? You better be glad she's straight. 'Yup?' You've been in Minnesota too long already, Tyler. You're starting to sound like one."

"You bet," I agreed, making Mary Sharon laugh. "What can I do, Mary Sharon? I'm a linguistic slut. Anyway, don't forget, Minnesotan is my mother tongue."

"You sound very much at home, Tyler."

"I feel very much at home. That's the truth."

"I miss you."

"I miss you, too. Truly, as soon as you're done with that stupid old Bar, you and Celia are on your way here, right?" Celia was the new love of Mary Sharon's life.

"Yup. We plan to be on the road August eighth. Of course, we're gonna go see my mom first . . ." I felt that familiar old lump in my throat. She *has* a mom to go see. ". . . so we'll probably get up there about the middle of August."

"Great timing, Mary Sharon. Everything should be done by then. Talk about going to extremes to get out of doing any work."

"Sounds good to me."

We talked some more—mostly catching up on California news. I was sitting on the porch, leaning against the wall, looking out at that great expanse of water that so made me feel like I was on an ocean. I'd found, in the past few days, that I could always quit whatever else I was doing and just gaze at the lake: at the constantly changing shades of color, at the endless motion skipping to the horizon, at the murky horizon itself—the evanescent line between water and sky, at the crashing waves, transforming the many shades of gray and blue of the lake into frothy white. I let the mesmerizing sight of the lake and the steady hum of Mary Sharon's voice (going on about the women at WINK, a domestic abuse agency where we both worked part-time; the latest gossip about who was getting together and who was coming apart; the strain her relationship with Celia was having because of her absorption with her studies) lull me. I came a little out of my trancelike state when Mary Sharon started listing my messages, and I realized I needed to write them down.

"Just a minute, Mary Sharon, I need to get something to write with. And on." The spell was broken as I walked, cordless phone in hand, back to my office.

I also found time, that first week, to go to an AA meeting. Back home in California, I didn't go to meetings all the time anymore. I went as I felt I needed them. That seemed to suit me. I had problems with the twelve-step approach, but I also had more problems with drinking. It had been hard for me to come to terms with that and even harder to acknowledge that

I didn't seem to be able to stay sober on my own. So, the "program" and I had worked out a compromise of sorts: I truly did "take what I need and leave the rest." And I'd learned to be grateful for the existence of this organization.

The meeting in Grand Marais was like all the meetings I'd ever been to in some ways and not like any meeting I'd been to—which, also, was like all the meetings I'd been to. Since Mom had died, I'd stepped up the amount of times I attended meetings. Some times in a drunk's life are worse than others.

After cleaning the office, my next main project was the porch. I borrowed Jerome's truck and went to Grand Marais to get needed supplies—only the first of many such trips: broom, dustpan, mop, buckets, brushes, scouring pads, hoses, detergent, cleaning fluids and powders, rubber gloves, a push mower, trimmers, rakes, a ladder, etc. The water had, indeed, just been shut off. Jerome turned it on again.

I took a hose to the screens in the porch and, consequently, to the whole porch. Then I scoured the screens with Brillo pads, again hosing them down to rinse them. The rest of the porch got scrubbed with brushes—ceiling, walls, and floor. And the windows opening into the living/dining room all got washed, inside and out. I dragged the metal cots outside and hosed and scrubbed them, too. A few flakes of paint came off, but the cots were just fine. The porch itself, I decided, had to be painted.

While Jerome built a new platform for the lift and then greased and oiled the tracks and checked all the mechanisms until the thing was working good as new, I mowed the lawn. I couldn't watch him crawling up and down that steep cliff face and the tracks that were pressed against it.

When Jerome assured me the lift was working and safe again, I coaxed Aggie onto it with me, and we rode down to the rocks below. It was about twenty-five sheer feet of craggy cliff from the top to the bottom. Aggie was very relieved to be out of that strange metal box and immediately began chasing seagulls. I understood her relief; my own hands had gotten clammy during the ride down. Something, I thought, that never happened when I was a kid! I walked out to the end of the rocky point lying at the foot of our cliff, found a reasonably comfortable ledge, and sat staring out to sea, letting the ebb and flow of the water cradle me, letting my mind drift like a paddleless canoe in this grand stretch of water and sky.

While Jerome started pulling the cupboards out of the kitchen, I scraped and sanded and cleaned the porch again, then painted it. I decided to paint it the same colors as I would be painting the outside of the house: ceiling and floor a dark green and walls a soft grey. It was terrific—both Jerome and Gertie thought so, and Charley agreed when I convinced him to come over and see it. I felt a sense of accomplishment I hadn't imagined.

Gertie began cleaning the upstairs rooms while Jerome finished getting all the cupboards out of the kitchen, and he and I scraped and sanded the floors. When neither Jerome nor Gertie could come because of other work, I borrowed Charley's pickup, left Aggie happily with him, and drove the hundred miles to Duluth to go shopping. I bought four undersized mattresses for the cots, two of which we wrestled into the back of the pickup, so that I would have them right away. I was getting excited to sleep on the porch again. The other two were being delivered with the mattresses I ordered for the bunk beds. Figuring I might as well go hog-wild (was this Minnesota-think?), I ordered two navy-and-gray-striped rockers to flank the fireplace and a couch in a dark navy corduroy.

Then I went to Target on the biggest spree I'd ever been on in my life. I filled cart after cart with sheets and pillows and quilts and rugs, wall lamps for beds, pots, pans, towels, washcloths, miscellaneous kitchen supplies, glasses, two wooden rocking chairs for the porch, bathroom supplies, a desk chair for Grandpa's desk—everything I could think of to make living in the house possible. I looked seriously at a compact stereo set but decided that was going too far. The music of the wind in the cedars and the waves was enough for now. My Visa's limits had never been stretched so far.

I drove back to Stony River with a happy smile on my face, wondering if I'd be broke by the time my mother's houses in Berkeley sold.

10

I began each morning—after my routine of outhouse, bath in the lake, and breakfast—walking the point road with Aggie. It wasn't that I felt I needed additional exercise, what with all I was doing at the house. Aggie needed to be able to count on our ritual of walking together every morning that began when she was a puppy. It was a pleasant two miles out to the end of the point and back to Chummy's, where—weather permitting—I would sit with Charley on the bench out front of his store, watching the sunlight shimmy across the lake as I pumped him for information.

Some days, Piggy and Nancy McDermott would be out walking at the same time and would persuade me to stop at their house for a cup of coffee. The old cabin on their property, they informed me, had been knocked down in the '80s, and they'd built their ultramodern house in its place, high on the cliffs like mine. The outside was modest, almost ordinary, but the inside was fabulous with floor-to-ceiling glass on the lake side that wrapped around corners with no frames, just all glass, and furniture that was both comfortable and contemporary, properly arranged to accommodate the incredible views.

They both chattered incessantly, but not odiously. I enjoyed them but was sorry they had not been in the area for more than ten years. They would have made excellent sources for old stories, if they'd just been around longer. As it was, they told me everything they'd ever heard about anyone in the Stony River area.

"'Course we never knew your grandparents," Piggy informed me. "They were dead before we ever moved here. But we've heard about them over the years."

"Oh yes," Nancy would interject. "We've heard all about what a great cook Alma was and how Holger worked all those years at the taconite plant, fixing those big machines. How he was pretty quiet and withdrawn while she was cheerful and outgoing." That's certainly how I remembered them.

"And we heard there were some problems at the end, too," Piggy added.

"Problems?" I asked, almost too eagerly.

"Well, but—" Piggy hesitated. "Maybe if you don't know, we're just talking out of turn."

"No, I don't think so. I knew there were some problems. I'm just interested in what you heard."

"It was, after all," Nancy said, "ten or fifteen years before we moved here. But, apparently he drank pretty heavily at the end."

"And then she went and gave the house to her daughter—your mother, I guess?" It was more of a question than a statement, so I nodded. "Anyway, that caused folk to buzz quite a lot. Just not the usual, you know, not leaving your property to your spouse."

"Did you ever hear anything about Alma's sister? Louisa?" I asked.

They looked at each other, then shook their heads. "Can't say I ever did hear anything about any sisters," Piggy said, and the conversation drifted in other directions.

Other days, I bumped into Lyle, who walked the road each morning with a gnarled walking stick and an equally gnarled, obviously ancient, black lab by name of Fred. The dog walked steadily but slowly by Lyle's side. At first, Aggie tried to engage old Fred in a little play, but Fred just ignored her. All of his energy seeming to be consumed by the mere process of putting one foot in front of the other. After our first encounter, Aggie would greet Fred respectfully by touching noses, then leave him alone.

"How old is Fred?" I asked.

"Well now, let me see," Lyle pondered. "Must be 'bout seventeen now."

"Pretty old."

"Yep," Lyle agreed. "His arthritis is worser than mine, but he can't stand to give up our walks."

Otherwise, Lyle was pretty taciturn, not seeming to mind my presence but not very interested in talking. Most conversations I broached with him seemed to end abruptly.

"Did you know my grandmother's sister, Louisa?"

"Never knew no Louisa."

"But you grew up in this area with my grandparents. Surely you knew there were two sisters in the Anderson family."

"Your grandparents were much older than me."

"But you knew my mom and her sister, Thalia."

"Yup."

"What do you know about the rum running done here during Prohibition?"

"Nothin'."

"But didn't you ever hear any stories, Lyle?"

"Nope."

He was more helpful, during our walks, about who lived on the point now. "Here, next to our place," he'd say, "is them Whites. Got a coupla kids, three maybe, mostly only come up for skiing. Except for the Fourth of July." There'd be several minutes of silent walking until we reached the next house. "Then this place? That's the Grangers. You met them yet?"

"No. Are they here year-round?"

"No. They go to Florida for a few months each winter. Otherwise, they're here." More silence until the next house. "And you know Piggy and Nancy, don't you?"

I'd agree. The Cedars was next, and then I asked, "How about the other side of me? Down in that hollow? Who lives there?"

"Coupla sisters. Retired."

"What are their names?"

"Hank and Ellie."

"How come I never see them?"

He shrugged. "Dunno."

"And this last house?" I'd ask, as we neared the land side of the point.

"Branches. Been there for years."

"Branches? They were summer folks when I was a kid up here. They're still coming in the summer?"

"Kids now. Grown kids with kids of their own."

If I asked Lyle more questions about the people who lived on the point, he didn't have much to say. Either Charley or Nancy and Piggy were agreeable to filling me in on further details, so I didn't try to press Lyle.

"Oh," Nancy said, when I asked them about my neighbors, "Hank and Ellie have been gone for a couple of weeks. Left right before you came, I think."

"Are they locals?"

"No," Piggy jumped in. "From Duluth area, I think. Spent summers up here as kids, then bought that place when they retired."

"Not true in Hank's case," Nancy contradicted gently. "She didn't retire. She was an engineer or something. Had a bad accident and is in a wheelchair now. Never able to work again. Ellie was a schoolteacher. She did retire. You'll like them, Tyler. They're loves."

"Oh yeah," Piggy agreed. "They're a hoot. Great storytellers. Very opinionated but equally likeable."

"Do they live here year-round now?"

"Oh yeah, when they aren't off visiting friends or family or something."

"I look forward to meeting them. How about the Grangers?"

"Now, there's an interesting couple," Piggy started. "Allen and Melanie. They built that place about five years after we did, isn't that right, Hon?"

Nancy nodded agreement. "Yup." She leaned forward conspiratorially. "He's only in his forties but retired already. He sold his business—some kind of trucking affair—to some big national conglomerate. But folks say it was the Mafia."

I looked skeptical. "Why would people say that?"

"You tell her what Ed Olesen says, Piggy."

"Ed Olesen was the contractor for his house. He insists there's an interior room in the lower level, no windows, bulletproof. Plus a walk-in safe and a couple of other hidey-hole places."

My eyebrows went up. "Very colorful." It made me want to laugh. "So, they're not from around here?"

"Yes and no," was Piggy's answer. "Melanie wasn't and Allen wasn't either, but he's got roots up in these parts. His family lived in this area at the turn of the century. Apparently, his grandfather moved to the Cities in the thirties, his father was born down there, and so was he."

"Mmm," I responded thoughtfully. "He might have heard some stories over the years."

"That's so," agreed Nancy. "Now you know, Tyler, we–all of us on the point–get together here for our Fourth of July celebration. You, of course, are invited to join us this year. It's very nice. Everyone brings food, and Piggy cooks a pig. In a pit, mind you! And we have hamburgers and hot dogs on the grill. We sing songs and catch up with one another. Why, Burt and Laverne even come all the way from Washington, D.C. They say they'd never miss it! Isn't that so, Piggy."

"Yup. That's so. When it finally gets dark, we all hunker down along the cliff's edge and watch the fireworks display from Grand Marais. It's quite special."

"It is indeed," Nancy said, almost dreamily. "Anyway, you'll have the opportunity, then, to meet everyone."

"It sounds wonderful," I responded. "Thanks for including me."

"Oh, don't be silly, Tyler. Of course, you're included. You're one of us now."

I both liked those words–"one of us"–and wondered about them. Was I one of them? Or was I really a Californian spying on them? I felt like I had a split personality.

Charley laughed when I told him the story about the Grangers. "Oh yeah, that's the favorite story these days."

"Any truth to it?"

"Who knows? No one has ever seen this bulletproof room, except Ed, not even the rest of his crew. Maybe it exists and maybe there's a perfectly acceptable reason for it. Who knows? The Grangers are nice but stick pretty much to themselves, so no one quite has the balls—or guts, I guess—to ask them right out if it's true. But folks don't want to know the truth necessarily. They like the Mafia story better; it's interesting."

"But Allen's family goes way back up here, right?"

"Yeah. Gramps knew his grandfather before he moved to the Cities. They didn't live on the point, just on the other side of the highway, actually. And they used to come visit when I was a kid. Like summer people."

"He might've heard some stories from his grandfather's youth then."

"Maybe. And Tyler? You're going to love those Anson sisters."

"Anson sisters?"

"Hank and Ellie. Live right next door to you. They're such characters. Just you wait."

"Piggy and Nancy told me they were from down around Duluth, right?"

"Yup," he agreed. "You know the type. Old maid schoolteachers."

A lot of the summer people, over the years, had been unmarried schoolteachers, women who had their entire summers off to spend up here and who had no families so had enough disposable income to buy a second home. "We don't call them 'old maids' anymore, Charley."

He raised his eyebrows. "Who's 'we'?"

I nudged him with my elbow. "Enlightened folks like you and me." He grinned, clearly liking it. "And the Branches still own the first cabin?"

"Sally owns it, I guess. Remember her grandma?"

"We all thought she was a witch?" Charley nodded. I guess all kids have a need for a "witch" in their lives. Corky and I used to make up some of our best stories about her, but how did we know, as children, that a "witch" was "bad"? The same

79

way we knew black was bad and white was good, I guess. Language development—fascinating and terrifying. "What I remember most about her was that she had white hair that stood out at odd angles from her head and thick, black eyebrows that beetled down over her eyes when she caught us cutting through her property or passing by on the rocks out in front of her place. Like she owned the world or something."

We both smiled with our shared memories. "Well," Charley said, "she's gone now. Dead, I guess. And her granddaughter, Sally, remember Sally?"

"Scrawny little kid, big glasses, pigtails?"

"That would be her. She either owns the place now or she's the only one that uses it. Remember she had a couple of brothers?"

"Yeah. Hellions. Even Corky and I thought they were a little too brazen."

Charley chuckled. "Well, they don't come up. But Sally comes up, all summer, with her kids. And she's not scrawny anymore. She's absolutely gorgeous. Filled out nicely—oh," he interjected. "I suppose that's sexist?"

"Pretty much," I agreed.

"Well. Anyway, she don't look like she did as a kid. She's a real looker. Suppose she wears them contacts, 'cause she doesn't wear glasses anymore. And she does something impressive. A psychiatrist, I think. Married to a lawyer. But we never see him much."

"Charley, your grandpa talk about the rum-running days?"

He shook his head, kind of frowning. "He was always kind of closed-mouthed about that. I never could get him to talk much about it."

"Grandpa was like that, too. Do you remember anything?"

"Just the stuff most everybody knows. It happened. He never did any of it, he said, but I never did find me one guy who'd own that he was a part of it. Someone must have done

it, but no one ever said they did. Isn't that peculiar?" I nodded. Charley scratched his chin, a gesture his grandpa always
did. It made me feel like I was straddling time zones. "Except
everyone pretty much agreed that the Johannsens did it, got
their first pile of dough that way."

After a moment's silence, I asked, "Who else could I talk
to this about? Who else is still alive?"

"Vera Johannsen is still alive. She'd be—I don't know—
about ninety, I guess. She lives in one of them caretaking
homes in Grand Marais. And Ole. You know, the old postmaster? Bjorn Olesen? He's still alive, definitely in his nineties.
He's in the nursing home in Silver Bay."

"Olesen?" I asked. "Any relation to this Olesen
contractor?"

"Sure. Ed is Ole's nephew."

"How old was your grandpa when he died?"

"Ninety-two. Just turned ninety-two a month before he
died."

"So he was really in the same generation as my grandparents, Alma and Holger?" I paused. "They just died a lot
younger than he did."

"When did they die, Tyler?"

"In the sixties. I was fourteen when Grandma died in '67.
And Grandpa died in '70."

"I was in the Navy by then, so I probably wasn't here
when they died."

"Charley, did your grandpa ever talk about Alma having a
sister? A sister named Louisa?"

He rubbed his chin again, then answered slowly, "Maybe.
He told a lot of stories about who was in love with who and
changing partners and running off with others, you know—the
stuff that endlessly fascinated grown-ups but bored us kids?" I
nodded and smiled, thinking of me and Corky on the porch.
"By the time I was old enough to be interested in those kind of
stories, I didn't know any of the people he was talking about,

so I still found them pretty boring. But," he stopped again, rubbed his chin enough that Aggie came and nudged him, believing that hand should be rubbing her chin, not his. "I remember something about a girl—a woman—" he amended, with a quick grin in my direction, "in that family who was, Gramps said, 'ravishingly beautiful.' I'm pretty sure this wasn't Alma. The reason I know it was one of your family, though, is that when I was mooning after Magda—back when we were in our teens?"

I nodded, feeling a little sadness that I couldn't tell Magda he was mooning over her when she was mooning over him and thought he didn't even notice her. I was pretty sure she wouldn't be interesed in hearing from me these days. Not that she ever had been—even before Mom died.

"Gramps once said something about how Magda 'sure was a looker, just like her great-aunt.' I can't remember her name but I do remember asking 'what great-aunt?' and he just said somethin' about her being long gone."

I leaned back against the store walls, squinted my eyes against the brilliant morning light on the lake, and sighed. Charley petted Aggie, leaving me to my thoughts. Then I told Charley the stories both Thalia and Sonny had told me about Alma's sister and the revelation about Thalia's mother.

"This Louisa must've been the one Gramps talked about being such a beauty," Charley posited.

I nodded. "Makes sense, doesn't it? I was just thinking . . ."

When I didn't finish after a few seconds, Charley pushed me a little. "What?"

"Oh, it's just speculation or fantasy at this point. But what if Louisa was Thalia's real mother? And Holger and Louisa had had an affair or something, then she died when she had the baby, and he eventually married her sister to raise that baby?"

Charley shrugged. "Possible, I guess. Intriguing, isn't it?" I nodded my agreement, silently turning over possibilities.

"The problem with that, though, is that it doesn't explain Grandma not leaving the house to Thalia . . . Oh, I don't know!"

11

Within a couple of weeks, I settled into enough of a routine that, when neither Gertie nor Jerome were able to come work with me, I sat down at my computer and wrote. I got a couple of columns done and sent them off to my paper in San Francisco. I tried to write a column about my mother dying, mothers in general dying, but I just ended up choking on sobs that were beginning to feel dusty in my mouth. I tried to work on the novel I'd begun, but that wasn't working so well. I just didn't seem to be getting into it. Mostly I just stared at a blank computer screen.

One day I played hooky and went into Grand Marais to the Cook County Courthouse. I was directed to the Court Administrator's Office. One of the deputy administrators had to look up the records in a large book, where everything was handwritten. I thought the book was beautiful and wanted to put my own hands on it, but Karen—the deputy administrator—insisted that wasn't allowed. And there it was: *Born, July 22, 1899, Alma Marie Anderson;* and *Born, March 3, 1904, Louisa Jane Anderson.* Alma's death was listed, but there was nothing for Louisa. When I asked Karen about it, she shrugged.

"Could be she's not dead yet. Or—more likely—that she died somewhere else. It's only in our records if it occurs in our county, or it's reported to us. If it occurred in more recent months anywhere in Minnesota, it would probably have been reported to us by the State. But . . ." she scrutinized the book again, before saying, "Let me check the main index." After a few minutes of perusal, she shook her head. "Nope. Nothing. If she's dead, we never found out about it."

Then I had her check Thalia's birth, and there she was: Thalia Mae Schmidt, born April 3, 1924, to Holger and Barb Schmidt, nee Larson. I was writing everything down. Karen checked further for me and discovered that they'd been married in 1923, and Barb died in 1924 on April 5. Two days after Thalia's birth. Well. So much for my theory about Louisa maybe being Thalia's mother. The marriage records were listed by the man's name only. I made a face at this, and Karen nodded her head, making a corresponding face.

But when I had her check on Louise Alma Schmidt (years later, my mother changed her last name to D'Alma, but that wouldn't show up in these records), she couldn't find a record of my mother's birth. She was not listed as being born in this county.

"What does that mean, Karen? I know she was born here."

She was very patient. "There's several possibilities. One: you have the wrong year. Two: the birth didn't take place in Cook County, even if the family lived here. Maybe there were complications, and they went to Duluth. There was no hospital in the county in 1926, you know. Well, old Doc Hicks had a small hospital of sorts, but most women still had their babies at home. Which leads us to Three: the parents may have never registered for a birth certificate. If that happened—and it did plenty—there'd be no record."

"But wouldn't that have to be rectified at some point? I mean, what if there was a need for a birth certificate?" I thought of all my mother's trips to Central America and knew she had a passport. "What would someone do if they needed, for instance, a passport?"

"Well, sometimes a birth certificate has to be made up after the fact when an adult needs it. They then have to fill out an 'Altered Birth Certificate Affidavit.' Let me check the index to see if such an affidavit was ever filed."

And there it was. 1958. I was five. What happened that year? Oh yes, my parents went to Europe to celebrate their tenth anniversary. Mom would have needed a passport, I suppose for the first time.

So a birth certificate was issued in 1958 to my mother, stating that she'd been born on May 12, 1927. Both her parents—Alma and Holger Schmidt—were still alive and so were able to sign the affidavit to this effect.

"Wait a minute," I interrupted Karen as she was reading this information to me while I wrote it all down. "1927? My mother was born in 1926."

Karen shook her head. "No, it says 1927 here."

It was my turn to shake my head. "How odd." My mother always said she'd been born in 1926. Was this a mistake, this 1927 birth certificate? Or had my mother been mistaken? I counted back and thought—but if she were wrong, why did she celebrate her birthday every year as if she'd been born in '26? I've heard of women shaving a year or two off, but I've never heard of one adding a year. Especially in Mother's generation.

I had Karen check for Alma and Holger's marriage license—under his name, of course, as if Alma herself didn't actually exist. She unearthed the fact that Holger and Alma Schmidt got married on September 14, 1926. Huh. If Mom was indeed born in 1927, the arithmetic worked out just fine: ten months later a child arrived. But if Mom had been born in '26, then she was four months old when her parents got married. So, I wondered, did they alter the birth year in 1958 because they were embarrassed that she had been born "out-of-wedlock"? Was Holger even my mother's father? That might explain it. Thalia wasn't Alma's child and, if Louise was not Holger's child, might Grandma have cut both Holger and Thalia out of the will, in order to keep the house in the family? This got curiouser and curiouser.

I thanked Karen for all her help. I was getting confused by all these dates, so I sat on the courthouse steps and made a list (Mary Sharon, the Queen of Lists, would have been proud of me).

1899	Alma born
1904	Louisa born (no records after this birth regarding Louisa)
1923	Holger marries someone named Barb
1924	Thalia is born, Barb dies two days later
1926	Louise born, May 12
1926	Alma marries Holger, September OR
1927	Louise born, May 12
1958	Louise has birth certificate made up with her parents' agreement, saying she'd been born in 1927, but she always said she'd been born in 1926
1967	Alma dies, leaving her parents' house to Louise but not Thalia
1970	Holger dies

I stopped and stared at the sky for a minute. What did I know?

1. There was a Louisa.

I'd have to see what else I could find out about her. I jotted down: newspaper office; church records; go see Vera Johannsen and Ole.

2. There's some discrepancy about Mother's birth.

I couldn't help but voice it, at least in mind: was my mother "illegitimate"? Although it would've undoubtedly been embarrassing for Alma, would it have embarrassed my mother? Why didn't she tell me? Was Holger her father?

The newspaper offices weren't far away. I asked a pleasant, middle-aged woman about archives. She directed me back to the library, where, she assured me, all the old newspapers were on microfilm.

The librarians were wonderfully helpful, and I settled down to work with the newspapers on microfilm and a couple of books and periodicals that gave me detailed information about Cook County in the early part of the century. They also informed me that the Cook County Historical Society had no storage room in its location, so all storage was at the library. They then brought me the card catalogs for the first thirty-five years of the century for the Historical Society.

I didn't really know what I was looking for, so I just started by skimming the newspapers for the whole decade of the 1920s. The only mention of Alma and Holger was their wedding in 1926. It was fascinating reading, but I found little to aid me. Then I went through three card files of Historical Society archives and jotted down any material or sources that might give me more information. By then, it was getting late, and I knew this was going to take more than one trip. I skimmed the books and periodicals that the librarians had provided me. By the time I had done all this, I knew I wanted to learn even more about this area. But none of it was helping me directly in finding out new information about Louisa and my other relatives.

I made one more stop, at the Lutheran Church that my grandmother always attended. I hoped they might have some records concerning my family members. The minister was in his office and informed me that they had records going back to the beginning of the church, some eighty to eighty-five years earlier. I did mental calculations: probably started between 1907 and 1912.

"What kinds of records do you have?"

"Births, deaths, when they joined the church, if they left, baptisms, confirmations, marriages. That's about it."

"Mmm-hmm," I responded. "Can I see these records?"

"No, we don't let anyone handle them. If you want to know something specific, we'll track it down for you."

"Okay. I'd like to know what you've got, if anything, on Alma Marie Anderson, later Alma Schmidt. She probably attended here as a child and got married here. I know she had her funeral here, in 1967."

"A little before my time," he smiled.

I would think that it would be hard to have a "spiritual mentor" be so much younger than you. I smiled back. "I could've guessed that. And I also want to know what you have, if anything, on Louisa Jane Anderson. Alma was born in 1899 and Louisa in 1904, so maybe before the church was actually in existence. But there might be some records later. And then, anything you have on Louise Schmidt and Thalia Schmidt. I would guess both of them grew up in this church."

"I'll see what we can come up with," this young minister agreed. "Leave me your name and number, and I'll let you know."

"Sure," I agreed and wrote down both on a piece of paper he handed to me.

"If I might inquire," he began diffidently, "why do you want this information?"

I smiled again. "I'm not really sure. These women are my grandmother and great-aunt. My mother died recently and . . ." I hesitated, and he jumped right in.

"I understand," he glanced at the paper I handed back to him, "Miss Jones. It's quite common, you know, that people start searching for their roots when they lose a parent. I wish you luck. We'll do whatever we can to help."

I smiled noncommittally and said, "Thanks. I appreciate it."

I finally headed for home, looking forward to a day of physical labor after having spent most of the day bent over books and computers, poring over words. I was startled by that thought; after all, bending over books and computers and words is my life!

I took Charley to dinner that night, to pay him back for all his help. He closed the store at seven, earlier than usual, and we drove up the Shore to Naniboujou. This resort had been built in the '20s as a private club for sportsmen from all over the country. Supposedly, some famous men were members. The only one I remembered was Babe Ruth. The Depression had closed the place down, and later it had been bought privately, refurbished, and opened again as a hotel and restaurant. I had not been there for nearly thirty years. The walls and ceiling in the towering, two-story dining room were painted in the wild and vivid colors and designs of the Cree Indians. The massive, two-story rock fireplace was famous for its rocky star-burst halfway to the elevated ceiling. I had been awestruck by this room's grandeur and romance as a child and felt no less dazzled by it now.

Our talk ranged easily from our childhoods to adulthoods and back again. He told me, in two or three terse sentences, that Viet Nam was a nightmare and totally off limits for conversation. I did, more or less, the same thing when he inquired about my love life while I tried not to shovel in the delicious food—a chicken, vegetable, cashew stir-fry served on basmati rice.

He cleared his throat a little nervously after I'd dismissed the subject of my relationships and said, "It's just that I, uh, wanted you to know, Tyler . . . I mean, I didn't want to lead you on or anything . . ."

He was so clearly floundering that I took pity on him. "Charley, it's okay. I'm not interested in you. Not that way, anyway. You're a swell fella, and I hope we can be friends but . . ." I hesitated slightly here, ". . . you're really not the right sex for me."

"What?" His fork, full of lemon mashed potatoes, stopped midair on the way to his mouth as he stared at me with the startled look of a deer caught in the headlights of a car. "You mean . . ."

He paused long enough that I finished his sentence. "Yup. I'm a lesbian." I continued eating, watching him intently.

"Oh," he said vaguely, completing the action he'd arrested and chewing unusually thoroughly, I thought. When he was ready to fill his mouth again, he said, "I don't know what to say. I mean, part of me wants to say—oh well, that's okay—but that's not right, is it?"

"Not really," I agreed. "It's not as if I'm asking your permission."

He nodded, a little pink creeping up his neck. "Well." He took another bite and chewed thoroughly again. "So what do I say?" he finally asked.

"Well," I said slowly, "that kind of depends on you. If you have a mind, I guess you could say you never want to see me again." He shook his head, frowning, at this suggestion. "But otherwise," I shrugged. "Nothing, Charley. You don't have to say nothing."

"Good," he said around another bite. "I'll choose that one." And we both laughed. "But . . ." he was attending to his thorough chewing again. "Can I ask you a question or two?"

"Sure," I agreed.

"Have you always been?"

He was so serious that I answered equally seriously. "Naw. Not until at least four or five." We both laughed.

"Was that a stupid question, Tyler?"

"No, Charley. There are just no easy answers. I guess I started to suspect, but didn't really know what it meant, when I was in high school. I fell in love, sort of, with one of my best friends, and—luckily for me—she returned it. But I was still not accepting it, seriously. I tried dating guys in college, but it just didn't work. Then I fell in love rather dramatically, and we were together for five years. That was it, then."

"And, are you happy this way?"

"Sometimes I'm happy, sometimes I'm not. Like anybody. But are you asking me if I'm okay about being a lesbian?" He nodded. "Yup. It's just who I am, Charley. I don't question it any more than you question who you are."

"Doesn't it cause you lots of problems?"

"Sometimes. Some people just can't handle it, you know. Like it makes me some kind of pervert or something. I haven't been closeted since I was twenty-four and came out to my family, and I never will be. I figure, if someone has a problem with it, that's their problem. But mostly I just assume people can handle it, and—not always—but mostly they can. Or they live up to my expectations. I don't know which. I've just found that it's easier being 'out' than living a pack of lies."

"I think you're very admirable, Tyler. And courageous. Not everyone would take the risks you take."

"Of course you're right, Charley, not everyone would, but I'm not sure that makes me courageous. I think it takes courage to do something that's really hard for you to do. This is not hard for me. It's just who I am. It's that simple."

Charley grinned and said, "I still think you're courageous."

When I dropped Charley off at the store, he leaned back in the car and said, "You know, you are one fascinating lady, Tyler Jones."

I winced about the word 'lady.' "Thanks, Charley. I have to tell you—I don't think I'm a lady, but that's probably a whole other evening of conversation. But you're not so bad yourself."

12

Whenever I could, in the next few days—while we were scrubbing and sanding the kitchen floor, moving stuff out of the garage before we had the local fire department torch the place to prevent it from falling down and killing someone, sharing the swing while we took lunch breaks—I pumped Jerome for information. He was my mother's generation, so many of the stories he told me were ones he'd heard growing up, much the same as I heard a generation later. He talked slowly, thinking things over before he even opened his mouth, and gave me neat, spare responses to my questions, sometimes laced with his quiet humor.

Like his language, he was a tall, lean man who moved with an economy of gesture. His blue eyes were pale and flat, and yet I discerned a spark of mischief occasionally glinting there. He'd lived here all his life. His wife, Gertie, had moved here when they got married, so her history only extended back to the '40s. I concentrated most of my efforts on Jerome.

"Did you know my mom?"

"Sure."

Sometimes his brevity was annoying. It was like picking burrs off a flannel shirt: it felt like it was going to take forever. "How'd you know her?"

"Went from kindergarten to graduation together, we did. She was a year older'n me."

"Did you ever date her?"

"Naw."

"How come? Didn't you like her?"

He frowned. "Wasn't that. She was older."

"Was she pretty?"

"Reckon."

"Smart?"

"Yep. Went to college."

I changed tacks. "How about my grandparents? Holger and Alma. Did you know them?"

"Yep."

"How'd you know them? Just because they were Weezie's folks?"

"Nope," his eyes glinted. "Everyone knows everyone here. It's a small place." That was true. "And of course my pop and Holger worked together."

"They did?"

"Sure. Early on. They both worked at Johannsen's. At first."

"And then what?"

"My pop opened his own business, doing the odd repair here and there, caretaking for them summer folk, the like. And your grandpop went to work at the plant they opened in Taconite Harbor." That's what I remembered. "He'd become a pretty fair mechanic, so he was their general maintenance man for them big machines they always had running there."

It was a pretty long string of words for Jerome, so I let him rest for a bit. The rhythm of our arms—as we scrubbed, rubbed, sanded, scrubbed, rubbed, sanded the kitchen floor—was hypnotic and soothing. It was like a physical meditation. I forgot about questions for a little while.

But eventually, "So your dad and my grandpa were friends?"

"Yep."

"Did you ever know of my grandma having a sister? Her name was Louisa."

There was a long silence after this question. I didn't break it; just kept working, glancing at Jerome from time to time who also just kept working. Finally he said, "Didn't know her."

"But you knew there was such a person?"

"Yep. But didn't know her. She was gone before I was born."

He'd said he was a year behind my mom in school, so that made sense. "Gone where?"

He shrugged. "Just gone."

"But did she die? Move away? Get married? What?"

He shrugged again and didn't elaborate.

One day, while Jerome was putting in the new cupboards in the kitchen, I cleaned up, dressed nice, and went into town to meet with Vera Johannsen. She was a tiny woman, seeming almost doll-like. Her white hair was sparse and wispy, but her blue eyes were crisp and direct in a face creased with the joy and pain of all her years.

"So you're Alma's granddaughter, mmm?" She did not seem vague at all. "You're one of them California ones, right?"

I smiled and agreed, "Yes. My mother was Louise."

"Mmm," she hummed noncommittally. "And what do you want with me?"

"To find out the truth about my family." I decided to be as honest as I could be.

"Mmmm," she hummed again, rocking slightly as she stared out toward the lake.

"Some coffee?" Frances Hawkins, the woman in whose home Vera was living, bustled about with a tray.

"Yes, yes," Vera agreed. "You run along, Fran. We'll take care of things ourselves." She looked shrewdly at me. "Won't we?"

I was startled. "Oh yes," I agreed. "Thank you."

Vera was waving her out of the room, and I saw a look of disappointment in Frances' eyes. She clearly wanted to visit, too, and Vera—just as clearly—wanted to be alone with me. I felt a ruffle of excitement. Something was going to happen here, I was sure of it.

"Pour the coffee—what's your name again?"

"Tyler," I supplied, pouring coffee and arranging sandwiches on a table next to Vera's elbow.

"Tyler?" she asked. "What kind of name is that?"

I sighed inwardly, not wanting the sidetrack. "My mother believed that Jones was so prosaic that we—my sister and I—needed interesting first names. So she named my sister, Magdalene. She named me after her best friend in college, Tyler. That was her last name, of course."

"Mmm. Odd name for a girl." She sipped some coffee and nibbled a sandwich. "Of course, people are funny about names. Knew a girl once named Fanny? That's not odd, of course, except her last name was Warmer. Can you imagine? Fanny Warmer? What were her parents thinking? And then the Olaf Olafssons and John Johnsons and the like." She looked at me over the top of her glasses. "Eat some food," she commanded.

I was drinking coffee. "Okay," I responded. "Thanks."

I wondered how much she was going to wander and how I could get her back on track, when she said, "You remind me a bit of Alma. She was a big-boned girl, too. Tall like you. Sturdy." Fat, I thought, but didn't say. She probably wouldn't understand that I thought *fat* was a perfectly acceptable word for describing a person's body: tall, short, thin, fat. How come only fat was considered a "bad" word? "But your mother was more like her mother than Alma. Smaller. More delicate."

I was immediately confused and thought she must be, too. "Alma was her mother," I corrected her.

Vera just looked at me for a couple of minutes while she methodically chewed unbelievably tiny bites of sandwich. "You said you wanted the truth, didn't you?" I nodded, afraid to speak and get her off on another tangent. She looked out the window again. "The truth," she repeated. "Very few people really want the truth, you know."

"I do," I said confidently, trying to imagine what kind of truth I wouldn't want.

"Mmm," she hummed again. After a small silence, which I worked hard not to break, Vera said, "Alma was not your mother's mother."

When she didn't continue, I said cautiously, "No? Who was?"

"Mmmm. Louisa was Louise's mother."

My god, I thought, Grandma didn't have any children? Again, cautiously, I said, "Will you tell me about it?"

"Are you sure you want to know?"

I nodded. "Yes, I'm sure. My mother—when she was dying—told me to come home and find the truth. So, here I am."

"Mmmm," it was almost a song. Vera closed her eyes for a few minutes, and I wondered if she'd gone to sleep. She started speaking before she opened her eyes. "Louisa was very pretty and gay. Everyone loved her, but especially the boys. She was a little too high-spirited, some would say. Never ready to settle down. When she was twenty-one, she got pregnant. The father was Holger Schmidt." My eyes grew large, but I didn't interrupt her. "Everyone expected her to get married, but she didn't. Holger, after all, was available. He was a widower, his first wife having died in childbirth a couple of years before. He had the little girl, Thalia—well, mostly his ma had her—and she needed a mother as well as him needing a wife.

"But Louisa was stubborn. And, after she got pregnant, she was uncharacteristically quiet and withdrawn. What she was doing was unheard of back in those days. Oh, girls got pregnant—that's always happened, you know—but they got married right away, and everyone counted months to that first baby, or went away and had the baby somewhere else and gave it up. Louisa just stayed around here, getting bigger and bigger, people talking more and more.

"Then, just before the baby arrived, she told me she couldn't marry Holger because he'd 'forced her.' We didn't use the word *rape,* but that's what she meant. I was her best friend. That's why she told me. I didn't know what to advise her. No one talked of such things. There were no places to go for help or advice."

She was quiet momentarily, rocking and looking out at the lake. I was trying to piece together what all this meant. My grandpa was a rapist? Did Grandma find out, before she died, that her husband had raped her sister and that's why she made certain that not Holger and not one of Holger's family, like Thalia, got the house? This made more sense than anything so far. But how would she find out?

"Then the baby was born. Louisa went away. She never came back. Three months later, Alma married Holger and raised Louise—as well as Thalia—as if they were her own. After a while, people kind of forgot about Louisa." Her lips pressed together in what I could only guess was anger and disapproval. "I didn't forget though."

"Where did Louisa go?" I asked, almost timidly.

Her eyes snapped away from the lake and fastened relent-lessly on me. "They had her locked up somewhere."

"What?" I felt a rising horror within me.

She nodded. "Yes, they put her in one of those places for crazy people."

"Alma did?" I asked, finally almost afraid of the truth.

She shook her head. "No, no. It was Holger. Maybe her parents—who, of course, did think she was crazy for refusing to marry Holger. For getting pregnant in the first place. It wasn't so unusual, you know, in those days to lock girls up for promiscuity."

Actually, I'd read of such things myself. She rocked furi-ously for a few moments, her silence only ruptured by the squeak and crack of the rocking chair. "When Alma was going to marry Holger, I was appalled. I went to her and told her what Louisa had told me, and she told me that she knew all about that. That Holger had told her that when the baby was born, Louisa had a complete nervous breakdown, was ranting about things that made no sense at all, accusing him of wrongdoings. That they'd had to put her in one of those places—on a doctor's recommendation."

"Wasn't Alma around when Louisa had her baby?"

"No. Alma was a teacher back then. She was twenty-five, you know. Something of an old maid, in those days. Of course, Louisa not being married at twenty-one was also pretty much an oddity, especially her being so pretty and all. I'd been married for four years at that point. But Louisa," she smiled, more to herself than anything, "she was a wild one, she was. Independent as all get out. And smart. I bet she read everything that came by way of the mobile library. Always talking about going to college and things like that, things girls rarely did in those days. Least not girls from 'round here." She hummed and rocked again.

Gently, I brought her back. "Alma? She was teaching somewhere?"

"Oh yes," she agreed. "That's right. She was teaching up on the reservation. Always doing good, Alma was. A heart of gold. It was too far to drive back and forth from the reservation plus the road was pretty primitive, this was before the highway was put in, so she lived in someone's house up there. The minister and his wife, I believe, put her up. So when she came back at the end of May, after school was out for the summer, Louisa was already gone." The tightness returned to the edges of her mouth.

Afraid that she would be getting too tired, I pushed her carefully. "Then Holger asked her to marry him?"

She snapped her head in a dismissive gesture, and for an instant, I felt I could glimpse backward all through the years to Vera's youth when she must've snapped her head like that frequently and impatiently. The déjà vu made me smile. "Well, he had two babies to contend with now. Alma was a good-hearted girl. A bit on the plain side and, well, big, you know, but I reckon he knew she'd take good care of him and the babies. And Alma," she pressed her lips together for a moment. "I imagine Alma was flattered and relieved that someone wanted to marry her."

"So she believed Holger's side of the story?"

"Oh yes. I mean, mostly people would've anyway. Louisa was just a little too wild, so most were willing to believe that she was a 'bad' girl. In those days—" she glanced sharply at me, "probably today, too—most people didn't believe that a man, especially a 'good' man, meaning someone who kept a job, ever forced a girl. It was, you know, considered to be the girl's fault."

I nodded, turning all this information over in my mind. "But you believed Louisa?"

"Oh yes," she agreed. "Without a doubt."

"Why?"

She scowled at me. "I told you. She was my best friend. She wouldn't have lied to me." She looked out again, rocking furiously. I didn't interrupt her reverie. After a couple of minutes that seemed like a couple of hours, she said, without looking at me, "Anyway, I don't think she actually liked boys."

Warning bells went off raucously in my mind. "What?" I asked, barely above a whisper.

She shrugged, still not looking at me, but repeated, "She just didn't, you see, like boys. We never talked about it. I just knew. And . . ." she turned toward me now, "and I always thought her folks probably knew, too, and that's why they were so easily convinced to have her put away."

My "real" grandmother was a lesbian? Is this what she was telling me? The horror of her rape and incarceration were momentarily obliterated as I turned this sweet possibility over in my mind. Then I asked Vera, "Did you ever go see her?"

Her head snapped again, in obvious anger. "No." she barked. "Never knew, for sure, where she was. I always supposed her to be in Fergus Falls because it was the closest. At least I think it was. It was the place our mothers always threatened us with. You know that threat? Where your mama says, 'You driving me crazy! I declare, I'm gonna end up in Fergus Falls one of these days. Just on account of you awful kids.'

"I once asked Alma, and she agreed that that was where she was, but insisted I mustn't go. Said that Holger had gone to visit Louisa shortly before Alma and him were married, and supposedly Louisa got wild and out of control and they told him to not come back and to let no family member come visit because it just distressed her too much. Hmmmph. Don't know as I ever believed that story. But then, I didn't ever believe much in anything Holger Schmidt had to say. I knew he had forced Louisa, raped her as you would say, and nothing was going to make me think that my best friend had lied to me about that.

"It caused problems between me and Joey—that's what they used to call my husband. Joey from Johannsen instead of Carl, because he was a junior. Holger worked for him, plus they were childhood friends. He thought we should socialize. I never talked to Holger again. Not once. For the rest of his life."

"And Alma?"

"Oh, I'd talk to her. She was just an unwitting partner with Holger, you know. I didn't hold that against her. It wasn't easy being a girl, then. Didn't have as many choices as you young ones do." I smiled; I was nearly forty. Youth is all relative, I guess. She abruptly changed gears. "Are you married?"

"Nope," I answered cheerfully.

She smiled. "See? That's an option for you. It wasn't much in them days. So Alma took the only chance she thought she was going to have. And made the best of it."

"Do you think she was happy?" I wondered.

Vera shrugged. "Mostly. She loved those girls, you know. Didn't matter they weren't hers. She just loved them to pieces. And Holger," she hesitated, "I guess she just mostly ignored him, after a while. Lots of wives do that, you know. Just keep movin'. That's all."

"And she always believed his side of the story?"

For a couple of minutes, Vera just rocked, looking out the window at the lake again. Then she turned back to me, a spark of anger in her blue eyes. "Not too long before she died, when she started having problems with her heart, Alma came to me and asked me if I remembered about Louisa and Holger. She said she felt she'd spent her life hiding from the truth and needed to go to her death honestly."

"She knew she was dying?"

"Well, the doctors figured she'd already had a couple of little strokes. I guess she thought it wasn't going to be long. And, she did go pretty fast. Anyway, Holger'd been drinking more and more as he got older." As an alcoholic, I always looked for the origins in my family—not to blame someone else or even genetics, but just to understand its source. I suspected my father was an extremely controlled alcoholic, but here was evidence that alcoholism maybe existed on my mother's side of the family. "When he was drunk, he got a little belligerent, said things that he wouldn't normally say or things that didn't make much sense. He talked, sometimes—or raved as Alma put it—about Louisa. She was scared and confused but wanted to know the truth. So I told her, again, what Louisa had told me all those years ago."

Vera was silent again. I waited. Tears glistened on her lashes. "She cried. Poor Alma. She cried. I think, this time, she believed me. Or maybe she'd always believed me but just couldn't let herself. I don't know. She changed her will. I do know that. And she started looking for Louisa. Least I think she did. But—seemed like she was dead in no time."

"Do you think Louisa is still alive?" I felt the thrill of possibility.

Vera shrugged. "Who knows? I am. She might be." I calculated in my head. She'd be eighty-eight now. It was possible. "But you don't think Alma found her?"

"No, she'd have told me if she did. It wasn't that long, really, before she was too sick to do anything."

For a few minutes, we were both silent, locked in our own thoughts. Then, Vera waved a dismissive hand toward me. "You have to leave now, what's your name again?"

"Tyler," I said, getting up.

She nodded. "Tyler. I'm sorry. I can remember things that happened in 1910, but your name is too recent."

"It's all right," I assured her.

"I'm tired now," she stated. "You come again, and I'll tell you more stories, if you like."

"I'd like that very much, Vera, thank you. Can I just ask you one more question?" She nodded. "Do you think Louisa did have a nervous breakdown?"

"Absolutely not!" Vera shot out with certainty. "I knew that girl better than anyone I ever knew. There's no way she broke down. Holger was just afraid she'd tell the truth, and so he locked her up. I've never once thought she was actually crazy!"

And yet, I thought with some astonishment, you let her rot in one of those places for the rest of her life.

13

I thought of little other than my conversation with Vera for the next couple of days. Was this "it"? Was this the "truth" Mom wanted me to find? Had I found the "skeleton in the closet"? It seemed as if I had.

The Fourth of July Gala was as wonderful as promised. People began arriving at Nancy and Piggy's around four o'clock. When I got there, Charley was unloading beverages out of his truck—coolers full of soda pop and springwater and beer. I brought the biggest fruit salad I'd ever made. Actually, it might've been the only fruit salad I'd ever made. I was pretty apprehensive, concerned that old-timers might expect me to meet my grandmother's reputation for cooking. I guess I would always think of Alma as my grandmother.

I put my offering on a table already heavy with at least three kinds of potato salad, baked beans, macaroni and cheese, wild rice hot dishes and salads, chicken and dump-lings, pasta hot dishes and salads, at least two kinds of green salad, meatballs, and a riot of odds and ends like pickles and olives and chopped vegetables with dips and potato chips and more dips. Piggy, with Charley's help, was digging out the array of pine needles and leaves covering the wrapped-up pig in the fire pit. The smell was indescribable, and people spon-taneously clapped when the layers of tinfoil got peeled back to reveal a steaming, juicy mass of tender meat.

"I'm putting the first batch of burgers and dogs on the grill," Piggy called out. "You all better start eating."

I felt weak with excitement at the thought of the taste delights about to enter my mouth. What could be better? Good food outdoors shared with good people? I met the Whites, Jackie and Bob, as I made my first trip through the food line.

"We're so glad," Bob said to me, "that you're fixing that old place up. It was getting to be kind of an eyesore."

I didn't much like that description but smiled politely any-way. "I hear you're mostly here in the winter?" I inquired.

"Oh yes," Jackie agreed. "We're devoted skiers." She waved at three teenaged boys ahead of them. "Our sons and us. In the summer, we usually only come for Memorial Day, the Fourth, and Labor Day."

"Those are the only long weekends I can get away," Bob said.

"Bob's a doctor," Jackie informed me. "And, of course, our boys are all into sports in the summer, in a big way," she made "big" sound bigger than usual, "so we just can't get up here much."

I said, "Uh-huh," and smiled politely some more. Well, I thought to myself, these are the first people I've met that I don't think I'd much care for. That's not too bad, actually. A couple out of how many?

Lyle and his brother and wife, Burt and Laverne, arrived a little late, bringing their mother, Vera, with them. They settled her in a comfortable chair, in a sheltered and shady corner. Lyle told her he'd get her some food while Burt and Laverne moved off to greet their neighbors (and constituents, I thought, uncharitably). I noticed that Lyle's usual face stubble had been shaved closer.

Lyle and Burt were a study in contrasts. While Lyle was grizzled and disheveled, Burt was distinguished and immaculate. His grey hair—the media would call it "silver"—was cut in a stylish manner, neither too long nor too short, swept back from his strong, arresting features. He smiled a lot, something Lyle rarely seemed to do, displaying even, white teeth. False, I thought, had to be to be so perfect. His clothes, although suitably casual, were noticeable in this crowd—neatly pressed, perfectly cut to fit his athletic body, nearly new. He looked the part, I thought, of an elegant actor told to dress in "regular" clothes to mingle with the "regular" folk. It was hard to believe he'd grown up here. He must've been thrilled to escape.

I switched my attention to Laverne, who had also grown up in the area. Although she, too, had a polished look that stood out in this crowd—clothes too perfect, hairdo that attempted to look slightly mussed but was clearly arranged to appear windblown, makeup, she still fit in better than her husband. There was a warmth in her manner and smile that seemed more genuine than her husband's clearly choreographed bonhomie.

Charley joined me, his hands and mouth engaged with a burger that made me realize I was ready for more food. "Observing our politicians?" he mumbled around his mouthful.

I grinned at him. "Yeah. Quite a difference between the brothers, mmm?"

At this point, Burt strolled toward us, his hand out to Charley. "Charley, good to see you again. How's everything going at the store?"

Charley wiped his hand on his jeans before shaking Burt's. "Fine, Burt, just fine. How's everything going in Washington?" I glanced at him quickly, trying to discern if he was mocking Burt. I was sure he was, just by the fact that he didn't return my look but, instead, stared seriously at Burt.

"Oh, you know Washington, Charley." A note of calculated exasperation crept into Burt's voice. "All those wheelings and dealings." He shook his head, a look of sad resignation resting there. "Just doesn't seem to be the way to run the best country in the world."

"So, Burt," Charley gestured at me. "This is Tyler Jones, granddaughter of Holger and Alma Schmidt. She's fixing the old place up."

"Nice to meet you, Tyler," he shook hands with me. "It'd be grand to get that old place looking good again. It was always real special."

"Nice to meet you, too," I responded. "It's a joy being here. I haven't been here much since childhood. I had a splendid talk with your mother recently. She told me a lot about the early days out here."

Charley, who'd heard all about my visit with Vera, pursed his lips, watching the Senator. Burt said, "That's nice. There's probably no one alive who remembers those early days as well as Mom does."

He moved on to other people, and Charley and I headed back to the food. There were a lot more people here than I knew, and Charley helped me sort some of them out. Besides the actual residents of the point, assorted friends and family members were here. With my second plate of food, including a burger and a dog, I walked around, meeting some people, visiting with others I'd already met. "Nancy," I asked her at one point, "aren't those Anson sisters here?"

110

"No," she said, looking about as if maybe they'd snuck in while she was busy. "They aren't back yet, I guess. You'll meet them soon, dear. You're going to just love them." I hope so, I thought, everyone keeps telling me that.

I visited for a few moments with Vera. Her eyes twinkled at me when she said, "Sure did bring back a lot of memories. Our talk. Seems like I can't stop thinking about them days since you came to visit. 'Course it's easier anyway. I remember all that stuff better than I remember things that happened two hours ago. The thing about age, you know, people think you just sort of lose your mind. It isn't true. What is true is that your mind is just so chock-full of stuff, you stop putting any effort into remembering the newer stuff. There just isn't enough time or energy. Do you get what I mean?"

"I think I do."

"I thought you would. You're pretty sharp. What do you do? If you're not married, you must have to make a living for yourself."

I smiled. "I'm a writer."

"A writer!" she exclaimed. "Oh I like that. Always did like to read. What kind of stuff do you write?"

When I left Vera, I nearly bumped into Lyle. "See you met my ma," he said.

"Yes," I smiled. "Actually, I met her a couple of days ago. She told me a lot of interesting stuff about my family."

He stared at me, unsmiling, the way he had that first night in Charley's store. "You shouldn't tire her out."

"Your mom? I think she'd be more likely to tire me out. She's quite indefatigable." When he seem disinclined to say more, I moved away from him toward the dessert table. As if the main meal hadn't been nirvana enough, here was a second table filled with new palate pleasers: apple pie, cheesecake, lemon meringue pie, cookies of infinite varieties, cherry pie, lemon bars, blueberry pie, raspberry tarts. How was I ever going to decide?

It was at this table that Allen Granger and I introduced ourselves to each other. "I've heard a lot about you from Charley and the McDermotts." I didn't think it was probably a good idea to ask him, right off, if he had a bulletproof room in the basement, although I was tempted.

"Well," he said slowly, seeming to pick his words as carefully as he picked his dessert, "I hope it wasn't too bad."

"Oh no," I protested. "Actually, I'm most interested in the fact that your family was originally from up here. I'm trying to find out all about the early part of the century here on the point. Especially my own family, of course, but I'm really interested in anyone's memories or stories they've heard." When his eyebrows went up in apparent question, but he didn't respond, I improvised. "I'm a writer, you know, and I'm thinking about writing a book about that period." Is that true, I wondered? Maybe. The novel I'm working on sure doesn't seem to be taking off. When he still didn't respond, I added, "So could we talk some time? This might not be the best place, but maybe we could have coffee or something?"

"I don't think I could be much help to you. My family hasn't lived in this area for a couple of generations, you know. Not since the '30s."

"But surely you grew up hearing stories. From your dad or your granddad."

"No, I really didn't. Sorry." He walked away.

Well now, that's curious, I was thinking as Charley came up to me with a woman a little younger than me. "Tyler, I want you to meet Sally Branch."

"Hi," I said, extending my free hand, the other one holding a plateful of devastating desserts. "I knew your grandma, sort of, when I was a kid."

"You mean she yelled at you if you ever came on or near her property?" We both laughed. "She was something of an old curmudgeon. It's a pleasure to meet you, Tyler. I feel like I already know you. I've read *The Undeclared War.* It was a wonderful book!"

I felt a rush of pleasure, the same I always felt when I met someone I didn't know who'd read my book. I expected all my friends to read it. I still hadn't gotten used to the idea that complete strangers would read it, too.

Before I could make a coherent response, Charley exclaimed, "See? You *are* famous!"

"Hardly," I laughed. "Thank you, Sally. It's nice to know people are reading it."

She snagged a couple of kids running by. "These are my children, Josh and Florrie." We exchanged "hi's," but they squirmed impatiently and made their escape immediately.

Sally turned her attention back to me. "I read your column, too, Tyler. They carry it in the Cities. It's very good."

"Thank you." I thought I was falling in love again. "Are you a writer?"

"No," she laughed easily, shaking her head. "I'm a therapist. But I work a lot with women on issues of violence. I'm always looking for material to share with my clients. What are you working on now?"

"A novel," I answered, feeling a distinct flutter of discomfort for the book that wasn't working for me.

"That must be different. Are you finding it more difficult or easier after doing nonfiction?"

"Both, I guess. You know, journalists almost always want to write a novel, a 'real' book—not just a collection of their journalistic pieces. That's kind of what *War* was: a bringing together of all the research and articles I'd written for ten years. Plus the first-person testimonials. I'm pleased with the results, and even more pleased when someone like you likes it, but now I want to write the Truth, with a capital T, without the limitations of the truth, without a capital T. Does that make sense to you?" I was finding this woman very easy to talk to.

She nodded her head and smiled, "I think so."

Charley interrupted. "Not to me. What are you saying?"

"It's hard to explain, Charley. I guess I'm saying that the literal truth—a set of facts—sometimes gets in the way of the larger context, the overall 'Truth.'" Charley looked puzzled, and I blundered on. "It's like this, Charley. If I tell you a woman's been raped or even that one out of four women will be raped in their lifetime, you might be sad or angry, maybe even horrified at the magnitude, but you wouldn't really be engaged, unless you knew the woman or women personally. But, if I tell you the entire story of one woman being raped—where you get to 'know' her in minute detail before she's raped and you're there while she's being raped and you're also there in the aftermath of her rape—then you experience her rape in a way that you don't when you read, with a great deal of distance, a 'true' rendering of a rape, in a newspaper, for instance. And, in a lot of ways, her story—whether it's literally true or not—is truer than the newspaper article because you have the WHOLE story, the WHOLE picture. Does that make any sense at all?"

He nodded slowly. "Yeah, it does. I think I see what you mean. That's really interesting."

I asked Sally about her practice, and we moved easily into talking about feminist activity in our respective cities, finding we both knew some of the same women. It turned out she'd worked on many projects, over the years, with Sonny. We parted with the promise of getting together again soon.

As the evening shadows grew longer, we started to clean up before it got dark. Piggy built up the fire in the fire pit, someone else brought out a guitar, and we sang camp songs while we waited for complete darkness and the fireworks display.

"There's the first one!" one of the kids finally shouted, and everyone hurried over to arrange themselves on chairs and the ground near the edge of the cliff, to watch star-burst after star-burst over the harbor in nearby Grand Marais. We were tired and full of food, but the fireworks display woke everyone up enough to do the usual oh-ing and ah-ing. It was a fine finish to a fine day.

14

My days fell into a soothing rhythm. When we got the new cupboards painted and my refrigerator was delivered, I left Charley's little cabin in the woods and moved down to The Cedars. I slept on the porch, curled against the night chill under a snuggly quilt. Aggie warmed my feet or else slept in the cot next to mine, if she wanted to stretch out or if I was too restless for her. In the mornings, we'd walk the point road—Aggie gleefully chasing a chipmunk here, a seagull there, jumping in the bay for a quick swim—followed by shaking all her excess water on me before she resumed her jaunt, and we ended up, as usual, at Charley's for a cup of coffee and conversation.

Meals were like a long string of picnics since my kitchen wasn't finished yet. Luckily, the new countertop had been installed at the same time as the cupboards, so I was able to make do with a toaster oven. Toast and cereal for breakfast, sandwiches for lunch and supper. Meals were augmented by frequent trips to the deli in town for soup or chili, potato salad, whatever was already prepared. I tried to use few dishes as I had no sink in the kitchen yet, and it was a decided bother to wash dishes in the bathroom sink.

Gertie and I managed to drag out all the debris upstairs, just leaving the solid old bunk beds. We moved them into the center of the room and scraped and sanded and painted them a bright, cheery yellow. Then, sometimes with Jerome's help, we scrubbed and sanded the floors and used the same soft grey that was already on the front porch. Gertie scrubbed everything down, from ceiling to floors, while I worked with Jerome on the kitchen floor. Then we started to paint the ceilings and walls upstairs, all a creamy white—simple and restful.

On days when Gertie or Jerome couldn't come, I went through and mostly discarded the papers that were stuffed into all the drawers in Grandpa's desk. I kept hoping for some surprise amongst all these old papers, but so far I had discovered nothing more than receipts, old newspaper clippings of people I mostly didn't know or had vaguely heard of, check stubs, returned checks, endless tax papers, and the like. I kept sorting through them, carefully and methodically, not giving up hope that some telling piece of information might be buried somewhere in this detritus. I began to think it odd that I found no papers relating to the incarceration of Louisa Jane Anderson. Wouldn't they have to pay something for her to be there? Shouldn't there be receipts somewhere? Monthly or yearly payments?

When I wasn't going through the desk, I worked at my laptop. I wrote first drafts of columns, shaped others, and jotted notes for ideas. I forced myself to pound away at the novel some days but found the characters slipping away from me, eluding me, refusing to aid me. Maybe I should let this be, I thought. It certainly doesn't seem to be working.

And some days, I played hooky—taking long walks with Aggie or drives to various state parks for hiking or just kicking back with a good book, sometimes neglecting the reading for long, meditative stares at the lake.

Once, when I was talking to Mary Sharon on the phone, she said, "What were you doing when I called?"

"Just looking at the lake."

"What?"

"Just looking at the lake," I repeated. "Mary Sharon, I can't believe you grew up in Minnesota and never came to Lake Superior."

"Tyler, don't start on me. I've been hearing this from you ever since we met."

Nearly twenty years ago, I thought, when I walked into my dorm room at the University. "Well. Be that as it may, Mary Sharon, I'm glad you're finally coming up here to see one of the Wonders of the World. Then you'll understand what I mean when I say that I was just looking at the lake. It's changing constantly, continuously. You'll see."

Part of every day, I spent some time either on the swing at the edge of the cliff or down on the rocks at the foot of the cliff, just drinking in the restorative powers of this massive inland sea. It mesmerized me—the way large bodies of water seem to mesmerize people all over the world. The constant sound of water lapping, sucking, roaring, the constant motion of the swaying water; the waves seemed to bring in peace while pulling away chaos. There was a continuous play of light across the heaving mass: all this sensual activity seemed to lull me and calm me in ways I can never describe. I cried, usually every day, at unexpected moments, in uncontrollable fits and starts. I began to think of grief as a presence who lived with me but mostly hid behind doors or around corners—sticking a foot out to trip me, tapping me on the shoulder, ambushing me from behind.

The Lutheran church minister eventually called me back. Alma's and Louisa's births were not recorded in the church records because they'd both been born before the existence of the church. But Alma Marie Anderson was confirmed on April 14, 1912, and Louisa Jane Anderson was confirmed on April 8, 1917. There was nothing more, ever, about Louisa. Alma's marriage and death were recorded, and also the births of both Thalia in 1924 and Louise in 1926.

"1926?" I repeated.

"That's right," the minister agreed. "May 12, 1926." That phony birth certificate, I thought. I guess, after never telling Mom the truth, Alma and Holger must've decided to change Mom's birth year in 1958—to cover up the fact that she was born before they were married and keep her from asking too many questions. By then, I guess most people had forgotten that she'd been born to Louisa just before she was "sent away."

Their baptisms, confirmations, and Thalia's wedding in 1948 were all recorded. Nothing really new. I thanked the minister and headed back to the library.

There was scant information about individuals, although the overall historical record of the white settlement in this area was fascinating and included many stories I'd heard growing up. The Historical Society card catalog listed several groups of "personal letters" by various families. I requested a packet of letters written by the Johannsen family between 1910 and 1930. It was hard making out the handwriting sometimes. A lot of the letters were filled with the kind of daily minutiae I actually loved because I thought it was a true record of "history," far more accurate in recapturing humanity at a given time than studying battles or treaties or governments.

Ingvar Johannsen wrote, in May 1913, to his brother in Winnipeg:

> The snow was so deep this winter, droves of deer stayed close to the shore, making hunting very easy. And thank the Lord, because transportation was impossible, and all of us were running low on stores. The deer, unfortunately, were so starved themselves that they made for poor eating, but it was better than nothing, easily obtainable, and absolutely necessary as I believed many of us would have died without that ready source of meat. Thank God spring has arrived and with it the *America* with all the staples we were all pretty much out of. Mrs. Johannsen, bless her heart, had not been able to make bread for more than a month! It was amazing, really, and scary—when the deep snow that so isolated most of us throughout the long winter receded—to see our neighbors, some of them we hadn't seen for months, thin as beanpoles, nearly as starved-looking as the deer had been. As far as I know, at this point, there were only three deaths—a hermit fella who lived alone in the woods and had nary a thing in his shack to eat when they found him, a tiny baby whose mother just couldn't make enough milk apparently, and old Mrs. Kari, who might have died anyway, she was so old. We're all rejoicing in our safe passage through this hard time.

In August of 1921, Christine Johannsen wrote to her sister in Illinois:

> I do believe I hate washing clothes more than any of my other duties. First, I have to carry, then boil all that water. Then I have to scrub with that strong soap whose prickly scent gets right up in my nose and, I swear, just sets there for another two days before leaving me alone again. Remember my hands? What they looked like when I used to play our piano? White and delicate and soft? They're as tough and rough as my washboard now and red as a sunset (but not so pretty)—what with hot water and soap and scrubbing and what all else. It's backbreaking work, leaning over a washboard, then carrying those dripping clothes to another barrel of hot water to rinse, then wringing and wringing 'til I'm sure there's no strength left, in my arms, in my hands, anywhere. Then I still got to get them heavy, wet clothes out to the clothesline (and pray there'll be no rain!). Actually, my favorite part is hanging the clothes on the line. At least I get to stand up straight and am only lifting one thing at a time. The warm sun on my back feels good while the wind almost sounds like it's playing the piano in Mama's parlor, skittering through those pine trees on the edge of our yard. Then the wind comes and fills up those clothes on the line, making them billow out so that it looks like ghosts are jumping into Ed's overalls and the children's things, too. Then they start waving and dancing, swaying and flapping, and I almost feel

like I'm just a girl again, at a church social
waiting for Jeremy Colter to ask me to dance.
Oh, I do go on, don't I? I don't know what
gets into me sometimes, and anyways, you
know all about washday. I miss you so,
Rebecca. I got to go to bed before it's time to
get up and start all over again.

Some of the letters were boring, but I ended up spending
hours reading them because, mostly, they completely caught
my attention. In a long letter to someone called Lydia, dated
1926, Vera Johannsen detailed blueberry picking, her second
child's first steps, picnics, home remedies for various ail-
ments, church activities, her older child's progress in toilet-
training, what she was growing in her garden that year, her
problems keeping her little house clean and even bigger problem of lack of desire regarding cleaning, and remarkably little
about her husband, Joey. At the end of her letter, she wrote:
"Lydia, Louisa is gone. There was a baby girl and then they say
she went nuts and they had to lock her up. I don't know. I feel
mad and helpless. I don't think we'll ever see her again."

Just as she told me. I looked sightlessly at the shelves of
books surrounding me, tapping a pen against my teeth, wondering what a mental institute would be like in 1926.
Wondering if I really wanted to know. I went back and looked
at the date on the letter: June 18, 1926. Then I flipped to the
end of the letter again. "There was a baby girl . . ." Presumably
this would've been my mother, Weezie. I guess she *was* born
in 1926.

I never found any primary information about the rum
running. There was some speculation in histories written
decades later, but nothing written during Prohibition. I
tapped my pen against my teeth again. It was, after all, I
reminded myself, illegal. Would they write in the paper or
even in letters about illegal activity? And why this intense

interest, anyway? I guessed it was two things, really. One, the rum running was the unsolved mystery of my own childhood, and it still intrigued me. Two, it occurred during the same decade in which my own family was setting itself, or so it seemed to me, toward its future.

Later, when I was talking it out with Charley, he said, "Maybe there is so little info because there was very little activity. Maybe there really is no secret about it, Tyler. Have you ever thought about that?"

"I guess," I agreed. "But Charley, why did it keep popping up when we were kids? And why did it always feel—to all of us—as if something was being swept under the rug?"

He shrugged, scratching the quiescent Aggie's ears. "Maybe because we wanted to believe there was more there than there was?"

I agreed again, "Yeah, maybe." But I didn't *really* agree. Something was there, I felt certain. Just what, I didn't know.

When the floors on the first story had been completely stripped and sanded to a smooth, soft gloss, Jerome and Gertie and I applied a thick coat of sealer. Then I told them not to come for a couple of days, so it could set properly. I decided to leave Aggie with Charley and go to Duluth to find out about the Mental Institute at Fergus Falls.

"Jerome," I asked him as he loaded some of his stuff on his truck. "Did you know that my grandma's sister Louisa had been put in a mental hospital?" An odd look moved briefly behind his eyes. It was too fleeting; I couldn't make it out.

"She was gone before I was born," he tersely replied, not looking at me.

"I know, Jerome, but didn't you ever hear anything about her?" I prodded.

He looked annoyed, something I had never seen on his face. "Maybe I'd heard somethin' about it."

"Do you know where it was?" I asked. He shook his head abruptly. "I'm going down to Duluth to see if I can find out about it." The odd look passed quickly behind his eyes again. I narrowed my own eyes, trying to identify it, but it was gone immediately.

"Tomorrow?" Jerome asked me.

"What?"

"You going to Duluth tomorrow?"

"No, I think the next day. I just want to relax tomorrow."

That night my dreams were flooded with images of a woman in a straitjacket, wandering through a rocky outcropping moaning and wailing. I came awake with an abrupt start, my heart pounding. Aggie's tail swished tentatively on the cot next to me. I listened for any sound besides her tail. Had I heard something that startled me? Had some noise awakened me with this thumping heart? I could hear nothing undo. I decided it was just the unpleasant dream. I shivered a little, remembering it.

I sat up in my bed, pulling the quilt around me, and gazed outside through the screens. A high, nearly full moon washed the landscape around me in a pale light. I could see the water moving, hear it whispering against the unseen rocky shore, while the leaves shifted and sighed against the air moving through them. The usual multitude of stars were paled by the brightness of the moon but still crowded against one another, trying to find space to twinkle out their message. Nothing sinister seemed to exist in my world. I snuggled back down in the bed, pulling the quilt up around my ears, and wondered about my real grandma, Louisa Jane Anderson.

15

The sky was sapphire blue, stretching cloudless to the horizon—almost merging with the equally blue-blue of the lake. At lunch time, after a few hours of writing, I took my tuna-fish-and-onion sandwich, an apple, and a thermos of coffee and went down the cliff. The rocks were warmed. I sat as close to the water as I could without getting sprayed and leaned back, soaking up the heat of the rocks. The waves were large, exploding against the shore with that singular combination of intense power and savage beauty.

Aggie looked at the water longingly, but clearly decided the thundering surf was too much even for her—Aqua Dog. She busied herself, instead, with chasing off the seagulls who moved in at the sight of my sandwich—dashing back and forth, barking madly, as they landed first on one side of me, then the other.

A sense of noise or movement—hard to imagine what, the breakers were clamoring so loudly—caused me to turn around. The lift was going up. There must be someone up there, I thought. I stood and looked up. The cliff was too steep for me to see anyone unless they hung precariously over the edge.

"Hallo!" I shouted. "Hallo? Is anyone there?" Stupid question. Of course, someone was there. The lift wouldn't be going up on its own. My words were snatched away by the din of the crashing water, and I knew they hadn't carried to anyone's ears.

It stopped at the top. Maybe whoever it was would lean over and wave, I thought, but no one did. And then the lift began its descent. By now, Aggie, too, had become aware of the movement and rushed over to the platform to greet the newcomer. I kept my eyes on the lift. It appeared to be empty, and I was beginning to feel a little uneasy. If someone were standing or sitting in it, it would be almost *required* that they lean over the side—to gape at the view, if nothing else.

I walked over to join Aggie. Even though the lift drew nearer and nearer, I still didn't see anyone in it. Reaching the bottom, the lift stopped with its usual thunk, and a limp hand fell out of the open side and lay still, palm up. I yelped and jumped back as Aggie started to bark. "Oh my god," I whispered, "Please let this be a joke."

I moved forward cautiously—partially expecting Charley to jump up and shout "Boo!" I leaned over to peer into the lift. I yelped again, putting my hand to my mouth, repeating over and over, "Omigod, omigod, omigod." Jerome was in the lift, on his back, his legs askew as if he'd been dumped unceremoniously. His lifeless eyes stared through me, and a large rubescent stain was spreading across the seat of the lift where his head rested.

I was still repeating, "Omigod, omigod," as I looked up again. Did I see a slight movement there? A shadow, perhaps? Or was it imagination born out of terror? I had to get out of there. But first, I clenched my teeth and put my fingers against the side of Jerome's throat. My shoulders hunched forward, and I felt a knot of apprehension between them. I half-expected a knife or some other projectile to land there at any moment. The carotid artery, I thought, the lifeline. Where was the pulse? There wasn't one. Relaxing and reclenching my teeth, I put my fingers against his wrist. I had to be sure. Still no pulse. I moved backward, slowly, away from that body.

Now what? I wasn't getting in that lift with Jerome, and—anyway—I couldn't go up with a murderer perhaps still lurking about. Or—could this be an accident? Was my imagination getting carried away? Was it possible . . . could he have started the lift on its downward descent, lost his balance, and fallen, hitting his head against the seat too hard? I arrested my retreat and stepped back toward the lift; I scrutinized the sprawl of his body. I wanted this to be an accident, but it didn't look as though his body were in a position that would indicate such a possibility.

Aggie continued barking."Will you shut up?" I hissed, but she paid no attention to me. "Come on," I commanded, as I headed north, staying as close to the cliff's wall as I could. The McDermotts were in the other direction, but they had no access down their cliff. Those sisters I hadn't met yet lived in the direction I was moving. I knew their place was down in a hollow, the cliffs sloping down to a rocky ledge. Hadn't Charley told me they'd returned? Hopefully, someone would be there. I glanced back at the lift. Jerome's hand was still laying limply, palm up. I shivered and swallowed, and swallowed again, thinking of the blood and the horror-stricken look in his eyes. I looked upward again. Nothing. I could see nothing. I had to stop a minute, lean over, and vomit—spewing my lunch at the cliff base. The seagulls would be happy, I thought irrelevantly, as I hurried on—brushing a shaking hand across my mouth. Those scavengers will eat anything.

16

I was entirely focused on not breaking a leg, maneuvering from one rocky slab to another. Suddenly, I heard Aggie barking again—sharply, insistently. I stopped and looked up. She was out of sight, apparently around the next point. That's when I realized there was no longer a cliff alongside me; it had sloped away, the rocks were edged by the woods. My skin prickled, thinking of someone who might be moving parallel to me, and now there was no cliff separating us. Aggie kept barking, and I hoped it was some live person at whom she was barking. And then I hoped it was some live person who was not brandishing a weapon of any sort.

Hastening forward, I heard a responding bark—more of a yip, actually—to Aggie's gruffer barking. Then it sounded like a chorus of yips, and as I rounded the bend, I heard a voice calling, "Bette Davis! Ann Sothern! Stop that racket right this minute! I'm warning you! Carole Lombard! You needn't join in with them, you know. Now all of you—stop this immediately or you'll be sorry!"

Aggie was barking at three smallish, white dogs, who were all standing between her and a cabin a few feet behind them. The voice was coming from a woman sitting in a chair on the deck in front of this cabin.

"Girls!" she was continuing to admonish as I came into view. "Oh, well, see! We've got company, and now you've made a terrible impression, I'm afraid." To me, she said, "Hullo. Do come up here, won't you? Don't mind the dogs. They won't bite, don't you know. Just have to flex their muscles occasionally. Do shut up, girls! You will have to forgive their manners. They're rather spoiled, I'm afraid. You must be the new girl next door."

"Hello," I said, approaching a ramp that led up to the deck. The dogs backed away from me, continuing to bark, but also wagging their tails tentatively. "Hush up, Aggie," I said, putting my hand briefly on her head, then squatting down to put my hands out to the smaller dogs. "Hello Girls," I inveigled them. "Aren't you nice girls? And good girls?" Aggie began to approach them warily. They sniffed at me but wouldn't let Aggie near them. They retreated up to the deck, and I ordered Aggie to stay on the grass. I leaned over for a couple of seconds, to properly catch my breath, which was a bit erratic after my fearful flight.

As I started up the ramp, I realized this woman was not sitting in a deck chair but in a wheelchair. "Hello," I said again, as I walked quickly to her. I stretched my hand out, saying, "I'm Tyler Jones, and yes, I am at the house next door this summer."

She took my hand and squeezed it, firmly and warmly. "Henrietta Anson," she announced, "and these ill-mannered snippets, our Westies, are Bette Davis and Ann Sothern and Carole Lombard." I wondered how she could tell them apart;

they all looked alike to me. They responded to their names by wagging their tails and coming over to sniff me again. "It is so nice to have someone next door," Henrietta continued as I fondled the girls, murmuring to them as Aggie looked on agonizingly. "That old place has been vacant all the time we've lived here, and I'd much rather . . ." She stopped and peered at me sharply. "Are you quite all right, Miss Jones? You look a bit ragged."

I couldn't help but smile; there was something so engaging about this woman. She must have been in her sixties—her round face was relatively unlined, but her hair, which stood out like a nimbus cloud around her rosy cheeks, was pure white. She reminded me of an aging cherub, her brown eyes soft but lively. "I'm sorry," I responded. "I don't mean to be so abrupt when we've just met, but I must use your phone. There's been a . . ." She didn't look delicate in any way, but does one just blurt out *murder*? ". . . an accident over at my place."

"You must go right in, dear," she said at once, gesturing behind her. "Right through there. The phone is in the kitchen." Saying that, she picked up a cowbell sitting on a table next to her and rang it heartily. "This is just to bring my sister in," she explained to me, as I undoubtedly looked startled. "She's out back somewhere, messing in the garden or woods or something. Go on," she urged. "Go right in."

"Thank you," I said, then hesitated just inside the door, turning back toward her. "Do you dial 9-1-1 here?"

"Yes, yes, that's right," she agreed. "For an emergency, of course. Ambulance or police or that sort."

The front room of the cabin was filled with somewhat shabby and mismatched but comfortable-looking furniture. The living room, kitchen, and dining area were one room, with knotty pine walls, and all overlooking the lake. I found the phone and dialed the emergency number.

I'd been distracted by the dogs and Henrietta Anson and the lovely setting, but now the memory of that hand falling flaccidly out of the lift rushed back into my mind. And Jerome, with that awful blank look in his eyes and blood oozing out of his body. I began to shake all over.

"Sheriff's Office." I didn't trust my voice for a minute, and the voice repeated, "Sheriff's Office. Can I help you?"

"Hello, this is Tyler Jones. I'm on Stony River Road, out on the point?" I said, all in a rush. "There's been a . . ." I hesitated. This was a murder, wasn't it?

"Hello?" The voice on the other end of the line said. "Hello? Are you still there? Are you all right?"

". . . a death," I continued. "A murder, actually." I heard a gasp behind me and turned around to see another older woman standing just inside the doorway. Her hair was graying brown and seemed to be chopped off in a more-or-less haphazard method. Her very blue, very intense eyes were very wide at that moment. I tried to signal an apology with my eyes to her. The woman on the other end was asking for my fire number. "Fire number?" I frowned.

The woman standing inside the door said to me, "Yours is W112. Ours is 113." I nodded and smiled my thanks, then relayed this information to the dispatcher, asking her to send them here to get me.

When I replaced the receiver, I turned and said, "I'm Tyler Jones," extending my hand, "and I'm really sorry. I didn't mean for you to hear like that. I didn't realize you'd come in."

She took my hand, another warm, firm grip, and waved with her other one, "Oh, don't apologize. We'd have had to find out now, wouldn't we?" She was putting water in a kettle and lighting the stove. "I'm Elinor Anson. Ellie, everyone calls me. Not much of an Elinor, would you say? Here now, I'll get you some tea, and we'll lace it with a little brandy. Just what the good doctor would prescribe. Sit down now and breathe deeply."

"No!" I said, altogether too sharply. She jumped a little. I put my hand on her arm and said, "I'm sorry. I didn't mean to snap at you. This has been quite horrid . . ."

"Of course it has, dear," she patted my hand affectionately, and I had to control myself to keep from falling right into her arms, sobbing. Good lord, I said to myself, you don't even know these people!

When she got a brandy bottle out from under the sink, I had to add, "I don't drink." It seemed so ungrateful that I added, "But thank you anyway."

"Oh well, that's it then. I see. Don't worry, we'll just make you a very strong cup of tea. It will do you up fine, you'll see." Suddenly she called, "Hank! Get yourself in here and have some tea. Miss Jones has a story for us, I expect." I looked around, confused by the name, and she apparently read my mind, laughed a little, and said, "No, no. There's no one else here. Hank is Henrietta, you know. Got that name when she was only three and she climbed the big white pine out front of our house. Got so far up she couldn't get herself down. I don't remember the incident, of course, but I can just imagine Mama! Oh my, she must've been beside herself, fit to be tied, I'm quite sure. Had to call this little itty-bitty volunteer fire department we had back then, so they could put their longest ladder up there, and then one of the firefighters still had to climb up further to get her down.

"They were just bringing her down when our Daddy came home from work in his fancy clothes—he worked at the town bank, you know. He swung Hank up on his shoulder and said to Mama, 'This here's no Henrietta, I want you to know. This here is a Hank!' And then I bet he laughed that big rich laugh of his, and it's been Hank ever since."

She'd been making my tea throughout this story. I watched horror-struck (feeling loathe to interrupt her) as she poured what appeared to be half a bowl of sugar into my tea. I never took sugar with my tea but didn't want to hurt her feelings, so I took the cup without comment.

"You telling that story about my name again?" the object of the story said as she wheeled into the house. "She didn't tell you why I went up that tree, did she?" I shook my head as I sipped the tea, feeling surprise that it wasn't as awful as I'd expected. In fact, it was quite good; maybe this is what shock demanded.

"I went up that tree because my mama brought this little baby girl," she gestured toward Ellie, "home, and I was thoroughly disgusted with her. I'd been told for months and months that she was going to be this fine playmate for me, and what do you think? She couldn't do a thing. Why, she couldn't even hold her head up without banging it down again right away. And she messed her pants. Dreadful smell. Really! She was quite useless, and when I suggested to Mama we might take her back and get someone a little more interesting, why Mama just about bit my head off! Hmphh. Wasn't much point in hanging around a household in which everyone was cooing and ah-ing over a drooling, stinky, weak little ninny." She shook her head as if the memory were yesterday.

I smiled, thinking how right everyone had been, how much I was going to like these women, while Ellie got me another cup of tea. Hank continued, "Daddy didn't give you a boy's nickname when you went up the same tree, now did he, Ellie?"

"No," Ellie said with a sigh, "but you know the answer to that one anyway, Sister. I was a great disappointment following you. I mean, after all, I was all of seven before I ventured up that tree. And Mama didn't have to call anyone to rescue me. By then, she was so used to our shenanigans, she just went in the house and ignored me."

Hank was sipping her own tea and said, "I think you were more of a relief to Mama, rather than a disappointment."

"I suppose so, but I still wasn't the 'little lady' she'd hoped for, and I wasn't quite the hellcat you were. I was just kind of milquetoast. Well, my stars, we do natter on, don't we? Miss Jones, dear, do you want to tell us what happened? By the way, I just want you to know, we would've been over sooner, to be neighborly you know, but we've been away. We just got back last night."

"Tyler," I corrected her, "just call me Tyler." I gulped more tea and felt a little dazzled by the day's events and their whirling dialogue. The dogs, mine and theirs, began to bark vehemently, announcing what I supposed to be the sheriff's arrival.

17

There were, at one time, three sheriff's cars and a couple of unmarked cars in my drive. Word got around quickly, of course, and the point road was crowded with other cars and people milling about, murmuring to one another, and accosting any law enforcement officers coming or going for information. Of course, in a county as sparsely populated as Cook County and a spot as small as Stony River, most everyone knows everyone else. Jerome's murder was not just an object of curiosity but also a source of grief and loss.

From the sheriff's arrival on, that day felt, to me, like a day spent underwater, where everything is both crystal clear and wavery. During what seemed like endless interviews, I remembered the minutest details while feeling like I was moving through molasses. What could I really tell them? Jerome had been working for me for about a month. We weren't working today because the wood floors were drying. I was having lunch down by the lake. The lift started to go up . . . At this point, I often broke down and started to cry. I kept seeing Jerome's dead, dead eyes. And I kept thinking of Gertie. And then seeing my own mother's dead, dead eyes. And it would all cave in on me, and I would begin to sob.

At several points throughout the afternoon, I was aware of Ellie's quiet but solid presence, as she patted my shoulder comfortingly and sometimes shooed the sheriff or his deputies away, insisting I needed a moment to collect myself. Late in the day, I realized that Charley had managed to break through the crime-scene barriers, and a sobbing, "Oh Charley," escaped my mouth before he put his arms around me and patted my back as I, once again, descended into uncontrollable sobbing.

"Can't you let it go now, fellas?" he demanded of the sheriff and his coterie. "Can't you see she's exhausted?"

"Yes," Ellie firmly echoed. "You can talk to her tomorrow. She needs some rest and quiet now." Aggie whined a little and licked my hand, clearly agitated at my crying.

What ensued was a good-natured struggle between Charley and Ellie over who was taking me in for the night. I remember this in very fuzzy pieces and only recollect feeling a warm, cared-for glow in their loving ministrations. I don't know how it is that Ellie won, but I do recall being encouraged to eat some very bland but comforting chicken noodle soup and collapsing into a bed tucked under the eaves in their attic loft, Aggie—at my side—letting out a long sigh before I fell dreamlessly asleep.

I was far more functional and coherent the next day. It was wonderful to get out and walk with Aggie in the morning, even though it was overcast and threatened rain. The combination of fresh air and physical activity further rejuvenated me. Crime-scene tape warned us off The Cedars. A squad car was already parked in the drive, even though it wasn't yet eight o'clock. When we passed Piggy and Nancy's house, they came out to query me. I gave them a brief rundown of the previous day's events.

Piggy shook his head. "Can't imagine. Can you, Nancy? Can't imagine a murder right here on the point."

She shook her head, too. "No. And Jerome!" she added indignantly. "Why, who'd want to kill him? He was the soul of kindness. 'Cept Gertie might've wanted to kill him sometimes. It was like pullin' teeth to get that man to talk." She giggled, and I couldn't help smiling.

Piggy frowned his disapproval. "No time for silliness, Nancy."

She swatted his arm. "Oh lighten up, Piggy. I was just havin' a little fun. God," she said conspiratorially to me, "aren't men just the dullest?" I smiled again. "Now you, Piggy McDermott, wouldn't have the least idea of what I'm talkin' about 'cause you never shut up long enough for a woman to get frustrated with your silence. But a lot of men—and Jerome was surely one of them—you just couldn't get them to talk at all."

Piggy decided to ignore her. "Have any ideas, Tyler, about this murder?"

I shook my head, wondering if it could be connected to my pumping Jerome for information. "No," I said slowly. "It doesn't seem real to me."

"He didn't seem upset or anything? Acting odd lately?" Piggy prodded.

I shook my head again. "No, I don't think so."

"For heaven's sake, Piggy," Nancy interrupted. "Think of Jerome. Would you even know if there was anything different about him?" I couldn't help smiling once more. "I mean Jerome was Jerome. Stoic is the word, I think. Is that right, Tyler?" When I agreed, she continued, "He's the kind of man who'd be dying and still working, being quietly pleasant. Why, if anything was bothering old Jerome, nobody else would ever know. 'Cept maybe Gertie."

Piggy harrumphed but said, "I reckon you're right."

They invited me in for breakfast or "at least a cup of coffee." I declined, assuring them that Ellie and Hank had already promised me a big breakfast.

"Oh, that's good then," Nancy assured me. "You're staying with them? They'll take good care of you. Such sweethearts, those two are."

I agreed again, recommencing my walk with Aggie. We ended at Charley's store. He had a cup of coffee waiting for me, and we sat—as usual—on the bench outside his front door.

"You better today, Tyler? You looked a bit puny yesterday," he inquired kindly.

I barked a little laugh before tears started to roll down my cheeks. When Charley started apologizing, I shook my head, explaining. "Oh Charley, everybody here is so . . . so nice, so kind. Who could've possibly've murdered Jerome?"

"Actually, Tyler, I can't imagine. No ideas of your own?"

I shook my head. "Do you think it could have anything to do with my asking him all those questions?"

He shook his own head slowly, reaching down to scratch Aggie's tummy as she slipped, in ecstasy, to a heap on the ground, "I shouldn't think so. Did you tell the cops about it?"

"No. They never asked me anything that would bring that up and . . ." I hesitated, my eyes staring out across the gray, restless lake. "I guess I don't really want to think it's connected. Do you think I should tell them?"

Charley took his hand off Aggie long enough to pat my arm. "Tyler, you have to remember—you didn't kill anyone. Don't get yourself all worked up feeling guilty. Asking questions is not a crime." I pursed my lips and barely nodded when he paused, then he finished, "As to telling the sheriff, I don't know. You're probably right. There's not much point."

Before I left, Sally Branch came by the store to get some eggs. "Tyler!" she exclaimed. "Are you all right? It must've been a terrible shock to find Jerome like that." We chatted for a few minutes, and then as I started back to Ellie and Hank's, Melanie Granger—whom I'd never actually met but we'd waved at one another a couple of times—stopped her car alongside me and leaned out her window.

"Tyler, isn't it?" I nodded, and she continued. "Melanie Granger. Heard all about the trouble at your place, of course. You let me know—and I mean this—if there's anything at all that Allen and I can do. A terrible thing. Just terrible."

I smiled and thanked her, then continued on.

18

Breakfast was waiting when I got back to Ellie and Hank's. I dug in as if I hadn't eaten for weeks. Huevos rancheros with mounds of hot salsa and sour cream and sausage that tasted like chorizo, thinly sliced fried potatoes mixed with red and green peppers and onions, and thick slabs of what-appeared-to-be homemade bread, toasted. A large platter in the center of the table was heaped with wedges of cantaloupe. Between shoveling and chewing I inquired, "Where did you learn to make this?"

"Hmpph," Ellie snorted. "What'd you think? Only Californians know how to cook Mexican?"

Hank shook her head. "Don't mind Ellie now, Tyler. She gets her back up regarding coastal people's attitudes about Midwesterners. Actually, I lived in San Antonio for a while and learned a lot of Tex-Mex cooking there."

"*You* cooked this?" I mumbled around a large mouthful of toast, then swallowed quickly, hastening to add, "I'm sorry. Now I'm being ableist, aren't I? Just assuming that Ellie does the cooking around here."

They both smiled back at me as Ellie said, "Don't know as I've heard that word before. Ableist? But I think that'd do it all right. Hank here, counter to most stereotypes, is the cook. Neither one of us, to Mama's huge grief and consternation, ever showed any interest at all in the so-called culinary arts while growing up. Hank was a committed tomboy, and I was a committed Hank-devotee. If Hank didn't like doing it, I didn't like doing it."

"So how is it you finally learned to cook?" I asked Hank.

She waved a piece of toast in the air. "You either cook or find someone to cook for you. Or starve. Most of my life, I lived alone. I didn't like starving, so I learned to cook. And I learned to love it, too."

"And you do it very well," I added gratefully.

She nodded her acknowledgment. "Thank you."

"You never married?" I asked, wondering about these sisters' histories.

"Nope," she agreed. "Never married. Had roommates from time to time, but that's about all."

Roommates. I wondered. "What did you do, Hank?"

She smiled. "I'm an engineer, mechanical engineer. Worked mostly on bridges, dams, commercial buildings, that sort of thing. All over the world."

"That must have been fascinating," I said, thinking there were probably hours of stories to go with her life. "What about you, Ellie, did you mostly starve or what?"

She tittered, and I was surprised to see two little spots of color appear on her cheeks as she busied herself clearing the table. "Oh, I ate out a lot."

Intrigued, I pushed gently. "You didn't get married either?"

"Oh no," she agreed. "I was a schoolteacher. In the early days of my teaching, I'd have lost my job if I got married. Later, when they changed those silly rules, I was used to not being married. My students were my children, don't you know? And I loved my job."

"And," Hank added, "you had Willa to cook for you."

"Yes, that's true," Ellie agreed, moving toward the kitchen with an armload of dishes. "Willa and I lived together all those years, and she was a fine cook. Made it easy for me not to learn much about cooking, don't you know? She and I taught together," she added.

I looked from one to the other, Ellie avoiding any eye contact and Hank gazing at me with that clear, unwavering look of her steady brown eyes. My god, I thought, have I got a couple of old-time dykes living right next door to me? Did Ellie dog her sister's footsteps so much that she even fell in love with women, too? I didn't quite have the cheek to ask directly so said instead, "Here, Ellie, you get out of the kitchen now, and let me clean up. It's the least I can do for all your kindness."

She shooed me away, saying firmly, "Don't be silly. This is our kitchen, and you're our guest. Don't you worry any, we'll find ways for you to reciprocate if you need to do that. Now you just go out on the deck with Hank and the girls, and I'll bring you some coffee in a minute."

"Come on, Tyler," Hank was heading for the deck already. "She's too bossy to argue with, take my word for it. Anyway, we have our little systems here. I cook, and she cleans up."

The sky was still overcast, and the waves were churning wildly. Aggie and their dogs had gotten friendly and immediately headed off the deck to gambol about with one another—Aggie seeming like a hulking monster in the presence of those delicate little dogs. But the four of them rolled around like puppies—nipping at one another's ears and feet, groaning, yipping. Both Hank and I laughed aloud when Aggie pulled away, and her long legs quickly distanced her from the others, but Bette Davis, Ann Sothern, and Carole Lombard gamely scampered after her on their stubby little legs—looking for all the world like three white cotton balls tumbling after a large golden sun.

Ellie came out with a tray loaded with coffee and fixings. After placing it on a table between us, she headed back into the house. "Aren't you joining us?" I asked.

"I'll be out in a minute," she said. "Go ahead."

As I poured coffee for Hank and me, I asked, "Did you and Ellie grow up in this area?"

"No. We grew up in a small town just south of Duluth. I went to college in Duluth first, then Ellie followed me, naturally, but our paths started diverging at that point. I was always interested in building things and doing things with my hands. And Ellie was always interested in reading, in knowing things. It was inevitable that I'd go into engineering and she'd go into teaching. I left the area after college, going wherever the jobs were, never coming back much until after my accident. In the meantime, Ellie stayed in Duluth, living with Willa for some thirty years. I never could have been that settled, and she never could have been as unsettled as I was. We were lucky, I think, both having lives we loved."

"And also lucky," I added wistfully, thinking of my own sister, Magda, "having this solid rock of love between the two of you to come back to."

"Well," she drew the word out and laughed a little. "We didn't always know we had that, you know." I looked quizzically at her. "We didn't talk to each other for some years, actually."

I couldn't imagine this. "You didn't?"

She laughed again. "Oh no. I lived what Ellie thought was a dissolute sort of life, never settling down to one place or one person. See, enough of Mama had rubbed off on her that she was just a bit judgmental of me. Part of her yearned to be conventional, ordinary, and part of her made that impossible." The Willa part, I wondered? "We had been joined at the hip, practically, as children. I guess, in a way, those years we were so apart were necessary—probably for both of us—in order for us to find our own selves, rather than being carbon copies of each other. Or, more honestly, I guess, her being a carbon copy of me. So, like a teenager rebelling against a conventional mother by getting wild, Ellie's rebellion against me was to become rather straitlaced."

"But, Willa?" I ventured carefully.

"Yes, well that did rather complicate things for Ellie." She glanced toward the house. "Ellie's never going to come right out and say this. Women our age rarely do, you know. But, yes, she chose women and so did I. And, if we're right, you do, too."

It was clearly a question, though not directly worded so. I smiled, thinking of the two of them discussing my sexual orientation, and nodded. "Yes, Hank. I'm a lesbian."

She smiled in return and merely nodded. "But Ellie and Willa were teachers. And, on top of that, Ellie was something of a prig—or at least worked at being one for some years—so they lived very careful, circumspect lives. I did not, and that made Ellie nervous. Her way of handling that was to separate herself completely from me."

"How did that change?"

"Well, first I had this accident," she gestured toward her legs, "and Ellie came down to help out. I lived in St. Louis then. That's when we first discovered that we still shared a lot. Not only our childhood memories, but also we had developed a taste for the same music and books over the years, had the same attitudes and values about politics and life in general. Then, about two years after my accident, Willa died. I knew Ellie was going to be completely devastated and basically nonfunctional. Her entire adult life had been spent with Willa.

"I didn't hesitate. I just packed up all my stuff and moved home to take care of my little sister. And, of course, she's taken care of me as much as vice versa. We bought this place and spent our summers here, making it wheelchair accessible a little at a time, until Ellie retired three years ago. Then we moved here year-round."

"Your accident." I asked. "What happened?"

She shook her head dismissively, "Just one of those things. We all think it's never going to happen to us. One misstep, and . . . poof! Your life is changed forever."

"Don't you let her brush that off, Tyler," Ellie said as she joined us. I wondered if she'd known that Hank was going to tell me all this while she was in the house. "You been telling Tyler about my stupid-years, Hank?" This was clearly an inside joke with them, and Hank nodded and smiled. "This here woman—" Ellie pointed a thumb at Hank, "—was what you'd call a rake. Don't let her tell you anything else."

At this point, Aggie charged onto the deck and slid to a collapse next to my chair. "Those ferocious critters tucker you all out, Ag?" I asked, smiling inwardly at my sounding like Hank and Ellie. The ferocious critters, actually, seemed more worn out than Aggie as they wearily clambered onto the deck and plopped down. The three of us laughed.

"But about her accident, Tyler. You should know, she fell off a girder, more than fifty feet to the ground. By all rights, she should've been dead. Her back was broken, both legs were broken—one in two places, one arm was broken, her skull was cracked, various other bones broken here and there, one punctured lung, internal bleeding. She was a mess. And this woman," she pointed to Hank again, "this rake was such a damn fighter! She just wouldn't give up, even when everyone else did. She was in a coma for weeks. They all thought there'd be brain damage even if she did come out."

"Lot they knew," Hank inserted. "So much brain damage in this family, wasn't room for any more." They both laughed.

Ellie continued. "She was so badly banged up, they just patched her up and said to wait for her to die. Huh! Imbeciles. It's true Hank can't ever walk again, but let me tell you—it's a damn *miracle* that this woman is even breathing, let alone being an almost completely functioning human being. A damn *miracle,* I tell you! And that miracle is this woman's indomitable spirit!"

I had tears in my eyes by the time Ellie had finished, and Hank was waving her hand dismissively again. "Now Ellie," she warned, "before you go canonizing me, let's not forget that part of this so-called miracle was you. A big part." She turned to me. "She loves to make me out to be this saint, but let me tell you, I think I would've probably gladly just curled up and died 'cept there she was, every which way I turned, poking me and prodding me, insisting that I live. She took a year's sabbatical from her teaching and spent that year, Willa joining us during the summer, in St. Louis with me. Never letting me rest, nattering away at me like a swarm of mad honey bees all the while I was in that so-called coma. Jesus, I was just trying to get some rest! Die peacefully, if you will, but there was Ellie—jabbering away like a line of birds sitting on a telephone wire. 'Remember the time Grandpa took us to the circus? Remember the time we followed cousin Adam to the cathouse? Remember the time we built that raft and went down the river and almost went over the falls? Remember the time we . . .'

"I had to wake up just to get her to shut up! Then, was there any respite? Huh, plenty of times during that year, how I wished I'd died and been spared the tyrannies of a natural-born teacher. I have no doubt her students are relieved she's retired, believe me. The woman is obsessed! She made special flash cards for me to work with my vision problems and to jog my lazy memory. She worked side by side with the physical therapists. She never let up, and she never let me let up." Hank turned back to Ellie and scolded, "No, don't you go running on about miracles. If there are any miracles in this family, it's you. Plain and simple."

At this, the tears in my eyes completely spilled over, and before I could stanch them, I was sobbing again. "Oh Tyler," Ellie said, "we didn't mean to . . ."

"I'm sorry, Tyler . . ." Hank began, but I ran in the house and closed myself in the bathroom, feeling flooded with the grief of losing my mother, having a sister who would never do for me what these two did for each other—and knowing that I would not take care of Magda either—and the pain and confusion of Jerome's murder. After a while, I felt drained and sufficiently embarrassed that I hated to rejoin Hank and Ellie. But then, I knew I couldn't spend the whole day in their bathroom, especially because it was the only one they had. So I dabbed at my red, splotchy face and puffy eyes with a cool washcloth, not that it made much difference, and left my haven.

"I'm sorry . . ." I started, when I got back to the deck.

"Don't be silly," Ellie interrupted. "You never have to apologize for feeling things, Tyler."

I smiled wanly. "If anything," Hank added, "we're sorry that we were being so insensitive to what you've been through."

"Oh no," I objected. "You weren't being insensitive. I loved hearing your story! It's just that it moved me a lot, and it seems, these days, that I can't feel anything without all of my feelings coming tumbling out."

With that, I told them my story. My family in California, the summers spent next door, my mother's dying request and death, her will and my own estrangement from my sister, the trip here, the slow unpeeling of the layers of my family's secrets, all finally culminating in the horror of Jerome's murder.

"So, do you think that Jerome's murder has something to do with your asking all those questions?" Hank asked.

I shrugged. "I don't know. In one way, it doesn't seem possible. I mean, what kind of sense can it make? In another way, what else was different in Jerome's life?" We all sat in contemplative silence for a few minutes, then I said, "I told the sheriff I'd go in and make a formal statement today. Do you think I should tell him about all this stuff?"

Ellie nodded firmly, and Hank said. "Yeah, I think you better. What could it hurt? And it might be important. Who knows?"

19

The sheriff was not particularly impressed with or interested in my information. I didn't blame him. It didn't make any sense that there would be any connection between Jerome's murder and my pestering him with questions about things that happened sixty-odd years ago. But then, as I pointed out to the sheriff, it didn't seem to make much sense at all that Jerome was murdered. Clearly not wanting to give me any false impression that I might be included in this investigation, he taciturnly conceded that it did seem odd. He told me that the state BCA boys were done with my house, so that I could move back into it, but I shouldn't go near the lift until the crime tapes were removed.

"BCA?" I inquired.

"State Bureau of Criminal Apprehension," he declared crisply. When I raised my eyebrows, he continued, "They're always called in for murders in rural areas. We don't have the sophisticated equipment necessary for this kind of investigation."

I nodded, thinking "or the sophisticated training?" but decided that such thoughts might be big-city prejudice on my part. I had to get home because my sink was being installed that day. The plumber and I arrived at almost the same time. He went to work in the kitchen, and I wandered through the house. Fingerprint dust covered everything on the first floor. I wondered what they were looking for. Obviously, Jerome's fingerprints would be everywhere. And mine. And Gertie's. I wondered if they thought I'd killed Jerome myself.

I stood on the porch and looked out toward the lift, where yellow crime tape, repelling nosy parkers, was still hanging. I noticed that the tape extended around a grove of pines next to the lift. I started to open the porch door before I reminded myself that the tape was a "keep-away" announcement. I called the sheriff and asked him why tape surrounded that group of trees by the lift.

"Can't rightly tell you, Miss Jones. Must be those BCA fellas found something in there. Just stay away from it until the tape is removed, hear?"

I agreed. The image of Jerome lying crumpled in the lift came to my mind again. This serene haven suddenly felt anything but safe. I called Sonny.

"You have to come stay with me for a while," I stated unequivocally.

"Have to?" she repeated. "What's going on, Tyler?"

I filled her in. "I'm afraid to stay here alone, and it'll be more than a month before my friend Mary Sharon will arrive. It would be great for the kids anyway, and you can help me."

"But Tyler," she protested, "you want me to bring six kids to a place where a murder occurred? Where a homicidal maniac is still on the loose?"

"Give me a break, Sonny. They live in a city where murders occur all the time, where homicidal maniacs lurk behind every bush!"

She chuckled. "You have a point, I guess. Let me check a couple of things, and I'll get back to you, okay?"

"You're a lifesaver," I breathed.

"Maybe, Tyler, maybe. I haven't committed to anything yet. Can you imagine what it will be like for me to transport six kids and two dogs—can the dogs come?"

"Sure. The more the merrier," I responded. Anything, anything, I thought to myself.

"—to the North Shore? This is a logistical nightmare! Do you have a crib?"

"No, but I'll get one. The cots are still on the porch, and the old bunk beds are here, too. I got new mattresses for all of them." Where were those new mattresses, anyway? "That means you'll have to sleep on the porch with me or in one of the bunks. Do you want me to get another mattress? For Grandma and Grandpa's room maybe or one of the other bedrooms?"

"No, no, Tyler. With the cots and the bunks, that sleeps eight. Right? I'll bring a portable crib for Annabelle—IF I COME—so that's plenty of beds. Don't get anything else unless you intended to anyway."

"Sonny, please don't say 'if.' I really need you. Please? Please come. It will be great for the kids, and you can bring your work. Don't bring a crib—it'll be one more thing for you to figure out. I'll get one, okay?"

"Jesus, Tyler, quit whining." She said it affectionately, but I knew she meant it, too. "I'll get back to you."

I called the furniture store in Duluth and found that the delivery for my furniture was scheduled for the end of the next week. I added a crib and mattress to the order. Then I called the appliance outlet in Grand Marais to make sure that my stove was also coming.

Next I called Mary Sharon in California. I tried to convince her to skip taking the Bar and come help me tickle out the truth here. As well as protect and comfort me, but I didn't tell her that part.

"Oh sure," she said agreeably, "just blow the past three years, not to speak of the intensive studying I've been doing this summer, and come out there to play Watson to your Sherlock."

"Mary Sharon," I pointed out, "you can take the Bar anytime. Twice a year, isn't it? Doesn't this sound like more fun?" I immediately felt guilty, referring, even kiddingly, to any part of Jerome's death as "fun."

"Tyler. Root canal sounds like more fun than studying for the Bar. Are you afraid?"

I nodded, even though she couldn't see me. "Yes. Even if it has nothing to do with me, it's pretty unnerving to have this happen here."

"Don't you think it's odd, Tyler, that you've now found two bodies in your life? I mean, most of us never encounter murder on any level—unless we're cops or something." Mary Sharon was referring to the fact that I'd stumbled across another body a couple of years ago in the park by my house in San Francisco. Actually, to be perfectly accurate, Aggie had stumbled across it.

"Of course I find it 'odd,' Mary Sharon, but what are you suggesting? That I live a life full of corpses on purpose or something?"

"No," she drew the word out slowly. "It's just odd. An observation, Tyler, a statement. Not a judgment. How likely do you think it is that it has something to do with your family stuff?"

"Actually, Mary Sharon, I've been thinking and thinking about that. And—this really creeps me out—I'm more and more convinced it *does* have something to do with me. The point is, if someone wanted Jerome dead, and it had nothing to do with me, wouldn't they just kill him and get out of here? But this killer took the time to figure out where I was, call the lift back up the cliff, dump Jerome's body in it, and push the lever to send it back down to me. Why would anyone do that?"

"Huh," Mary Sharon puffed. "Obviously to scare the shit out of you, yes? That's the only thing that makes any sense."

"Exactly. And, by the way, it worked very well. So why would anyone want to scare me? The only answer I can figure is: to get me to stop asking questions."

"Again, makes sense. What did the sheriff think?"

"He wasn't impressed, but I didn't exactly put it to him this way."

So, after finishing my conversation with Mary Sharon, I called the sheriff and filled him in on these new insights of mine. "Yes," he agreed, "I'd thought along those lines myself. Maybe you better tell me again this story about your family?"

I gave him the details once more, thinking "we could've avoided this if you'd paid attention to me the first time I gave you this information." When we were done, he warned me to lay off my research "for the time being" until they had a better picture of what had happened but also insisted that I fill him in on any new info I ran across. I thought that was a pretty contradictory message but assumed he understood human nature.

The sheriff's suggestion notwithstanding, I next called information for the Fergus Falls area and got a number for the mental hospital there. "This is Tyler Jones," I informed the woman who answered the phone. "I'd like to know if you have a Louisa Jane Anderson there or if she ever was there." She put me on hold. In a couple of minutes, I repeated my request to another person. She wanted more information, so I gave her what scanty information I had—including the whys about my inquiries and the probable year of incarceration. I was put on hold again. Yet another person, a man this time, came on to hear my story. Once more, I was put on hold. Finally, the middle woman came back on and informed me that a Louisa Jane Anderson "was not and never had been incarcerated at this institution."

I was surprised. Before she got off the phone, I managed to get names of two other such institutions in the northern half of the state and a phone number for the State Mental Health Department to get more information about existing facilities in the state and any that no longer existed. I spent the next three hours on the porch, calling one place after another, being put on hold endlessly, checking out every possibility, getting promises to check long-buried records, and came up with a big zero. Although I was expecting at least two callbacks in the next day or two, it looked as if my grandmother had never been in a mental institution in the state of Minnesota. Would they have taken her out of the state? That didn't seem likely.

I looked at my watch. Ten to five. I got in my car and drove into Grand Marais, to the house where Vera Johannsen lived. She was glad to see me again and shooed Frances out of the room once more. I told her about my phone calls.

"Vera," I asked, "is it possible they took Louisa out of the state?"

She shook her head. "I guess it's possible, but I don't think they did. The more I think about this, the more certain I am that Alma told me that they'd put her in Fergus Falls. You're sure she wasn't there?"

"Well, as sure as I can be. I talked to three people–they kept putting me on hold–but they seemed absolutely positive."

"Strange."

"Vera, do you know if Alma ever saw Louisa after they put her away?"

She shook her head. "I don't think so. Alma told me that Holger had visited Louisa, and she was ranting and raving and out of control. I told you this already, didn't I?" I nodded, and she shrugged. "Alma said that place didn't want anyone to come visit her. That she'd be better off if everyone left her alone." I wondered if an institution would do that. Forever.

Vera insisted, "Tell me about Jerome." I was startled, just assuming, I guess, that maybe she wouldn't even know about his murder. I told her what little I could. "Were you asking him a lot of these questions, too?" I nodded. "So? Do you think there's any connection between your questions and Jerome's death?"

I suddenly felt a shiver of fear pass through me. What if Vera got killed, too? "I don't know," I responded. "Mostly it doesn't make any sense why they would be connected but . . ."

"But why would anyone take the time to put Jerome's body in your lift if they weren't trying to scare you?"

God, she's quick, I thought, and answered, "I know. I thought of that, too." I stood up. "Vera, this makes me nervous. I don't think I'd better be asking you any questions for the time being. I mean, what if Jerome knew something and someone didn't want me to know that something? What if you know it, too, just don't realize its importance?"

She nodded slowly. "Yes, you're probably right."

I couldn't resist one more question, though. "Do you know anything about the rum running that went on around here during Prohibition?"

Her hands moved in an agitated sort of way for a moment, then settled back into her lap as she sighed. "Oh, I don't know what difference it makes anyway. You know about my son, Burt, the Politician?" She put a capital P on that word as if she were making fun of it. I agreed that I did know about him. "Well, he never wants us to talk about it. Might spoil his chances for the Presidency." Another capital P. I suppressed a grin.

She was silent again, and I didn't push her. "Don't know why it bothers him so much. Didn't them Kennedys make their fortune offa bootlegging?"

I did smile this time. "Seems to me that's the story."

"Well. Isn't much, actually, for me to tell you. It was Men's work, you know." There was that capitalized word again. "So, we women were never privy to much of it. Besides, men are just big boys, you know. They liked it to be all cloak and dagger, Secret stuff." She snorted. "There was some activity early in the '20s, right after Prohibition started, and they all did it . . ."

"Who's 'they'?" I interrupted.

"Oh, Joey—my husband, you remember—and Holger. Eugene Chummy," I could not remember anyone ever calling Old Man Chummy, Eugene. ". . . and Ole—you know, Bjorn Olesen? The postmaster?" I nodded. "Your great grandpa, it seems to me, you know—Alma and Louisa's daddy. And a couple others, I guess. Gerald Granger, I think." Granger. I had an image of wrinkling my brain as I tried to remember why this sounded familiar. Oh. Granger. Allen and Melanie. The man who insisted he'd never heard any stories about this area. "All dead now. Except Ole."

"Do you know anything else about it?"

She shrugged. "Like I said, not much. You should probably go talk to Ole. He might know more. 'Cept I heard he's not quite all there anymore." She tapped her index finger lightly on her temple. "He's still alive, isn't he?"

I nodded. "I think so. Charley suggested I go talk to him."

"Charley?" she asked. "Charley Chummy?" I nodded again. "Oh, a good boy, that Charley. Are you and Charley keeping company? What's the word you use nowadays? Dating?"

"No," I smiled and shook my head. "We're just friends."

"Humphh. Anyway, they did it for a while. Whatever 'it' was, presumably they were smuggling in booze from Canada, then transporting it to Duluth and beyond to sell for big bucks. But then, all of sudden, they quit. Abruptly. Never

162

would talk about it. Any of them. I don't know what any of the others did with their money. Joey used ours to expand the mill. It was a smart move."

"When did they quit? Do you remember?"

She squeezed her brows together, thinking, shaking her head slightly. "Can't remember exactly. It was a long time before Prohibition was over. Middle '20s, maybe? I once kidded Joey about how much money we could still be making, and he just told me to forget it. That it was 'just kid stuff.'" She snorted again. "Like all of a sudden they all growed up?" She shook her head.

"When I was a kid, we always heard there was a cave or something where the stuff was unloaded. My cousin Corky and I used to look for it but never found it. Do you know anything about that?"

She looked thoughtful and didn't answer for a minute. "That's weird because it rings some kind of bell in my mind, too, but I can't think where it'd be. I know that point as much as anyone. Grew up within spitting distance of it and don't remember anything like that. Maybe it was somewhere else?" I shrugged.

I got some food for dinner and sat down by the harbor, eating while turning over everything Vera had told me. I needed to go talk to Ole. But would I be jeopardizing his life then? Maybe Charley would go with me. I needed to clean my place again, remove the fingerprint dust. But I wasn't ready to clean that night. Nor was I ready to stay there. I gratefully accepted Hank and Ellie's hospitality and slept at their cabin again.

20

The next morning, after another delicious breakfast, Hank and Ellie and I sieved through all the information I'd garnered up to this point and examined various ideas and theories. It was stormy, the wind off the lake driving the rain hard against the windows of their cozy cottage. Ellie built a fire, and its warmth and sizzling light cast a rosy glow on the four dogs and the three of us.

"Well," Ellie said firmly, "I think it's pretty obvious that you, or at least your questions, have something to do with Jerome's murder. It's the only thing that makes sense." Hank and I nodded our agreement. "But why? What is it you're uncovering that could make such a difference to anyone? Your grandmother was probably raped and unfairly incarcerated in a loony bin, but who would that affect today? Holger is dead. Alma is dead. It seems as if this story of yours has more secrets to disclose or else nothing makes sense." Again Hank and I nodded.

After a moment of pondering, Hank said slowly, "Has it occurred to you, Tyler, that your grandmother, Louisa, was never actually put away?"

"Yeah," I agreed. "Ever since those phone calls yesterday, I've started wondering."

"But what else could've happened to her?" Ellie asked. I shrugged, but Hank and I were looking into each other's eyes with understanding. "You think she might have just took off? Women have done that when they can't face motherhood or feel they can't give their baby enough."

"And then Holger made up the story of having her institutionalized? Why would he do that?" Hank asked.

"Pride?" Ellie said, tentatively.

"Mmmm." Hank looked unconvinced. "Maybe."

"Or . . ." I glanced at Hank, who was still gazing at me with those deep, penetrating brown eyes, "maybe she never left Cook County at all."

Ellie frowned. "What do you mean? If she never left . . ." she trailed off as she became aware of Hank and me looking at each other. "What?" she demanded. "What are you two thinking of?"

Hank shrugged this time, and I said, "It just doesn't make much sense. If Louisa ran off, I don't think Holger would have had to make up another story. It would be sufficient, for his purposes, to just point out that she was completely irresponsible: first she refused to get married, then she ran off. So . . . If she didn't run off and if she wasn't put in a mental hospital, what's the alternative?"

"What?" Ellie pushed, clearly not making the leap herself.

"Well, maybe she never left Cook County, and maybe no one ever saw her again because she was dead."

Ellie's hand flew to her mouth, "Oh! Do you think? . . . " She looked from Hank to me and then finished, "Do you think Holger killed her?"

"It certainly seems to be one of our options," I said as Hank nodded.

"Look at all the pieces," Hank said. "Holger rapes and impregnates Louisa. She refuses to marry him. She has her baby and disappears. Everyone's told she went off her rocker and 'had to be locked up for her own good.' They believe it mostly, because it seemed so crazy not to marry Holger in the first place, and she always was a little 'different.'

"But—what if she has the baby and tells Holger to 'get lost' while threatening to expose him to everyone. He kills her, disposes of the body, and convinces her parents first, then everyone else, that he was forced to have her locked up."

"Shouldn't be too hard to hide a body here. Weight her down and slip her over the side of a boat out in the lake, yes?" I inserted, feeling a little sick to my stomach.

"Something like that," Hank agreed. "Then Alma is convinced it was all a great tragedy, and she marries the rounder, in spite of Louisa's best friend attempting to warn her off. Although Alma might not be deliriously happy with Holger, she has a home and two daughters she loves. Forty years later, Holger starts drinking a lot and talking too much. She finds out—between his drunken ravings and another tête-à-tête with Louisa's best friend—the truth about the rape. And starts wondering about the incarceration."

I picked up the thread at this point. "Here, the story line gets a little murkier, but let's suppose she tries to find Louisa and runs up against the same dead ends I've encountered. Let's suppose she interrogates Holger. Does he tell her he killed Louisa? Does he let just enough slip that she figures it out? Or is it sufficient—knowing he raped Louisa? Maybe that's all Alma had to know to cut Thalia out of the will because she

167

couldn't stand the thought of anyone but Louisa's child inheriting the family home."

"So," Ellie said, "her making the decision about the will *might* have happened regardless of this murder theory."

"Yes, that's what I'm saying. I'm not sure what she knew. Maybe she just suspected or wondered. Like I'm doing. Or maybe she had no idea. The reason I'm looking at this possibility is it makes no damn sense that Holger told everyone she went to a 'snake pit' if she didn't. And, the other piece that still eludes me is that I think this whole secrecy about the rum running is somehow linked to this."

"Why's that, Tyler?" Hank asked.

"I don't know. It just keeps coming up. Maybe because I keep bringing it up. I can't seem to tickle this out. But the timing is right and . . . it seems odd to me that a little rum running almost seventy years ago is still so shrouded in mystery. And now, Vera tells me they just quit doing it about the time Louisa disappeared. I just *know* there's a connection. I know it. I *feel* it, in my bones."

Neither of them contradicted me. For a couple of minutes, we watched the rain sliding down the windows. Ellie put another log on the fire and stirred it up. "Well," she said, turning to us and clapping her hands lightly together. "What can we do to help?"

I looked at her with surprise. "You really want to help?"

"Of course," Hank echoed. "What's next?"

"I thought I'd go to Silver Bay today to talk to Ole. Hank, if you want, you could get on the phone and see what you can find out about mental hospitals in Wisconsin. We're so close to Wisconsin, I guess it's possible that she got taken over there."

"Okay," she agreed.

"What about me?" Ellie asked.

I frowned a little. "Well . . . would you be willing to just hang around next door? I'm expecting a couple of callbacks

168

from some places in regard to records in their archives. It would be good if someone was there for them to talk to."

"That's fine," Ellie agreed equably. "And it's probably a mess from those lab people, yes?"

"Yeah, but Ellie . . ."

She waved my objections away. "I've got to do something while I'm sitting around. Might just as well tidy the place up."

I felt a rush of warmth and affection for these two women. "You two are pretty special, you know?"

"Nonsense," Hank remonstrated. "We're just busybodies who are very happy to be in the center of things."

21

I couldn't convince Charley to go with me to visit Ole in the nursing home in Silver Bay. "But Charley," I entreated, "he knows you. He's more likely to talk to you."

"I know, Tyler. I just can't get away today."

"Why don't you call one of those women who help you out on weekends? They could cover for you for a couple of hours, couldn't they?"

He shook his head. "I'm sorry, Tyler, really. The women around here do a lot of cooking for a funeral. Especially this one. I just can't get anyone to cover for me."

He looked so sorrowful, I backed off. "I'm sorry, Charley. It's a huge loss, isn't it?"

He nodded tersely. "How about you? You doing okay?"

"Yeah. Hank and Ellie are feeding me like there's no tomorrow. And we're all three brainstorming like mad, trying to figure out what's going on. You know what's odd, Charley?"

"What?" He stopped wiping counters and shelves and gave me his full attention.

"I called Fergus Falls yesterday, and they have no record of Louisa ever having been there. I spent the rest of the day on the phone, trying to find some institution in Minnesota that had a record of Louisa Jane Anderson. Nada. A big zero. It's like she disappeared off the face of the earth."

"That is odd," he agreed.

"Then I went and talked to Vera again? She's pretty certain Alma told her Fergus Falls was the place they took Louisa. And I asked her about the rum running? And, you know, she told me that they just quit doing it, abruptly, in the mid-'20s and would never talk about it again. More of the same stuff we kind of sensed when we were kids."

"Mmmm," he responded, going back to unloading a box of canned goods.

"So, that's when I decided that I needed to talk to Ole. He seems to be the only one alive who was involved with that stuff."

Charley stopped his activities again and came and leaned toward me over his counter. "You know, Tyler, maybe you ought to quit this nosing about." My eyebrows shot up as I stared at him. "Hey! Someone's gotten killed. Until you know what happened, it might be dangerous to keep poking around in stuff that's none of your business."

"Charley," I protested, forcing my voice to stay calm. "It is my business!"

"Okay, okay," he conceded. "I just think you oughta let the sheriff do the checking for a while."

"He didn't seem too interested in my family stuff. I don't think he's convinced there's a connection between Jerome's murder and my 'nosing about,' as you put it. But Charley," I leaned back over the counter toward him, "if they weren't connected somehow, how come Jerome's body got put in my lift? Why wouldn't the murderer just take off?"

"Exactly my point," he agreed. "It seems like that must've been—I don't know—a warning. Why don't you back off for a while?"

I shrugged. "After I talk to Ole. See you later, Charley."

On the drive to Silver Bay, some forty-five miles along a curvy, narrow road, I thought through everything that I'd heard or made up, and everything that had happened. There was something missing, I was sure, but what? And I was equally sure it had something to do with the rum running. I didn't doubt I was on the right track, but I wondered if I'd ever know the whole truth. It didn't seem like anyone, so far, knew the whole truth.

The rain continued down in a steady rhythm, spattering my windshield and limiting my visibility. I kept my wipers on high, but I could see little out of the back window. I drove slowly; this curvy road could be dangerous in clear weather, it was definitely hazardous with a wet surface. I kept trying to see if anyone was following me. If this were a movie, now would be the time and place that someone would attempt to murder the hero. I chuckled a little at my dramatics and wished I had a drink. "Jeez," I thought to myself, "Give it a rest."

Ole was in a tiny room with two beds, a small TV that was blasting, institutional green walls, and a torn shade on a window that overlooked some garbage cans. There was another old man in the other bed who looked more interested in me than Ole did.

"Ole?" a nurse nearly shouted. "Someone's here to see you! Isn't that nice?" In a quieter voice, she said to me, "He's hard of hearing, and you have to be prepared: he doesn't make much sense most of the time." Ole was staring at the TV but didn't seem to really be seeing it. He had a few strands of white hair on his head, his lackluster eyes were sunken into his almost-visible skull, and his crooked hands kept mindlessly clutching and unclutching each other. I would not have recognized him as the Stony River postmaster of my childhood.

"Hi Ole!" I yelled. "I'm Holger Schmidt's granddaughter, Tyler!"

He didn't respond, but the other guy turned the TV off and said, "Hi. I'm Elmer. Elmer Seward. Old Ole isn't much here, you know."

"Hi Elmer," I said pleasantly but turned back to Ole.

"Ole! I want to ask you about the old days."

"Used to be the postmaster at Stony River," he suddenly blurted out.

I felt a leap of excitement. That seemed to make sense. "I know. I used to spend my summers in Stony River in the '50s and '60s. At my grandparents place on the point? The Cedars?"

"The Cedars?" he peered at me. "Who are you?"

"Tyler Jones. My mother was Weezie Schmidt. You know, Alma and Holger's daughter."

"I broke my arm when I was six, you know. It never did heal proper. That was the winter the wolves got so hungry, they even ventured into Grand Marais."

"Uh . . . really? What year would that be?"

"They was here again last night. You know? They was."

"Uh—who was here?"

"Them. The same ones as always comes. I tell them and tell them to get out, but they don't pay me no mind."

"Oh, that's too bad." This wasn't going to be easy, I could tell. I glanced over at Elmer, who was grinning lopsidedly.

"We got too greedy," Ole rambled on.

My ears perked up. "Did you? Back when you were running rum in from Canada?"

"Whiskey mostly. Never rum. How's come they always call it rum running?" I started to answer, but he just kept talking. "And then, when my brother drowned that year in the big lake? My mother cried herself to sleep every night that whole winter."

"That must've been so hard for her," I agreed. "Ole, can we talk about Prohibition? The years that you and your friends smuggled booze in from Canada?"

"They closed the post office, you know. I'd already retired by then, thank God, but they closed it—just like I hadn't even worked there all those years. Like it didn't count. Just up and closed it!"

I tried another track. "Do you remember Louisa Anderson, Ole?"

"My wife's name was Jenna," he said. "She was from Duluth. Came up on the *America* one year and spent the summer with her aunt in Hovland and never went back. Jenna. She was one in a million. She never liked Louisa. Never liked her at all. Said 'good riddance' when Louisa was gone. 'Good riddance.' It didn't seem very Christian, but she never liked her. Thought she was too peculiar."

"So you do remember Louisa?"

He shook his head. "Never heard of her. Louisa? Don't know anyone named Louisa. Who are you?"

And so it went for the next hour while I tried to elicit some clear information from Ole. All I got was frustration. He rambled, seemed perfectly lucid, but made statements that had nothing whatsoever in common with one another, contradicted himself, contradicted me, but—actually—rarely connected at all with me. Just made statements that stood alone in the morass of his rambling. Elmer put in a word occasionally, but mostly he watched us.

I finally gave up and turned to Elmer. "You've been listening to all this, Elmer. Does any of it make any sense to you?"

He shrugged. "Sort of interesting. He's rambled before about that rum running, but I thought he'd just made it up. Old man's bravado, you know? So, it really happened?"

"Oh yeah, it really happened. As much as I know, Ole's the only one still alive in this group that did it. He ever say anything to you about a woman named Louisa?"

Elmer shrugged. "Might have. Mostly talks about his wife, Jenna. You know how it is. He rants so much, I don't pay much attention."

I sighed and looked at Ole while he was telling some story about his uncle who came over from the "old country." I shook my head and said, "I give up," then shouted, as I stood, "Thanks Ole! It's been nice chatting with you!" And dropped my voice to an ordinary register to add, "Sort of. Nice to meet you, Elmer."

"Yeah," he said. "Sorry I can't be much help to you. I only moved up here in the '50s. Never knew many of those fellas down Stony River way." He shrugged again.

"Bye Ole!" I shouted.

And he said, "She was already dead, you know."

I had started to walk to the door, stopped, and turned around. "What?"

"Lost a dog the big blizzard of '43. 'Course lots of folk lost livestock and even loved ones. Still, I loved that old dog. Big lab. Name of Sanders. We found him in the spring."

"Ole! Who? Who was already dead?"

For a moment his eyes focused on me. "Who are you?"

I repeated myself. "Who was already dead?"

"Lots of folk died in the wars. Lots of them. I woulda gone to that second one, but I had the bad foot from the first one. So Jenna was glad. I was, too, I guess."

22

The next day was Jerome's funeral. When we had the memorial service for my mother, I entertained the notion of never going to a funeral again. Here I was, just a few months later, at another such event. To not go would have been disrespectful. Charley and I and Hank and Ellie went together. I was glad to be with friends, and even more glad to put my attention to getting Hank in and out of a church that was not wheelchair accessible, so that I didn't have to focus on our reasons for being there. I'd had enough of death for a while. Forever, actually—as if any of us have that kind of choice.

My mother was cremated. I know some people think it is essential to see the loved one dead, that we don't really believe in death unless we view it. My mother thought the idea of gazing at a dead body was barbaric. I don't know where I stand between these polarities. Having been with my mother when she died and having already seen quite enough of Jerome's body, I didn't really want to see either of them again. But that made it impossible to imagine how I might have felt if I hadn't seen both bodies already. Would I need the closure of viewing someone dead to round out my grief?

I don't know. I just know, at Jerome's funeral, I avoided looking at his body laid out in splendor at the front of the church, reposing in a coffin. Grisly. My mother might've been right. Lots of people commented, afterward, on how wonderful Jerome looked. That was confusing to me. With my one quick glance at him, I just thought he looked dead. Was that "wonderful" to some people?

Jerome's wife, Gertie, was distraught but quietly so, with silent dignity. I put my arms around her and murmured a handful of meaningless but well-meant words, and she responded by smiling and patting my back, as if I had lost my husband instead of vice versa. My guess is that most of us are far more at ease with comforting others than we are being comforted.

There was a meal following the service, in the church basement. Luckily, there was an entrance to the lower level from the parking lot, so we didn't have to abandon Hank or carry her downstairs. There were tables loaded with enough food to feed the proverbial army. In contrast, our Fourth of July feast looked like scant pickings.

We ate well, people talked to one another, even laughed. It was a party, albeit a subdued one. Charley and Hank and Ellie knew more people than I did, so they were busy visiting all the time. I sat back and let my eyes roam the room. Was the murderer here? Probably. Almost everyone in town seemed to be here, more likely the whole county.

Vera Johannsen was sitting in a wheelchair near the punch. Several women clustered about her, chattering avidly. Lyle was standing nearby, stiff in an ill-fitting suit, nodding occasionally to someone or other but otherwise not talking.

Burt was also present, as resplendent in an impeccably tailored suit as Lyle was uncomfortable. He was, of course, "working" the room. I looked around but didn't see his wife. Piggy and Nancy bustled over and chatted with me for a few minutes before they moved on to other friends. I noticed the sheriff, his eyes moving around the room much as mine were. Our eyes met momentarily, then moved on.

Sally came and sat next to me. "Oh Tyler. This is so dreadful, isn't it?"

I nodded. "You knew him, too, huh?"

"Oh sure. Jerome worked for all of us on the point. A really dear man. I can't quite believe he's actually gone. I mean, why would anyone want to murder him?"

I shook my head. "I wish I knew. I'd feel a lot safer at The Cedars if this were all cleared up."

She nodded. "Yeah, I suppose that must be difficult."

"Plus I . . . I feel responsible. Like maybe it's my fault."

"Why would it be your fault, Tyler? Just because it happened at your place?"

"No, it's not that. It's because I was asking him a lot of questions and now I wonder . . ." I ended up telling her a shortened version of the whole story.

She was spellbound. When I was finished, she said, "That's fascinating! I wonder how many secrets all of our families are hiding? My grandmother knew most of those people, you know."

"She did?"

"Sure. She might have been cranky with kids, but she got along reasonably well with other adults." We both laughed a little. "She spent six months every year up here. These people were her neighbors, her friends. You know, she used to talk about pulling all her notes together and writing a memoir. I wonder where those notes are now?"

"You've never seen them?"

"Nah. I couldn't imagine, as a kid, what could be interesting enough about her life to write a book." We both smiled and shook our heads at our child selves. "But, you know, there's a lot of stuff pushed into drawers and such at that place. Every summer I say I'm going to go through everything and get rid of stuff, and every summer I get up here and," she threw her arms out and her head back, "die. Oops." She grimaced. "Wrong word today. God, I'm tacky. But you get the idea—I collapse, and when the end of summer has come, I still haven't gone through all of Grandma's stuff. I'll look around, Tyler, and see if I can find anything."

"That'd be great," I said, changing the subject. "Say, Sally, have you got a husband?"

She laughed, this time wholeheartedly, then clamped her hand over her mouth. "God, is that tacky, too?" I shook my head. "Yeah, Tyler, I've got a husband. We just spend most of the summer apart from one another. He comes up once in a while, but he's not really crazy about it. No fax. And it's a nice break for both of us each year."

"That seems sensible," I nodded, then changed subjects again. "Did you say Jerome worked for everyone on the point?"

"Yeah. At some time or other."

"So the Grangers would know him, too, then?"

"Oh sure."

"Have you seen them here today?"

"No," she looked around. "Doesn't look like they came. Well, they sort of stick to themselves, you know."

"Yeah, but you'd think . . ." I shrugged.

After the funeral, I got caught in a flurry of activity getting ready for the arrival of Sonny and her gang. I had known she would find a way to come. I continued to spend my nights at the Ansons', not yet ready to sleep at my own place, and worked all day at my house. The stove arrived, completing the kitchen that Jerome had worked so hard on. My eyes filled with tears, admiring this splendid kitchen and feeling his absence acutely. The upstairs was almost finished, too.

As I began to prepare the rest of the house to paint, Gertie showed up and—when I remonstrated—she said, simply, "I'd rather be working, Tyler, than sitting home alone." I nodded, and we hugged wordlessly.

Together, we finished scrubbing and cleaning the downstairs, then painting the ceilings, walls, and woodwork. While I worked at Grandpa's desk, getting some writing done, Gertie painstakingly painted the new stair railing and posts that Jerome had installed before he died. There was very little furniture yet—except for on the porch. Inside were only the desk, table, and bunk beds—and no curtains, but the house shone with pride. I'd told Sonny to bring blankets, then found a shop in Grand Marais that had beautiful quilts. I bought one for each bed.

One day I drove to Duluth again, to go to Target to get those household items I'd forgotten—more kitchen stuff, bathroom stuff, a handful of books for the built-in bookcases in the living room (I couldn't bear those empty shelves any longer), a wicker table for the porch so I could more easily eat my meals out there, a couple more rockers for the porch, some end tables and lamps, and various and sundry other items. I stopped in a couple of gift shops on the way home and bought two more quilts and a few other decorative items: baskets, a soapstone bear, a wooden carving of an old woman.

Again, my Visa was getting dangerously stretched. I was lucky, I thought, to have enough savings to allow me this freedom of buying before I actually realized the cash from the sale of my mother's houses. Even though I had a stable income from my newspaper work and a little extra coming in from my book as well as from the rental of the studio apartment in my house, I was really more comfortable than those incomes would have allowed because I lived in a house I'd inherited, mortgage-free, from my aunt. Without the huge bite of housing costs every month, I'd been able to save quite a lot.

When I knew the furniture was actually arriving, I invited Ellie and Hank and Charley for dinner. I wished Grandma had left me a cookbook, but—of course—she didn't use recipes. She just did it: put together whatever she had and whatever she instinctively or experientially knew worked. I wasn't going to pretend I could reproduce that skill. I'd found a cookbook at one of the gift shops, so I decided to live dangerously and cook something I'd never done before. Because I used to love my grandma's wild rice dishes, I made a chicken/ wild rice hot dish and salad and almost-homemade bread: frozen. The raspberries were starting, so I told Charley to bring some ice cream, and I went out and picked raspberries for dessert.

I fussed over the furniture when it came and made beds. I wasn't yet certain why I was furnishing the place to this degree. When everything was arranged the way I wanted, I realized how badly I needed more books and paintings or photos, something on the walls. And dressers. And knick-knacks. Well, I reminded myself, you only need those items if you intend to live here. Do you intend to live here? And I replied in the negative—only it felt like a tentative negative.

The dinner was a great success. The back stoop was a low one, so it wasn't difficult to get Hank into the house. I made a mental note that I needed to find someone like Jerome to be my handyperson now. I wanted a ramp built for easy egress. Everyone properly ooh-ed and aah-ed over my house. We all shared a collective sadness that Jerome wasn't here to see how well it had turned out. My cooking was adequate, maybe even slightly better than that. And, for the first time in days, I had a chance to talk over everything again. The callbacks from Minnesota institutions as well as Hank's calls to Wisconsin had revealed no new information. It did not seem likely that Louisa had been in a mental hospital anywhere in the area. Charley was not surprised to hear of my useless visit to Ole.

"I heard he was drifting a lot," Charley said. "I'd just hoped that you might have caught him on one of his good days."

"Well," I responded, "according to his roommate, that's about as good as it gets."

"Too bad," Ellie said, and we all agreed.

"The sheriff have any new ideas?" Hank asked.

I shook my head. "No. I talked to him yesterday. He was very vague. Any of you hear anything from your local buddies?" We all looked at Charley.

He laughed. "Sorry. Not a thing on the grapevine that I know of."

"You know," I started slowly, "all these days that I've been doing all this physical work—and driving to Duluth and back—has given me a lot of time to think and turn things over. The day before Jerome was murdered, I told him I was going to Duluth to try to track down Louisa. Find out if she'd been put in Fergus Falls or wherever." I paused.

Hank prompted me, "And?"

"And—now that I think of it—he questioned me about what day I was going. He wanted to know if I was going the next day or not. I don't know. Maybe I'm just looking for something but . . . it wasn't Jerome's style, it seems to me, to ask many questions of other folk. He was intensely private himself, and so it wasn't like him to pry much."

I looked around the table, and everyone nodded. "Anyway," I continued, "I got to thinking. What if he was coming to tell me something that day? I'd told him I was going to just take the day off and relax, go to Duluth the day after. So, what if he decided he had to tell me something before I left? And what if someone else didn't want him to tell me?"

"Makes sense," Hank agreed.

"But who?" Ellie inquired. "Who didn't want you to know what? I'm sorry. I'm not dismissing this thought of yours. It's just so frustrating because it doesn't make any difference whether you're right or wrong if we don't know who, what, why?"

We all nodded and lapsed into silence. Then we took our ice cream and berries and coffee to the porch—I was glad I'd picked up the additional rockers. Tired of mystery talk, we entertained one another with childhood stories as we appreciated the reflected lights dancing on the horizon from the sunset behind us. It was relaxing and made me almost feel we'd achieved a sense of normalcy.

I slept alone in the house that night, with some apprehension. Stronger than my misgivings, though, was my need to overcome my sense of alienation from this place I loved so much. After everyone left, I padded around comfortably—washing dishes, cleaning the kitchen, touching the new couch or a book on one of the bookcases, turning the lights out.

Finally, I sat—with all the lights out—on the porch, Aggie at my side. The slightest noise made me hyperalert, then I would breathe deeply, talking myself toward calm. When I was absolutely certain I was hearing the careful placement of footfalls, one after another, I was not able to talk myself out of the adrenaline-rushing grip of fear coursing through my body. I did not move, however; I just waited. I felt the same still tension in Aggie, next to me. Suddenly, a doe with a very young fawn came into view—about twenty feet in front of the house. Aggie let out a low growl, and I placed my hand on her head, shushing her. Relief ran giddily through me, and I almost laughed out loud—except I didn't want to scare them away.

The doe picked her way cautiously through the open space, supremely alert, stopping frequently to listen, to observe. The still-spotted fawn stumbled slightly behind, clumsily attempting to keep up with her mother, bumping into her when she stopped. It was a soothing scene and made it easier for me to let go and sleep.

23

The next morning, I felt as if I'd come a long way toward reclaiming my space. I walked around the house with its new furniture, its freshly painted walls, its stunning kitchen, its cozy quilts, its new dishes, its fabulous views out every window—either of lake or woods or bay or more woods—and I felt a deep sense of contentment. Aggie followed me, her tail wagging whenever I made a comment. I was puzzled. This was home in a very real way, a huge chunk of my childhood all tied up in this place. And yet. San Francisco was my home, too, had certainly been more of my home—just in terms of time—than Minnesota ever had been. And cities. I loved cities! Didn't I? What was this strange pull I was feeling?

Aggie and I finally went out for our morning walk. It was chilly, a soft fog moving in and out of the trees, a ship somewhere out in the mist, letting its foghorn lead the way. I donned a sweatshirt and clapped a hat on my head, in case it started to rain. I thought of the doe and her baby last night and felt a bubble of elation rise within me.

The coffee was hot and ready by the time we made it to Chummy's. "Morning, Tyler," Charley greeted me as he poured me a cup. We didn't sit out on the bench; it was too clammy.

"Hi Charley. Have a good night?"

"Oh yeah. I almost always do. I'm tired come bedtime. How about you?"

I told him about the deer. "I don't know, Charley. I've got this funny desire—well, funny isn't the right word—to just stay here. Not go back to San Francisco."

"Doesn't sound funny to me. Makes perfect sense. Going back to a city that's full of pollution and crime and too many people and not enough parking spaces. Now that seems funny."

"And all that's true, Charley. But it's also my home. The place I was born and raised. A city of immense beauty, astonishing light, all kinds of people speaking all kinds of languages, water dancing all around it, excitement, a dazzling array of options, culture, movies. I don't know. Can I give that up?" He shrugged, not arguing with me. "Have you ever been there, Charley?"

"Once. Briefly. Just before shipping out to 'Nam. It was pretty, I'll grant you that." He grinned. "For a city."

"Yeah . . ." I felt a pang of homesickness. For the rolling streets, for coming around corners to amazing vistas, for the smell of eucalyptus trees, for the unbelievably sharp color of deep purple or blazing scarlet bougainvillea rambling across the face of a house, for the quaint, European look of the houses nestled into hills and one another, for the sound of conversations spoken in languages that aren't even faintly familiar, for the smell of the saltwater of the ocean, for the hustle and bustle of a large city, for my very own little house perched high on one of the western hills, overlooking the ocean rollers—at least for the two or three weeks that it was not completely enshrouded in fog. How could I even consider leaving that endlessly fascinating city?

Charley was patiently waiting for me to return to the present, here and now at Chummy's in Stony River, Minnesota, on the North Shore of Lake Superior. He was looking at me intently. This time I shrugged and shook my head. "I don't know," I said.

He appeared to understand and responded, "You'll figure it out."

At that point, Nancy came in, as usual exuding energy. "Good morning, you two. Have they figured out who offed Jerome yet?" I winced, but Charley seemed to take her style in stride.

"Not that we know of, Nancy. Do you know any deep, dark secrets about Jerome that maybe the sheriff ought to hear about?"

She tittered. "My stars, no. But there must've been something we none of us knew about, don't you think? I was over to see Gertie yesterday. She's holding up well, all things considered. But then, she's Scandinavian after all. Ice water for blood, I swear. Now me, if it were Piggy, well I'd be all to pieces I would. 'Course some days I must admit I do wish he'd up and croak, he's such an annoyance. But you know how that is, has nothing to do with what you *really* want. No sir, I'd be a complete wreck if someone did my Piggy in. 'Course that's the Latin blood in me."

When Charley and I just stared blankly at this revelation, she explained, "You know my family's mostly German, but there's some Spanish—from way back, something to do with them Crusades, I think—on my ma's side. Makes me a little more emotional, you know."

Expressing my gratitude for this insight, I eased my way toward the door, glancing at Charley, whose lips were puckered into a silent whistle that almost made me laugh. "Tyler," Nancy caught me before I made it out the door. "Are you okay? Isn't it just terrifying being there all alone after Jerome's murder?"

"I'm okay, thanks, Nancy. I admit, I was a little jumpy, so I stayed with Ellie and Hank for a few days. My cousin and her kids are arriving today, so I won't be alone."

"Oh good. Let me know if there's anything I or Piggy can do, won't you?" This was sort of shouted after me as I sidled out the door, practically knocking Sally Branch down.

"Hi Sally," I said. "Sorry."

"No problem, Tyler. How're you doing?"

"I'm fine, thanks. Sonny's coming today, so I'll have you over soon. Your kids are probably the right age for some of her kids."

"Great! It'd be good to see Sonny again. I look forward to that."

It was midafternoon before Sonny and her gang arrived. She had borrowed a friend's aged VW bus, and it was full of kids and dogs and luggage and pillows and favorite stuffed animals and balls and bats and toys and books. Hanging on the outside were more luggage and bikes. Suddenly, my yard was filled with hollering kids and barking dogs and two adults trying to make contact. Aggie was delighted to see Reuben and Alfie again, who were barking their exultation.

I hugged Sonny and said, "I'll never forget you did this, Sonny."

She laughed as Alfie—or was it Reuben?— crashed into the back of my legs, almost knocking me down. "Oh, I know you'll never forget it, Tyler. But will you forgive me?" We both laughed.

"I need to get Annabelle into bed, Tyler," Sonny said as she lifted a sleeping baby out of the bus. "Crib? Then I just want to walk around and see the place."

"Come on." I picked up some of the bags that were emerging from the bus. "I'll show you."

"Patsy? You and Ghia and Maya make sure the dogs and the little girls don't go near the cliff's edge. Start bringing everything inside." Sonny's eyes swept over the house. "It's been so long since I've been here. This is a real treat, Tyler. It's a little worse for wear, isn't it?"

"Just outside. Haven't gotten to that yet. Wait until you see the inside." My head was swiveling, counting kids, already worrying about that cliff.

As we entered the house, Sonny said, "Tyler! This kitchen is beautiful! You've done a wonderful job!" I glowed in her praise.

I set the crib up in Grandma and Grandpa's room, so we took Annabelle in there. "I thought it'd be easier to have the baby on the first floor," I explained to Sonny, "but we could put the crib somewhere else if you want to."

Sonny deposited the still-sleeping Annabelle in the crib and replied, "No, this is fine. But where are you sleeping, Tyler? This is your house now, you know."

I smiled. "I sleep where I always slept. On the porch."

She grinned. "Some things never change, huh? Maybe we better find Corky to keep you company."

"I know. I miss him. But I think Charley has become a kind of surrogate Corky for me."

The kids were in the house now, voices raised as they claimed space. "I get the top bunk!" someone shouted, "No, I do!" someone else protested.

"Hey!" Sonny commanded attention. "Outside. I don't want to see any of you again until the VW is emptied and all the inside stuff is brought in here. Got it?"

"O–kay," was the general response, as they stampeded down the staircase. I felt enormous relief that Jerome had replaced the entire railing. "Can we go down the elevator when we get everything unloaded, Mom?"

"Yes," Sonny agreed, to general shouts of approval. She turned to me. "Charley? Charley Chummy?"

"Yeah," I agreed. "He runs the store now. His grandpa died."

"Charley!" She shook her head a little. "Is he still so cute?"

"He's older, Sonny. But yeah, he's pretty cute still. You know, he's not exactly my type." She rolled her eyes. "But he's been very good to me since I got here. A big help. He's a really sweet guy. But then—it seems like almost everyone up here is."

I gave Sonny a tour of the house, and we ended up on the porch with cups of coffee. "Where should we put this stuff?" one of the girls asked, arms full.

"Just dump it on the dining room floor for now," Sonny said. "We'll sort it out later." We gazed out across the yard at the lake and the horizon, and Sonny sighed. "I'm not glad one of your neighbors died, but I'm glad you pushed me to come. It would've been so easy to come up with a million excuses for why I couldn't make it, and then I would've missed this. I forget how heavenly it is. I'm glad to be here, Tyler." We squeezed each other's hands for a minute. "The old swing is still there."

"Yeah. It wasn't out there when I got here. It was still in the garage, but Jerome and I moved it out there."

"What happened to the garage?"

"Oh, I had it burned down by the fire department as a training exercise. It was about to fall down, and I didn't want to worry about anyone getting hurt." I barked a facsimile of a laugh.

"What?" Sonny asked.

"It's just kind of ironic. I was worrying about someone getting hurt, then Jerome . . ."

When the girls finished unloading, they got in the lift to ride down the cliff, calling, "Is this safe? Is there a weight limit on this? Do you want to go with?"

We assured them they were safe, and we walked around the property to the edge of the cliff to watch the girls scramble on the rocky point below. "Wow, it sure brings back memories, doesn't it?" Sonny commented.

"Yeah," I agreed. "I think I've been in a memory bath for weeks now."

When the girls came back up, Sonny enlisted their services again. She had sorted out the piles into toys and books, clothing, and bathroom items. "Okay," she said. "Rose and Lily? You stack all the toys and books and coloring stuff on the shelves in the living room. Is that okay, Tyler?"

"Sure."

"Then Maya and Ghia? You take all this other stuff upstairs and put it in the bathroom or the bedroom." Just then we heard Annabelle wail. "Patsy, take the baby's stuff into the bedroom on this floor and change her before you bring her to me. Let me see your hands." She looked at Patsy's outstretched hands, turned them over and said, "Okay. Put my clothes and stuff in the bedroom with Annabelle. You can all figure out the bunks whatever way you want." Patsy was already on her way with diapers and a bag full of clothes and a diaper pail.

She stopped and said, "Mom? Can't Ghia and me sleep on those beds on the porch?"

Sonny looked at me. "Sure," I said. "That's what they're for. When we were kids, your mom and I and my sister and your Uncle Corky always slept out there."

"Cool," Patsy asserted as Ghia echoed her sentiment.

"Me too, me too!" Rose and Lily clamored.

"There aren't enough beds on the porch. Don't you want to sleep in the bunks upstairs?" Sonny asked.

"Oh yeah!" they acquiesced. "On the top, on the top!"

Maya looked a little dejected. "Maya," I said, "do you want to sleep on the other end of the porch with me?"

She pushed her glasses further up her nose and nodded, shyly. "Okay!"

"Good," I said. "I used to sleep there with Corky, so it's kind of lonely to sleep there alone." Actually, I had been thinking Sonny and I would maybe sleep together out there, but I didn't want Maya to feel left out.

As the kids hauled the stuff upstairs, Sonny said to me, "You didn't have to do that, Tyler."

"Didn't have to do what?"

"Give up your space alone to sleep with one of my kids."

I waved my hand in dismissal. "It's temporary, Sonny. I don't mind."

We took all the kids to Chummy's to meet Charley and get more food until tomorrow when we'd have to go to Grand Marais for a major grocery expedition. The kids pretty much filled up Charley's store. He looked amazed when we all trooped in. I was even more amazed as the food quickly piled on the counter.

"Cheese, Mom," Rose said as she brought it.

"Frozen pizza." Six got plunked down by Ghia.

"Can we get ice cream?"

"Ice cream! Ice cream!" chanted both Lily and Rose.

Peanuts, potato chips, crackers, cream cheese, cottage cheese, tons of milk, peanut butter, jam, more bread, more cereal, bagels, yogurt, candy bars that got put back from whence they came, macaroni, soup, honey, eggs, lettuce, carrots, onions, potatoes, green pepper, hamburger, hot dogs, chops, mounds and mounds of food.

I tried to put it on my account, but Sonny intervened. "Don't be silly, Tyler. This is an invasion. You don't have to feed us."

"But I want to," I insisted. "It's my way of showing my gratitude that you came."

She smiled grimly, patting my hand. "Tyler, putting up with us will be gratitude enough, believe me."

24

It was hours before the chaos in the house quieted to a few murmurs, and I began to understand what Sonny meant. A huge dish of macaroni and cheese and equally huge salad disappeared quickly into six hungry mouths. The younger girls cleared the table while the older girls did the dishes. I retreated to the relatively quiet front porch where Aggie lay in an exhausted heap with Reuben and Alfie. Her tail moved slightly when I came on the porch, but she didn't make any attempt to rise.

Sonny bathed Annabelle and got her ready for bed while the others were cleaning up. While Rose and Lily bathed themselves—with a little help from Ghia, Sonny settled into a rocking chair on the porch and read a book to Annabelle. Annabelle listened and gazed with a rapt intentness that I wouldn't have expected in a baby. Every now and then she would bang her chubby palm on the page and announce, "Gog!"

"That's right, sweetie," Sonny would agree. "That's a dog."

Or, "Mow! Mow!" and Sonny would say, "What does a kitty say?"

"Mow!" Annabelle would shout. "Mow, mow, mow!"

"Can you say 'kitty'?" Annabelle would respond with something that sounded like, to me, a word with all consonants, and Sonny would say, "That's right. Kitty."

After Annabelle went to bed, Sonny sat on the new couch in the living room and read from a Laura Ingalls Wilder book to Rose and Lily. I assumed they were working their way through the series. Tears sprang to my eyes as I remembered my mom reading the same series to Corky and Sonny and Magda and me for a couple of summers running. I noticed that the older girls lounged around the living room, too, while Sonny was reading, although it was clear from their commentary that they'd already heard or read these books.

Patsy and Maya and Ghia began their baths while Sonny put Rose and Lily to bed, both on different top bunks. "It doesn't matter where I put them, anyway," she told me when she rejoined me on the porch, "They always end up in the same bed."

"Cling to each other, do they?"

"Oh yeah. They are the only constant in each other's lives."

"What's their story?"

"They were found in a barely-heated room in the dead of winter with no food when they were both under two. They had apparently been there alone for some days. A neighbor had complained to the police of constant crying. Lucky they had enough strength to cry or they would have just starved or frozen to death. They were both malnourished and extremely dehydrated when they were found."

"God," I shook my head.

"Rose, she's the older, had been physically abused. They found her on the floor with the baby in her lap, kind of rocking her and crying."

"Breaks your heart, doesn't it?"

"Yeah. They were able to find out who the mother was but never tracked her down. She was white, by the way. Everyone assumes, because the girls are clearly part black, that it must've been some black welfare mother who abandoned them. But color doesn't matter. Can you imagine how desperate or messed up that mother must've been to just leave them there? Maybe she killed herself. Or maybe she just left town with some boyfriend or other. The girls have been in foster homes ever since."

"How long have you had them?"

"Two years in September."

"Will they stay with you?"

"I think so. We certainly want them to, and this is probably the stablest home they've had."

"Tell me about the other kids."

She laughed a little. "I wasn't going to have kids. Oppression of motherhood and all that, you know. Plus I had Things-To-Do." She shrugged. "I was really involved in AIM—American Indian Movement?—back in the '70s and equally in love with a native man who was also active. I knew it was never going to work out between us. He was smart and funny and so damaged—I just knew it wouldn't work. I decided to have his baby, so I'd always have some of him with me."

"And named me," the object of her story entered the porch, "after my grandmother. Patricia Two Feathers."

"I guess you know this story," I smiled at Patsy.

She rolled her eyes. "Oh yeah. Listen. My father was an alcoholic, he beat Mom up, he abandoned her and me when he found out she was pregnant with me, but Mom! She just goes on talking about him as if he were Black Elk or something. I keep telling her, it's racist to expect less of a person because he's Native American. But she wants to romanticize him and forgive him and put him on some stupid pedestal. You'd never do that, Mom, if he were white. You know you wouldn't."

I was stunned. "How old are you, Patsy?"

She just grinned as Sonny said, "Fourteen going on forty-four. She thinks she's the mom here."

Patsy rolled her eyes again, and I said, "She makes a very good point, Sonny."

"Yeah, yeah, I know," Sonny agreed. "You two don't have to gang up on me, you know. And anyway," she swatted Patsy's bottom, "you never knew your father, so you don't really know what you're talking about. I've told you before, and I'll probably tell you again—your father had awful problems and did awful things. I'm not denying that. But he was also a very special person." Her eyes softened. "Very special. I don't want you to just know bad things about him."

"Yeah, yeah," Patsy echoed her mother as she started back toward the sunset porch. "Luckily I know my Grandma Patricia, otherwise I would've made a shrine to the great man by now."

Maya and Ghia crowded in the doorway at that moment. Maya said, using her pajama tops to wipe her glasses. "Are we talking about that ghost man again?"

"Don't you start," Sonny leveled a warning finger at her, which both girls immediately parodied.

"Now we have to do *my* father," Maya said. This apparently was not a new conversation with them. "A-basically-good-man-who-simply-couldn't-handle-the-responsibility-of-a-family."

"So," I asked Maya, "would this be the official version?"

She curled her lip, made a clucking noise, and nodded. "Ask the mother." She curtsied in her mother's direction. "She'll tell you all."

Sonny shrugged. "There's not much else to tell. He *was* a pretty decent man, but I already had Patsy and Ghia, and when Maya came along, poof! He was outa' there. He sends money once in a while."

"Do you ever see him, Maya?" I asked.

She shrugged with the studied nonchalance kids think they do so well, although astute adults can easily discern the pain. She put her glasses back on, almost seeming to use them to distance herself. "Oh, once a year or so. *He's busy, you know.*" She didn't try to hide the pain with those final words, dripping in sarcasm.

"I'm sorry," I said.

"Oh, that's okay," she seemed to recover quickly. "At least I see him once in a while."

The girls decided to move one of the sunrise cots down to the sunset end of the porch, so the three of them could be together. Maya said, shyly, "I hope you don't mind, Tyler. It was very nice of you to offer to sleep with me on the other end, but I just kinda would like to be with my sisters."

"No, no," I assured her. "I understand perfectly."

Three beds didn't really fit in the alcove, but they managed to squeeze them in even though they could no longer walk back there but had to crawl across one another's beds now to get in and out. Then they had to rig up some lighting, so they could all read a little before they went to sleep.

When that was done, I asked them what they were reading. "I'm reading a book on computers," Ghia said. "I really prefer books that educate me."

The other two grimaced and bobbed their heads as they said, to each other, in hoity-toity voices, "I-really-prefer-books-that-educate-me." Ghia pushed them and said, "Come on, you guys. You know what I mean."

"We do know what you mean, Ghia, but geez—do you have to sound so stuffy?" Patsy said while Ghia made a face at her. "I'm reading *Black Elk Speaks*. Mom's been after me forever to read this book. Then one of my friends read it and loved it, so I'm finally reading it."

"Didn't count when *I* thought you should read it," Sonny said in a pouty voice.

"Yeah, I know," Patsy said. "Motherhood's tough."

And Maya just held up a Nancy Drew book. "Oh, I read all those when I was a kid," I told her. "In fact, your Uncle Corky and I used to read them aloud to each other before we went to sleep. And I've read *Black Elk,* too, Patsy. It is good."

They all retreated to their beds, and I said, lowering my voice, "I think your girls are terrific, and I admire the relationship you all seem to have. You're really doing a good job, Sonny."

"Did you all hear that?" she called to the girls.

"Yeah, yeah," they chorused.

"Just remember that when you're so pissed at me. Tyler says I'm doing a good job." Then she picked up the thread of our conversation about the girls. "Ghia was adopted by a white American family when she was a baby and brought here from her native India. They, her adopted parents, were killed in an automobile accident when she was two, and she came to live with us. She's been with us ever since. I legally adopted her four years ago, but that was just a formality. She's been a family member since she arrived."

"And Annabelle?"

"We don't know anything about her, really. Other than her mother probably had AIDS when she was carrying her. Maybe even is dead now. This is getting to be a pretty common problem—babies being born with health problems created by their parents and then being abandoned. So, we just love her until she's gone."

"There's no chance she could survive?"

"Probably not. We can't hold on to false hope about this. She's going to die in a year, maybe two."

"What about the AIDS? I mean, changing her diapers, the drool, wet kisses. Couldn't any of you get it from her?"

"It's not quite as communicative as people think. We use surgical gloves to change her if any of us have hangnails, open cuts, or sores on our hands. Otherwise—not much to worry about. The drool? Nah."

"I'm really impressed, Sonny. I don't know how you do it."

She shrugged. "It's hard for me to take credit for something that comes so naturally to me. I mean, I appreciate your praise, Tyler, it's just that we all have different talents. And I was lucky enough to find mine."

25

The next weeks flew by. Patsy and Ghia and Maya and Sonny scurried across the face of the house on borrowed ladders, scraping and sanding and repairing, preparing the outside for painting. I supervised but rarely ventured up a ladder. I didn't like the fragility of tall ladders, but also my "physique" was unsuited for such activity. The fatter you are, the more uncentered your balance seems to become. So I was in charge of the littler girls. We all pitched in for meals and cleaning inside.

And some days, we just played. I took them all up to Charley's fishing shack to go swimming. We had picnics at nearby state parks. Charley begged, borrowed, and stole some fishing rods, and we all went fishing in the upper reaches of Stony River. We hiked up the river trails of Stony, Temperance, and Cascade Rivers. One morning, we stumbled up the Oberg

Mountain Trail with flashlights in the pre-dawn so that we would be eating breakfast on its crest when the great ball of the sun came up over the far edge of Lake Superior. We went to Canada, stopping at every public beach and river and trail and other scenic sight along the way.

Other days, we just hung around home. Sonny and I stayed with the younger kids so the three older ones could strike out alone—exploring the shoreline in both directions, riding their bikes up into the hills or into Grand Marais. Whenever she could, Patsy loped over to Chummy's and enticed Charley to go out back with her and throw baskets at his hoop. She was going to get a basketball scholarship to college, she assured me.

Sonny smiled and nodded. "She probably will. She's very good." Sonny and I laughed about girls and sports in our youth. Girls could be cheerleaders or play intramural sports. "GAA!" Sonny shouted.

"What's that?" I asked.

"Didn't they have GAA in California?" she asked back. "Girls Athletic Association. All the so-called 'hefty' girls were in GAA."

"That would have been for me, then," I agreed. "I was definitely 'hefty.'"

"Not that *I* did anything like that," Sonny stated. "I would've worried too much about breaking a fingernail." All of her girls, even Maya who was the least athletic, sneered at such a notion.

"You were such a priss, Mom," Ghia said disgustedly.

"That I was," Sonny cheerfully agreed. "But I've made up for it." They all looked skeptical about that last statement.

"You have to understand," I said pedantically. "When we were girls, there were pretty much three choices: you could be brainy or brawny or glamorous. But not all three or even two of those."

"And I chose glamorous while Tyler vacillated between brawn and brains."

I laughed. "I'd never thought of it that way, but I guess you're right. I was never in sports, but I was real outdoorsy."

The older girls just rolled their eyes, and Maya said, "You two are weird, you know?"

On cold, rainy days, we stayed inside, sometimes with a roaring fire—reading, playing games, coloring in color books, or just drawing pictures. Everyone was accumulating treasure troves of rocks, gull feathers, pinecones, leaves.

On these occasions, I would sneak off to the office and get a little work done. I had begun to make notes about the possibility of a completely different novel, one about a woman who gets institutionalized unfairly. I felt that flare of dread, anticipation, thrilling potential that all writers feel at the beginning of a new project.

The girls discovered Sally's kids, Josh and Florrie, before I invited them over, and they immediately became members of our merry troupe, joining us for many of our outings or just hanging around. Sally joined us, too—we three "big girls" enjoying one another's company as much as the kids. Rose and Josh organized baseball games whenever they could. Both discovered they intended to play "pro" ball when they grew up. None of us told Rose that Josh had more possibility than she did for this particular goal.

Maya often begged off on these sports activities. "My glasses might get broken," she'd protest, and Patsy would retort, "That's just an excuse, Maya. You're too lazy."

At which point, Sonny usually intervened with a quiet, "Everybody gets to be who they are here with no shaming, Girls."

Lily, like Maya, was more interested in activities other than sports. She was young enough though, at six, to just wander off with no one paying much attention.

It wasn't entirely idyllic. Lily had earsplitting tantrums, often precipitated by nothing discernible, in which she shrieked and threw her body forcefully against floors, walls, furniture, trees, anything available. It was terrifying because she seemed intent on hurting herself. Perhaps the most wrenching part was watching Rose's calm ministrations to her baby sister's hysteria. I wondered how long before seven-year-old Rose exploded with the pent-up emotions that were being denied as she so capably played "mother" to Lily's "baby." Rose already had headaches that made tears roll down her cheeks.

And the older girls—being eleven, thirteen, and fourteen—were, after all, in the early throes of that dreaded passage called adolescence. In time-honored ways, their moods were mercurial and capricious. One moment, one or the other was cheerful, the next moment that same one might be yelling at one of her sisters or at Sonny or me. There were a fair amount of flounces and sneers and pouts. Some nights, one of the beds on the sunset end of the porch would be empty as one or the other chose to sleep upstairs rather than "with those unbearable creeps."

Annabelle had a remarkably and achingly sweet nature, but even she had her fussy periods. Sonny handled all of this with unbelievable (at least to me) equanimity while I, more and more, enjoyed the near-solitude of my morning walks with Aggie, Reuben, and Alfie. An occasional encounter with other adults was easy to take compared to the upheaval back at my house.

And yet, I found myself surprisingly comfortable with all of them—enjoying the girls' sharp minds, quick wit, lively interplay. It was true, night was always a welcome respite when the girls settled down for bed and Sonny and I, depending on the weather, sat on the porch or in the living room. Sometimes we walked out to the swing and stargazed.

I filled Sonny in on all of the information I'd gathered, uncovered, surmised since my arrival. We'd talk on the porch in ordinary, quiet voices, and I would fill with an extraordinary wash of déjà vu as I became aware that the sound of turning pages from the end of the porch had ceased. I knew the girls were listening more than reading. Rose and Lily were too young—and, in some ways, too enclosed in their own world—to pay much attention to any of the adult conversations, but the older girls were intensely interested in all the details of the family saga, asking endless questions.

"They locked your grandma up in a place for crazy people just because she had a baby without getting married?"

"Well, maybe. We're not sure she ever was locked up, but yes—if she was, that's essentially why."

"But I don't get it. Mom was never married. Could they lock her up?"

"Probably not, although I don't know for sure. Times are different. There are still people who think your mom is an awful person because she didn't get married before having kids, but not so many as there were in Grandma's time."

"But why lock her up? Why not just ignore her or be mean to her if they thought she was a bad person? Why lock her up? Did they really think she was crazy?"

"Well, some people really believed that young women who were promiscuous—"

"What's that mean?"

"Mmmm. Sexually active, you know, having sex with one or more men when you're not married."

"What about the guys? Weren't they promis-whatever, too?"

"No. Sexual activity was considered 'normal' for men. It just wasn't 'normal' or expected behavior of well-brought-up young women."

"That hasn't changed that much. Girls who sleep around are considered sluts while boys who sleep around are, you know, studs."

"So your grandma maybe got locked up in a crazy place just because she was, like, a slut?"

"Sort of. And it did happen to a lot of women. In Grandma's case, we think they were easily convinced that she was 'crazy' because they thought she was promiscuous and because she wouldn't marry the father of her baby and—maybe—because she didn't really want to be with men."

"Like you?"

"Yeah, like me. Maybe. We don't know for sure."

"But we do know for sure in your case?"

"Yup."

"I like girls a lot. Does that mean I'm a lesbian?"

"Maybe. Maybe not. Your mom likes women a lot, but she's not a lesbian."

"So it's just about who you sleep with?"

"Sort of. Women can love women but want to make love with men—and they are not lesbians."

"Like mom."

"Yup. And women who love women—and sometimes even love men—but want to make love with women are lesbians."

"Who you sleep with, like I said."

I didn't argue, although I know plenty of lesbians who would. At this point, Sonny inserted, "Let's talk a little about this word 'crazy.' I don't want you all using that and not being respectful of what it means to be labeled crazy. Especially if you're female."

I loved these long, convoluted conversations with the girls. Sonny didn't seem to think any subject was inappropriate for them to hear about or discuss, so I could entirely relax about what I said in their hearing. All the family stories intrigued them, and they began searching for the lost smuggling cave.

Early evenings, when the girls scoured the point, with Josh and Florrie in tow, Sonny and I and Annabelle sat on the swing. "Wouldn't it be fun if Corky came to visit? Watching your girls do all the same things we did, it just gives me such a satisfying sense of continuity. I've never really wanted children—and I don't regret that—but I'm sure enjoying getting some of the vicarious pleasure of motherhood being around your kids."

"So, Tyler," Sonny asked with annoying regularity, "are you staying in Minnesota?"

I waved a hand impatiently. "I don't know. Some days I think I must. Others, I know I can't. I've gotten to the point of feeling I can't possibly sell this place. Maybe I'll spend three or four months here each summer, and the rest of the year in my other home in San Francisco."

"That sounds pretty good."

"If I do that, will you and the kids spend part of each summer with me up here?"

"Of course! I love it here, and look at these kids—" she gestured at Rose and Lily piling rocks to produce boundaries for a just-pretend house while the older girls were off somewhere, "—this is a marvelous experience for them."

"Well," I had a sudden inspiration. "Why don't you and the kids just move here, Sonny? You can do your work wherever you are, the house is plenty big enough to hold you all, it would be fantastic for the girls, and I could come to visit you each summer. You could buy the place from me—cheaply—or I could just rent it to you, cheaply." I was really getting excited thinking of this possibility. "What do you think?"

Sonny smiled at me, shaking her head. "It's very tempting, Tyler, don't think for a minute it isn't. It's just not the right place for me. At least not now. We have our routines, our rhythms. I need the help and support I get from the women who act as 'big sisters' to these girls. Patsy's grandma is on a reservation, and Patsy spends a month with her each summer. This is wonderful for Patsy because it keeps her connected to her native side, but the other girls need to be exposed to their own cultures, too. Rose and Lily already go to a Black Baptist Church, primarily because of the music, which is such a huge part of the black half of their heritage, and spend time with a couple of African-American families who are willing to help me in regard to their cultural/racial identity. Ghia goes to a South Asian women's support group. Granted, they're mostly adults, but it's essential that she doesn't get raised "just white." She needs to hear the languages, be introduced and exposed to the cultural differences, to remember and understand her roots. I can't raise these girls as if they're just like me. None of this would be possible up here."

I nodded. "I understand. It was just a thought . . ."

Sonny hugged me. "I think it was a great thought. Just not right for now. But Tyler, I think you should move back here. You seem so perfectly at home here. And you, too, can do your work anywhere."

"Yeah, maybe . . . "

I turned the options endlessly over in my mind. Could I leave San Francisco? Of course, I'd lived in Minnesota for seven years already, for college and three years after, but that was in the Twin Cities. Could I be happy year-round in a place as isolated as this with so few people I might be able to deeply connect with? After a while, it felt like my brain just needed a nap, so I quit thinking about it.

We included Hank and Ellie frequently on our wanderings, whenever we could. The little kids adored them—it got to be usual to see Annabelle sitting contentedly in the wheelchair with Hank, who she called something like "Gapa." Rose and Lily, for some reason, personally adopted Ellie as their "Gamma." Of course, Sonny's parents weren't active grandparents to these kids, so I expect they felt a certain hunger for that presence in their lives (with the exception of Patsy, who was lucky enough to have her Indian grandmother). I thought about how alone I'd felt driving out here to Minnesota—Mom dead and my dad and sister as good as dead—and now I'd acquired this enormous extended family.

Charley came by a few times, and once brought his two-year-old granddaughter to play with Annabelle. One night, Charley and Sonny went out to dinner. I raised my eyebrows, and the girls pestered and teased her, but Sonny just ignored all of us. Most of the other neighbors on the point stopped by to say hello, at least. Some stayed to visit. Sally and Hank and Ellie were the only ones courageous enough to invite the whole crowd to dinner.

"Why don't you stay longer?" I said one evening to Sonny, a couple of days before they were scheduled to leave. We were sitting on the swing by the cliff with Annabelle, in her p.j.'s, between us. The other kids were around somewhere. "It's not like you have a job waiting for you."

"But I do, Tyler. I've got deadlines to meet, meetings to attend, things to do. This has been great, but I really do have to get back. Besides which, you've got to get writing, too. You can't do that with six kids running around."

"I know. But . . . I'm going to miss you."

"We'll miss you, too. Are you still afraid to be alone here?"

"Not so much anymore. And it will only be another week or two until Mary Sharon and Celia arrive. They're probably in Rocky Ridge with Mary Sharon's mother as we speak. It'll go fast. I wish you could meet them."

"I'm sure I will sometime, Tyler."

"Brd!" Annabelle announced as a gull sailed by.

"That's right, Annabelle. Bird." Sonny said as she picked her up and stood. "It's time to go to bed now, honey."

Annabelle, the picture of cherubic innocence, put her head down on Sonny's shoulder and said, "Ni-ni," before putting her fingers in her mouth.

I got up, too, and patted Annabelle on the back while kissing the top of her head. "Night-night, little love."

She sucked on her fingers for a moment, gazing solemnly at me. Then she pulled her fingers out of her mouth and said, "Ni-ni, Ty." Oh yes, I thought, I was going to miss them a lot.

I walked aimlessly around the property, then took the lift down to the point below. I was alone because, except for our morning walk, Aggie had pretty much abandoned me for the kids and Reuben and Alfie. She seemed to have made the transition from only dog to huge family with no problem. She would probably miss them more than I would. I sat on the rocks, which were being barely kissed by the water tonight, and gazed out over this immense sea at the striations of color on the far horizon. When the lift started to go up, I felt a finger of apprehension run down my spine. "Ohmigod . . . " was my thought, and I was flooded with relief when Patsy and Maya and Ghia leaned over and waved to me as they got in the lift.

A moment later, they were scrambling over the rocks to where I was sitting. "Tyler, Tyler," Patsy was calling. "We found something!"

26

The girls led the way: back up the cliff, across the yard, across the road, and finally down on the rocks by the bay. The shore on this side of the point was a cobblestone beach, full of rocks that ranged in size from small stones to enormous boulders. It was agonizing to walk on (unless you were younger than twenty), with rocks shifting constantly underfoot. The bank, sloping down from the road, was mostly bolstered by boulder-sized rocks. Aggie immediately headed for the bay, standing in chest-high, lapping water. Alfie was rolling on a dead-fish carcass, while Reuben was clearly waiting her turn.

"Alfie," I shouted, "knock that off!" She, of course, ignored me.

"We got to thinking," Patsy said. "What if the smugglers' cave was on the bay side instead of on the lake side? It makes sense. Loading and unloading would be easier because it's sheltered in here, more protected." It did make sense; I was impressed. I didn't remember Corky and I ever looking for the cave on the bay side. We were totally convinced that it would be on the lake side. "Well . . . " Patsy stopped by a large pile of three- to four-foot diameter rocks leaning against the bank, and dramatically pointed to them.

I saw nothing but this handful of boulders that looked as if some ancient giant had dropped them in a haphazard manner on the shore. I frowned. "Look here," Ghia insisted, clambering over the rocks and pointing to something I couldn't see.

I followed her, more gingerly, and looked in the direction she was pointing. At first, I still didn't see anything but rocks. As I looked dutifully and scrutinized more closely, I realized that behind the rocks—where there should've been a dirt bank or a rocky ledge, there was a wall of concrete. I felt a tremor of excitement.

"See?" the girls were practically jumping up and down on this jumble of boulders, and I feared broken legs or worse.

"Girls," I remonstrated. "Be careful. These rocks aren't flat ground." How did my mother let Corky and I risk our lives every day?

"But Tyler," Maya said, "you see it, don't you?"

I squatted as best I could, given the uneven ground and my own bulk, carefully examining this patch of ground. "Yes, I see it. Someone clearly cemented up something here."

"The smugglers' cave!" the three of them shouted in unison. "We found it!"

I shooed them back before I attempted to shift the rocks that were resting against this cement "door," assuming it was a door. Mostly, every rock had another rock leaning against it—making it pretty impossible to move any of them, plus the size of these rocks made them too heavy.

"We can help," the girls moved in closer again.

"No," I motioned them back once more. "I don't want anyone to get hurt." I managed to move a couple of smaller rocks, revealing part of a cement wall. It was crumbling and yellowed, appearing to have been around for a half-century or more.

"We did it!" the girls were still shouting. "We did it, didn't we, Tyler?"

"Yeah," I agreed. "I think you did." I was inspecting the whole pile of rocks, peeking through them wherever I could, to determine the width of this cemented area. You would never notice this, I thought, if you weren't specifically looking for it. As I followed the perimeters of the cement, I realized that part of it was obscured by a large ninebark bush, now covered with its usual summer flowers. It was an old bush, a bit on the scraggly side, and I figured that it was probably bigger in its youth—maybe even big enough to hide the mouth of a cave.

The girls were still dancing about, still shouting, "We found it!"

"Found what?" a male voice said, and I jumped.

Lyle Johannsen was standing at the top of the bank with his gnarled walking stick, peering down at us, Fred stalwartly by his side. "It looks like maybe the girls found the entrance to the long-lost smugglers' cave."

He harrumphed and said, "What makes you think so?"

"There's a fairly large section here, behind this tumble of rocks, that's been cemented in. What else could it be?"

"Come down and see," Ghia trilled out.

He smiled one of his rare, craggy grins, and shook his head. "No, not too surefooted on them rocks anymore. A doorway or opening?"

I shook my head. "No, it seems to be securely closed. It's just that it's cement where there should be just rocky ledge or soil. What else could it be?"

He shrugged. "Sometimes, over the years, portions of the banks along the shore have been cemented to keep them from eroding away."

"Mmm," I nodded noncommittally. "I suppose. But this seems pretty contained, not like part of a whole attempt to preserve the bank here."

He didn't respond.

"Lyle?" I asked, looking up at him. "Who owns this land? The county?" I'd never thought, before, about this strip of land between the point road and the bay. It wouldn't belong to the individual owners, being separated from each piece of property because of the road.

He shrugged again. "I never thought about it. The road is county. Probably the shore along here is county, too." He waved as he resumed his evening walk along the road with his dog.

I nodded and waved, wondering if we could convince anyone to blast this open. I persuaded the girls into going back to the house. They were all for getting tools—pickaxes, knives, hammers, whatever—and tearing this barrier apart. Sonny had Annabelle, Rose, and Lily in bed when we returned to the house.

"We found it!" all three girls sang out again at the sight of their mother.

"The smugglers' cave!" shouted Maya.

"Over there!" Ghia pointed.

"We found the smugglers' cave on the bay side!" Patsy concluded.

All three of the dogs were whirling and jumping, infected by the girls' exuberance. At the sound of the ruckus, Rose and Lily came clamoring down the stairs. Sonny laughed and looked at me. "Really?"

"It looks like it," I agreed. "All those years we looked for it, Corky and I never thought to look on the bay side."

"Tell me about it," Sonny said, and the girls gathered around her and began telling the story while I went in for a Coke.

Later, when the girls were tucked in bed but obviously listening for every word that passed between their mother and me, Sonny and I talked about it. "What now?" she asked.

"I have to find out who owns that strip of land between the road and the lake. The county or the state, I'd guess. Then . . ." I hesitated. "I don't know. See if we can get them to open it."

"Why?" Sonny asked.

I sipped my Coke, staring out at the inky lake in silence for a moment. "I don't know," I finally answered. "Maybe Lyle's right. Maybe there's nothing to open. Maybe it's just a precautionary layer of cement, protecting the bank."

"Uh-uh," three voices protested in unison from the far corner of the porch. Sonny and I, in the pale light reaching us from the lamp in the living room, smiled at each other.

I continued. "But I think the girls are right. I think it's the cave. As much as I can make out, the cemented area is very contained—maybe six or eight feet wide. And anyway, the waves are not so big in the bay, so it seems unlikely that there's been much need to protect from erosion on that side."

"But the shore—from the top of the bank to the water's edge—is narrower than when we were kids, don't you think?" Sonny asked.

"Yeah, but Sonny, the lake is higher now. You know, since they put in the locks that opened the St. Lawrence Seaway? It's affected the level of all the Great Lakes." I was informed on this subject only because I'd already made the same observation to Charley and gotten the same history lesson.

"Oh. But, still, why do you want to open the cave up? If it is that."

I was silent for a minute or two again. "I don't know. It's just a feeling I have. Or maybe a need. Somehow, I want to see inside that cave. Maybe it has nothing to do with our family, but . . . I don't know. I feel like it does."

"Mom?" Patsy called. "Can we stay until it gets opened?"

"No, Patsy, I'm sorry. Tomorrow's our last day."

"Please?" Ghia pleaded. "Just a couple more days?"

"Please?" Maya echoed.

"Girls," Sonny said softly but firmly. "I said we have to go."

"But Mom . . . "

"Enough." The subject was closed.

27

Although we talked a lot about the cave the next day, it was secondary to doing all our favorite things with one another, one more time. In the morning, all five of the girls (except for Annabelle) got up to walk with the dogs and me. Even Maya, who definitely did not like getting up in the morning. She preferred staying up half the night, reading, to mornings.

We ended up, of course, at Charley's. The girls excitedly poured out the story of the smugglers' cave to him. He listened intently, nodding gravely and appreciatively. I smiled, watching Patsy and Ghia, and even Maya a little, preen and flirt with Charley. It was like watching their mother and Magda all those years ago. Some things, I thought, never change. I could worry, I guess, that they'd get stuck with this basically demeaning behavior, or I could assume, which I did, that they were just practicing and, especially with their mother's influence, their practice would lead to an entirely different way of operating in the world.

When Nancy and Piggy came in the store, the girls quickly shifted their storytelling dramatics to them. The McDermotts also listened carefully and were persuaded to go and take a look at the "find."

Patsy said, "Charley, why don't you come, too? Don't you want to see it?"

He waved them on. "Some other time, kiddo. I gotta stay here, you know. My customers need me."

After the girls dragged Piggy and Nancy off, I turned to Charley and said, "What do you think, Charley? Could this be it?"

He shrugged, returning to a box he'd been unloading when we descended upon him. "Might be."

"How would I go about finding out, do you think? Who owns that land?"

"Never thought much about it." He stopped for a minute, scratching his chin. "I suppose the county does. Probably the first thing to find out is whether it really is a cave or not. Could be just shoring up the bank, you know. Or even a simple accident. Where a bunch of cement rolled off a truck at the wrong place."

"Mmm," I agreed. "I never thought of that. How could I find out?"

"Shouldn't be too hard. Get a heavy-duty drill and drill a hole through. If it's hollow behind the cement, it'll be apparent. If not . . ."

"That's brilliant, Charley! Do you have a drill like that?"

He was scratching his chin again. "I don't think mine'd be strong enough. We'll find someone who has something you can use."

"That's great!"

"Might be a coupla days, Tyler . . ."

"That's okay. The kids and I have today pretty well filled. See you tonight."

He agreed as I went in search of the explorers. Piggy and the older girls had been able to shift a couple more of the boulders, exposing more of the cement. "Piggy, do you have a heavy-duty drill?" I asked. "One with a bit strong enough to drill through cement?"

He shook his head. "No, but I'll ask around. See what I can find, okay? That's a good idea: find out if it's hollow behind here, huh?" I nodded, as he picked up a small rock and tapped the cement. It made a thwonk noise, something that sounded strangely familiar to me. "Sounds hollow, doesn't it?"

"Yes, yes!" the girls were dancing around dangerously on the loose rocks, even Rose and Lily were excited, though they had little idea of what this was all about.

"Girls!" I spoke a little too sharply. "Calm down. We don't want to spend your last day in the hospital with a broken leg or something."

After gathering up Sonny and Annabelle, the whole troop proceeded over to Hank and Ellie's for breakfast. Hank had fixed a breakfast that was fit for gourmets: fruit with crème fraîche, cheese-and-onion omelettes (except no cheese for Ghia, who was a strict vegetarian, and no onions for Lily, who wouldn't eat anything with onions), Canadian bacon, moose sausage, and a massive pile of blueberry muffins and sticky buns. There was not enough room for all of us to eat inside, so we ate on the deck—banishing all six of the dogs to the grass. We ate with relish and delight, while the girls regaled Hank and Ellie with the story of their discovery of the smugglers' cave.

After breakfast, we left Annabelle and the dogs with Hank and Ellie and picked up Sally and her children, and we all went to the slide at Lutsen. This was a cement track swerving down the side of a mountain, the ski resort's attempt to make money in the summer. We rode down the track on sleds with rubber wheels and hand brakes. Lily and Rose and Patsy eased up on their brakes while Maya and Ghia and Josh and Florrie whooped loudly and coaxed as much speed as possible from their sleds, racing one another down the mountainside. We grown-ups were pretty sedate, more interested in the view than in speed. Everyone got two rides—that cost us enough to buy a cabin in the woods.

We came back to Stony River, picked up our dogs, and hiked up the trail along the river, ending at Charley's cabin on Deer Yard Lake. Here Ellie and Hank joined us with Annabelle, and we had a picnic Sonny had made in the morning when we were walking. We swam some more, some of us napped and some explored, and others read. It was a splendid day. I think none of us ever wanted it to end.

When we got back to the house, the kids took over. They had planned a final weinie roast down on the rocks. They insisted that we had to wait until late to have our meal so we could sit around the campfire and sing songs in the dark afterward. All the children went down the lift to collect driftwood for the fire.

I got Annabelle ready for bed the last time. She babbled and cooed, and I felt tears welling up inside of me—knowing that this adorable, innocent baby wasn't going to live. Nor was I going to see much of her before she died. When she was in her jammies, I took her downstairs. The kids were starting to take loads of foodstuffs down to the rocky ledge at the bottom of the cliff. Charley arrived and helped Sonny get Hank's wheelchair down the lift and wedged safely on the rocks below. The girls brought a lawn chair down for Ellie, expecting the rest of us to fend for ourselves.

I sat on the swing at the edge of the cliff, rocking Annabelle and watching the activity of the girls as they scrambled up and down the cliff with all their food and utensils. Charley joined me.

"You look pretty natural sitting there with that baby, Tyler." It was already past Annabelle's bedtime, and she was placidly sucking her fingers and watching the water. I rubbed my cheek against her silky hair. "Do you ever regret not having kids?"

I smiled. "I never even gave it a moment's thought, Charley, until this horde came into my life. I guess I still don't want any kids. But I'm sure gonna miss them when they leave tomorrow."

"Mmm-hmm," he agreed. "I can see that."

"Come on!" Rose and Lily had been sent to fetch us. "It's time to eat. Come on!"

When I got up, shifting Annabelle to my hip, her plastic bottle slipped out of my hand and fell to the stone patio beneath the swing. It made a noise, and I paused. There was something this made me think of . . . thwonk. I looked down at the patio below my feet. It had been there all my life. It had always made that noise. Thwonk. Then I remembered: Piggy knocking that rock against the cement this morning. Thwonk. I looked at the patio again. Was it hollow underneath this stone patio? I let my eyes follow back from this spot, past the house, behind it, across the road to the bank where the girls found the cave entrance. Was it about even with this spot?

"Come on-n-n-n!" the littler girls entreated. Charley was looking at me strangely. "Come on!"

The weinie roast was a great success. There were turkey weinies for Sonny who didn't eat much red meat and real weinies for the rest of us, while Ghia just ate the other food. There was an unusual potato salad with wild rice that Patsy had learned to make from her grannie on the reservation. There was also a large mixed green salad—"We made this, we made this!" Lily and Rose bragged—and a fruit salad with whipped cream. Potato chips and pickles and carrot sticks rounded out the meal. And we still found additional room for s'mores.

By the time the moon started rising above the lake to a chorus of oh's and ah's, Annabelle had long since fallen asleep on Hank's lap. We sang songs—the old classics I'd grown up singing while crossing the country each summer with my mother and sister, some newer women's movement songs that Sonny and Sally and I had learned in the past twenty years, some old labor songs that Charley had learned as a kid from his union-activist family, others the kids knew from their various cultures, songs Ellie had sung with her schoolkids, and an odd mélange of songs that Hank had picked up on her travels around the world.

It was a happy and weary group that finally fell into bed that night. On my end of the porch, I could hear the girls murmuring for a moment or two before they quieted down. I lifted my head and looked out toward the swing sitting on the cliff's edge. Thwonk.

28

Sonny and I had a quick coffee on the swing before she had to shift into high gear, mobilizing six kids, two dogs, and all their belongings for the trip home.

"Sonny, if nothing else comes out of my trip here, I'll always cherish this opportunity to get to know you again."

She looked alarmed. "You sound as if we're never going to see each other again!"

"No," I shook my head. "I didn't mean to sound that way. At the end of the summer, when I head back to California, Aggie and I will stop to visit you in the Cities. And . . ." I hesitated, not wanting to say it aloud, then swallowed, and finished, ". . . and I'll be back for Annabelle's funeral." Tears sprang to both our eyes, and we squeezed hands, not needing to say anymore. "Sonny. I feel like I've gained a whole new family these past weeks. I have no intention of losing you all again."

"That's good," she replied, "because I have no intention of letting you out of our lives." We had no need to say more as we rocked the chair gently, leaning lightly against each other.

And suddenly, our moment of quiet appreciation was ripped away as Patsy called, "Mom? Annabelle's up."

Before we made it to the house, Rose was shouting, "Mom? I can't find my blue shorts. I want to wear my blue shorts today!"

And Ghia was interrogating, "Has anyone seen my box with all my rocks in it? It was right here in the dining room last night!"

"Mom? Did you pack the toothpaste already? I need to brush my teeth!" Lily wailed. Lily would hardly get out of bed in the morning before she brushed her teeth.

"Maya, get up!" Patsy insisted. "We've got to get the porch beds back where they belong. Mom! Make Maya get up!"

The silence was deafening when they were all gone, having dictated their last-minute instructions to me from the bus windows as they pulled out of the driveway. "Tyler? Call us the minute you get the cave opened up. Okay?"

Aggie and I walked down to Charley's. He placed a cup of coffee in my hand, saying nothing.

"Thanks, Charley."

He leaned over and scratched Aggie's ears vigorously. "You gonna miss that mob, too, aren't you, old Ag?"

When I was leaving, I asked Charley, "You got a crowbar I could borrow?"

His eyebrows shot up. "Crowbar?" He hesitated, then shrugged. "Sure. What're you gonna do with it?"

I felt an odd reluctance to talk. "I need to move some rocks."

SILENT WORDS

He disappeared in the back, reappearing a few moments later with a crowbar in hand. "Gonna try and pry some of that cement loose, Tyler?"

"No," I shook my head. "This is for something else." When he looked puzzled, I added, "I'll tell you all about it when I find out if I know what I'm doing."

"Okay." He looked oddly serious. "Be careful . . . "

Allen Granger came in the store just as I was leaving. He nodded politely, eyeing the crowbar in my hand.

As Aggie and I walked back to The Cedars, Nancy and Piggy stopped their car next to us. "Your gang all leave this morning?" Piggy asked.

"Yep," I agreed.

"Aww, you're gonna miss them, aren't you, Tyler?" Nancy inquired kindly. I nodded. "My stars, Tyler, what're you gonna do with that crowbar?"

"Oh," I hefted the heavy bar a little, "just some work at my place."

At home, I got gloves and went out to the swing. It wasn't easy, but I moved it off the patio by moving one side a few inches, then the other, and continuing this action alternatively until the whole swing sat on the grass. By then I was ready for a nap. I went back to the house and got a sandwich. I ate it on the porch, looking out at the swing—trying to quell the tension inside of me. That thwonk. I felt almost certain that it indicated that it was hollow under the swing. What this meant or what I expected to find, I didn't know for sure. I just knew it was significant in some way. There was never any reason that a small rock patio had been set out next to the cliff. We just took it for granted because it'd always been there. A convenient place for the big swing.

After my lunch, I scrutinized every inch of the patio. I wasn't surprised to find a small hole along one of the edges, almost obscured by grass that had been growing over it. I found an even smaller stone and slipped it in the hole and—

sure enough!—it was silent for a couple of seconds before I heard a faint ping as it landed somewhere below me.

I worked the end of the crowbar into the hole, making it bigger by forcing the bar in further, and began pumping the handle so the end banged against the rock from underneath it. At first, the rock just began breaking off in small pieces, then slightly larger chunks—until I had a hole about the size of a softball. I gaped into this hole, but all I could see was a fathomless darkness. I ran back to the house to get a flashlight; I shone this in the hole. It was clear there was a large, open space below, but I couldn't see anything through this little opening.

I began pushing and pulling more vigorously with the crowbar, to open it up more. Sweat was running down my face, neck, and back. My breath came out in uneven puffs. Suddenly, several of the rocks in the patio began to move upward together. This was it! I'd tapped the secret trapdoor, and I was lifting it up—almost in one piece. I felt shivers exploding throughout my body as a large hole in the ground came into view. I wanted to go to a phone somewhere, call Sonny and tell her to bring the girls back. They'd want to see this!

The "door" broke a little but mostly remained intact as I flopped it backward on the grass. A shallow set of steps was cut right into the rock wall of the cliff, descending into this hole. A great whoosh of cool, musty air came whirling up. I waited a moment until the cloud of murky dust settled, then instructed Aggie—who'd come over to investigate when I dropped the trapdoor—to "stay." Flashlight in hand, I began the descent into this netherworld very cautiously.

There were no handrails, and the black was almost impenetrable. The air smelled damp and moldy. I could almost taste it, it was so strong. The flashlight emitted a dim light in a tiny radius that seemed to have millions of dust motes floating in it. I almost felt as if I were underwater. One hand held the almost-useless flashlight, and I let the other one brush lightly against the walls. They were slick and somewhat fuzzy. I could hear, as I went lower, the sound of water lapping loudly—probably on the other side of the cliff, I thought, but apprehension still crept up my spine.

I kept the flashlight down as I took each step, almost afraid the steps would cease and I would step off into a void. Suddenly, in this black-black chamber, something white appeared in the spot of my flashlight. I steadied myself by touching the wall again. I looked up to the hole that now only showed me a patch of sky with wispy clouds trailing across it. I focused my attention downward again, slowly moving the flashlight around to get some kind of bearing.

I realized that I'd reached the bottom; one more step and I would be on a rocky surface, one that was littered with several white objects. I played the light around the walls until it disappeared into a dark hole. I assumed that was where this tunnel—if that was what it was—went further along. I looked up again and oriented myself: the opening down here moved away from the open lake, toward the bay. Probably, I thought, toward that cemented spot on the bank by the bay. I refocused on the white rocks on the cave floor.

I think I knew—even before I looked closer—but hadn't wanted to know. There was a skeleton sprawled at the foot of these steps. They were not white rocks but bones, in a mostly orderly fashion—one or two in a kind of disarray suggesting they'd been broken in the fall. I looked up, again, at the entrance and calculated the distance: maybe twenty feet. I was assuming a fall or a push? Probably a push. Otherwise—why all the secrecy? In my mind, I had no doubt that this was my own grandmother, Louisa.

I examined the remains, as much as I could in the dim light created by my flashlight in this underground tomb. It was a fairly small frame, surely a woman. She was lying on her back, arms and legs splayed the way they would be if one had fallen. I stepped gingerly over the bones and, again, played the light across the floor and walls and especially into the spot where there was no wall, trying to see what else—if anything—was in this tomb.

Once again, I trained the light to the floor as I moved cautiously into the cave that seemed to stretch beyond. I wanted the light on the floor, to make sure that I wouldn't step off into an abyss that I assumed mostly existed in my mind but nevertheless was terrifying me just imagining it. I thought I heard a noise above me and stopped, looking back and upward. A shadow came across the opening as something—perhaps the trap door itself?—was coming down and blocking my only escape.

"No!" I shouted, as I leaped for the stairway. "No!" In my haste and fear, I dropped the flashlight and heard the sound of breaking glass as the light extinguished, plunging me into dense darkness. "Omigod!" I scrambled up the steps on my hands and knees, using my hands to guide me upward and keep me in the middle of this steep, sideless staircase. There was only a little light coming in around the edges of the impediment at the top of the stairs.

I heard a voice shout and Aggie bark. Then I heard a muffled bang—a gunshot?—and a yelp from Aggie. "Aggie!" I shouted in vain. "Aggie?" I'd reached the top of the stairs and was pushing against the obstruction. I heard another shout and another bang. Then nothing.

"Aggie!" I was still shouting. "Let me out! Let me out!" I was pushing against this solid barrier, but nothing was moving—not even a little. It was more than the trapdoor, or something altogether different, I didn't know which, but I did know—from lifting that trapdoor up—that it would've moved from underneath if nothing was on top of it.

"Hello?" I continued shouting. "I'm in here. Please let me out!" As if—some calm part of my brain was thinking—my would-be murderer was going to take pity on me now and let me out. But I persisted. "Hello? Hello? Let me out!" Was Aggie dead? And who was it? I pushed and shouted for a ridiculously long time before I reached both physical and emotional exhaustion and, with them, enough wisdom to know that—if there was anyone up there—they had no intention of letting me out.

I huddled on the narrow steps against the very top, whimpering a little. What could I do? I certainly couldn't go down to find my flashlight. I was pretty certain, from the sound of that breaking glass, that it wasn't usable. I had no intention, anyway, of feeling around in the dark for a flashlight and coming up with Grandma Louisa's fibula instead. I almost giggled at such a thought and then worried that I was getting hysterical.

I couldn't explore the rest of the cave to search for another way out because I couldn't risk moving in this unknown space with no light. Maybe if I waited awhile, my eyes would get used to this murkiness, and I'd be able to see a little.

I'd never, in my memory, been in any place that was as blindingly black as this. Was blindness, I wondered—trying to calm myself with distraction—this black? It seemed to me that I'd read somewhere that it was more grey than black, sometimes even had streaks of color in it. There was no greyness, no color here. Only a chilling, completely black darkness.

I felt panic rising within me and attempted, futilely, to move the barrier above me again. I thought of Louisa at the bottom of these steps and knew that history was reliving itself somehow, that my skeleton was meant to join hers, that the family skeletons were meant to be entombed here forever. I comforted myself with the thought that Sonny would never accept my disappearance. She'd keep digging until she found out what had happened. Anyway, I further comforted myself, it wouldn't come to that. Someone would miss me. Hank and Ellie. Charley when I didn't show up for coffee tomorrow morning. Tomorrow morning? I suddenly started whimpering again, then shouting, when I thought of having to spend an entire night here.

On some level, I knew that shouting was useless. I stopped and took several deep, slow breaths—again trying to quell the panic. I knew I couldn't think clearly or decide what to do next unless I calmed myself.

I did something I hadn't done since my childhood. I started to sing—chant was probably more accurate—the name-places that distinguished the North Shore. This was a competition that Corky and I had done for years, trying to remember—before the other one did—every town, river, and cliff along the shore. Sometimes, when we were alone in our porch bedroom and had thoroughly terrified each other with scary stories, we calmed ourselves down by repeating this game. Later, when I had a nightmare or some other terror in my life, I would start that chant again.

Lester River.
French River.
Knife River.
Larsmont.
Two Harbors.
Silver Cliff.
Encampment Forest.

I'd continue this until I reached the last river, Pigeon River, at the Canadian border, then go back to the beginning and repeat it—adding place-names I'd forgotten.

Sucker Creek.
Agate Bay.
Stewart River.
Crow Creek.

And then I would begin once again, stumbling over the names a little: did I say this one? How about that one? It had the calming affect I needed. It lulled me. I didn't even know I was dozing until I woke with a start, having heard, or dreamt I heard, a shout.

29

"Hello?" I shouted back, almost instinctively. "Hello? Is anyone there? I'm here! This is Tyler! Hello?" I began to pound on the underside of the cave door again. "Hello?" I was fully awake now and desperate to catch someone's attention.

Faintly I heard voices, then, "Tyler? Wait a minute. We'll get you out."

I breathed a sigh of relief and leaned back into my uncomfortable perch at the top of these stairs. I could hear the sound of someone grunting and groaning and a lot of scraping noise right above me. There was a loud thud followed by some more scrabbling noises, and suddenly, the door above me was open, and pale light flooded into my would-be grave.

I sprang out of the hole with an exuberance I hardly expected my cramped body to display. Ellie and Piggy were standing by the patio, and I grabbed them, dancing with exhilaration. A shout of elation escaped my throat, only to be blunted at the sight of a crumpled Charley lying on the ground nearby, his shirt soaked with blood.

"Charley?" I knelt on the grass next to him, touching his cheek. His face was ashen-colored and contorted. I looked up at Ellie and Piggy.

"Ambulance is on its way," Ellie said.

I repeated, "Charley?"

He opened his eyes with obvious effort. "Tyler." He was whispering, and tears sprang to my eyes. I was reminded of my mother's last moments of life. "Tyler," he repeated. "I'm sorry. It's all my fault. I should have just told you . . ." I looked at Piggy and Ellie again, but they shook their heads.

"Charley, who did this?"

He gasped a little, then said, "Lyle. But it was me that killed Jerome." My eyes widened. "It was an accident . . . Everything was an accident."

The sound of a siren bellowed as the ambulance pulled into the driveway. I held Charley's hand tightly. "It's okay, Charley. You're going to be okay. Just hang in there." He shook his head slightly, grimacing.

When the ambulance attendants moved in, I wheeled around to Ellie and said, "Aggie?"

"Hank's taken her to the vet." My eyes widened again. "We think one of her legs was nicked by a bullet, Tyler. She crawled through the woods to us, exhausted and bleeding. I wrapped her leg up and got her in the van with Hank, then called Piggy and the cops to meet me here." On cue, the sheriff's car pulled into the drive next to the ambulance.

They were carrying Charley away, but his hand reached toward me. "Charley?" I was surprised, as I reached to take his hand, to see that my own hands were raw and bleeding.

"You'd better come along, too, miss, and get those hands treated," one of the attendants said.

"I'll drive her in," the sheriff announced.

"Tyler?" Charley whispered. "I'm sorry."

I felt the weight of sorrow and years of pain and secrecy descend upon me. I looked around me in pain and confusion. The sky was still blue, dotted with lazy white clouds, and the lake pounded away at the rocks, exploding in a welter of water and foam. The swing was on its side; apparently Lyle had just tipped it over to secure my tomb. I stared down the hole I'd just exited.

Ellie put her arm around my shoulders. "Tyler?" she said in a soft voice.

"I guess you found the smugglers' cave, mmm?" Piggy asked.

I nodded and added, "I found my Grandmother Louisa, too." Then I fell to my knees, shaking and sobbing.

30

It was a week before everything was sorted out. Charley was still in intensive care but doing well. The bullet with which Lyle Johannsen had intended to kill him had barely missed his heart, and he'd lost a lot of blood. The doctors were confident he'd recover fully. Fully enough to go to jail, I thought. Probably for manslaughter. Lyle was already in jail. He was charged with attempted murder on two counts—for me and for Charley. Aggie didn't count as an attempted murder, except with me.

I'd managed to track Mary Sharon down at her mother's place in Rocky Ridge, Minnesota, where she and her sweetie, Celia, were visiting. I think I was nearly hysterical when I called, so it didn't take much to convince her that I needed her. Mary Sharon's flamboyant fashion style often led people to believe, erroneously, that she was kind of flaky. The opposite was the truth: she was "Minnesota" through and through, which meant—in my experience—that she was strong, stable, and competent. I felt a wave of relief wash through me the minute she told me that she and Celia were on their way.

It was evening, and we were on the porch: Mary Sharon and Celia, Sally and Ellie and Hank, and me. Just that day we had Louisa's bones transferred to the family plot—next to her sister, Alma. I almost wished Mom were here with them, the three of them together. I guess, if there's life after life, they're together somewhere now. Aggie was lying on the floor next to my chair, obsessively licking her naked leg with the stitches in it.

The fog was hanging low over the lake and now creeping up over the edge of the cliff, moving toward the house. "Come on," Mary Sharon insisted, "time to go inside and have a fire."

"And some hot chocolate," Celia added. "You take care of the fire, Mary Sharon. I'll take care of the chocolate."

"Can I help?" Ellie asked Celia.

"No, you relax. I'll be just a minute."

Mary Sharon looked almost ridiculous, in this north-woods setting, in her raspberry-colored, floor-length culottes topped by a tunic resembling a Jackson Pollock painting with splashes of raspberry and blueberry and watermelon and plum and cantaloupe—all a little more vivid than in real life. Still, she clearly knew her way around a fireplace.

I wrapped myself in a blanket, feeling relatively safe and happy to be amongst friends. I hadn't felt quite warm since my sojourn in the cave. Celia, a quiet contrast to Mary Sharon's flamboyance, in jeans and sweatshirt, returned with hot chocolate and an array of sweets the neighbors had dropped off—treating Louisa's burial as an ordinary funeral rather than the bizzare ending of a tale that stretched over a seventy-year period. We all groaned, having partaken of a huge meal, also provided by neighbors, but managed to reach for one more sweet anyway.

"Mmm," Hank said, after sipping the hot chocolate. "What's in here? It's delicious."

"Raspberry syrup," Mary Sharon smiled fondly at Celia. I watched the two of them, feeling a little pang of jealousy that I was on the "outside" of this relationship. Mary Sharon and I had the kind of close friendship that qualified us as a "couple," without the complications of romance. But their romance altered our closeness. Mary Sharon insisted it didn't, but of course it did. Mostly I felt a great well of affection for both of them and happiness for Mary Sharon's obvious contentment, mixed with a little sadness. "She always puts raspberry in her hot chocolate. It's scrumptious, isn't it?"

We all agreed. Mary Sharon poked a little at the sparking kindling, then added a couple of small logs. "So, Tyler, give us the details slowly now. I'm still not sure I get all of this."

I'd poured out some of the story in a rush to her over the phone when I'd first gotten hold of her. The two of them had arrived yesterday, and I'd given them more parts of the story—a piece here, a piece there—since then. I took a deep breath and hesitated for a moment, contemplating the fire and feeling—once more—my own losses. No one hurried me.

"Okay," I eventually said. "You all know that my mother, as she lay dying, told me to come home to 'shake the skeletons in the closet.' At first, I had no idea what she meant. I'm reasonably certain she *didn't* mean there was going to be, literally, a skeleton. I was surprised to find out that she still owned what I thought was my grandparents' home in Stony River. I was even more surprised to find out that she owned it herself, not with her sister, Thalia. So, I came home to Minnesota to look for something—I didn't know what that something was, but something.

"I talked to a lot of people and got a lot of pieces of the puzzle, but some pieces were always missing. I think, now, I have them all. One thing is that my Grandmother Louisa was probably a lesbian."

"Yes!" Mary Sharon chimed in enthusiastically. Sally and Hank and Ellie smiled politely.

"I guess I'll never know for sure, but her best friend, Vera Johannsen, clearly thinks she was. And that's good enough for me. What it meant, however, was that she had no intention of getting married. Which made her an oddball. It seems that people were very aware of her, watching her, paying attention to her. She didn't want to get married and settle down and do what a 'good girl' was supposed to do. She wanted to go to college.

"Instead, she got raped by a local man—my grandfather, Holger. She got pregnant, and eventually that became obvious. Holger was a widower with a small daughter, Thalia, and he wanted to marry Louisa. She refused. Everyone assumed she'd just gotten a little wild and ended up in trouble, but she had no intention of marrying a man who'd forced her, and she didn't want to get married, anyway. This was 1926, and no one talked about rape. At all. She figured there was no point in telling anyone, because people wouldn't believe her anyway. Except her best friend, Vera, whom she did tell.

"Her refusal to get married and 'do the right thing' just increased people's view of her as an oddball, an eccentric, maybe even a little crazy. So when the baby was born and Holger told everyone she'd gotten completely hysterical, had—in fact—had a nervous breakdown, people believed him. Even Louisa's own parents, apparently. He told them that he took her to the state hospital in Fergus Falls. No one really questioned this story.

"Except Vera. Though Vera did believe that Louisa had been incarcerated. It wasn't that uncommon for young women who were viewed as promiscuous or out of control to be put away in mental institutions."

"It wasn't?" Ellie asked.

I shook my head, pursing my lips in anger. "I wish I could say I'm exaggerating, but really, Ellie, this was a common occurrence. I don't guess we'll ever know how much it happened."

"That's awful!" Ellie protested. We all nodded in agreement.

Hank said, "We knew a girl like that. Got sent away to one of them places. Remember, Ellie? Dallas Farley."

"Oh yeah, but Dallas Farley? She really was pretty wild, you know. They say . . . Oh, my goodness!" Her hand flew in front of her mouth as she stared at us with troubled eyes. "I just bought it, didn't I?"

"Probably," I agreed. "Anyway, everyone believed that Wild Louisa Jane Anderson had 'snapped' and had to be put away 'for her own good.' The thing about her friend, Vera, is that Vera didn't believe—for a minute—that Louisa had actually gone crazy. She truly believed that Holger just had her shut up to keep her from telling everyone he'd forced her." I paused for a minute. "She believed that and yet—she never made any attempt to rescue Louisa." No one said anything. What could we say? "To be fair, I guess she believed she had no power to do that. Still . . ." I didn't talk for a couple of minutes, just stared at the flames. I'd gone to see Vera after I had most of the truth, but she'd refused to see me. I can't imagine what it's like to be the mother of a son who attempted to murder two people, but I guess she felt seeing me was just too much.

"What really happened was somewhat different. A group of local men—Charley's grandfather, Joey Johannsen, my grandfather, Ole the postmaster, my great grandfather who owned The Cedars in those days, and some others—had been engaged from the early days of Prohibition in rum running. There was a cave and tunnel that came in under the point, running from the bay nearly to the cliffs on the lake side at The Cedars. It was the perfect setup for their operations.

"Late at night, boats would come into the bay with contraband from Canada. The boys would unload it and store it deep in this cave. Eventually they cut steps coming up the inside of the cliff to the top of the cliffs. This enabled them to store the bottles of booze the night they were delivered and then go back another night through the trap door out by the cliffs to retrieve them. This way all the activity was not centered on the more public access at the cave mouth on the bay. The opening they created on the cliff top and the trapdoor were not visible from the road and gave them a great deal more privacy."

"How'd you find this all out?" Mary Sharon extricated herself from the arms of her lover to dump more logs on the fire.

"When Charley was well enough to talk, he spilled the beans. His grandfather, shortly before he died, told him the whole story. Lyle is still not talking, but Charley's testimony will probably hold up in court—seeing as how he's incriminating himself to tell this story."

"So Louisa? . . . " Hank asked.

"Most everyone in the area knew some rum running activity was going on. The locals all pretty much knew who was doing it. But the feds just didn't have the 'man-power' to police these rural areas. So, this group of fellas made a good deal of money doing this for a couple of years. And no one really knew the details of how they were doing it. Nor did they want to know.

"Apparently Louisa was up late with Weezie, my mother, one night. Some of this is guesswork. Maybe she was rocking her on the porch with no lights on. She must have seen some activity near the cliff. So, obviously she put the baby down—otherwise I guess the baby, too, would have ended up on the floor of that cave, and I wouldn't be here today—and went out to actually catch the boys in their deed.

"That probably would've been all right. Their activities weren't exactly secret. But Louisa demanded something from them. It was just Joey Johannsen that night and Old Man Chummy. Louisa wanted to get away from Stony River. She wanted to go to Duluth and go to college. She needed money, so she told them—now that she knew the where and the how—that she'd call in the feds unless they gave her enough money to do what she wanted."

I paused at this moment, thinking of Charley telling me this part with tears rolling down his cheeks. "I should've told you, Tyler," he insisted. "I should've told you. Then every-thing else wouldn't have happened. But Tyler—can you understand, can you ever understand?—people adored my grandfather. He was respected and revered. And for me? For me, he was the only 'father' I had. He'd always been there for me, taught me how to be a man. I couldn't stand for his mem-ory to be sullied, his name to lose honor for an accident. An accident!"

"But Charley," I argued, "this 'accident' took my grand-mother's life. Her life! And what? *Her* memory, *her* name didn't count? Just your grandfather's did? It's this kind of arro-gance that ruins women's lives. It took her reputation. It made people believe lies about her. These kinds of incidents create the mythology that makes people believe lies about *all* women. But mostly, it deprived Louisa's parents and sister and friends of a loving memory. It deprived her child of her own mother. How can you talk to me about your grandfather's name and memory?"

"It was so long ago, Tyler. I just wanted it to . . . die down. Who cared, after all these years? No one, hardly, even remem-bered Louisa. Why did it matter?"

"Well, Charley," I said coldly, feeling immense anger, "it mattered enough to you and Lyle to make sure that Jerome didn't tell me the truth. It mattered enough that Lyle tried to kill both of us. The only thing that *didn't* matter here was that Louisa died. Died, Charley! And my family was riddled with debilitating secrets that have reached down through the generations. I'm sorry, but your family honor just doesn't stand a candle next to my grandmother's right to live!"

He closed his eyes, his face was the color of dirty dishwater. "You're right, Tyler. None of it was worth this. I'm sorry."

There was no more to be said. In a way, I did sort of understand his desire to protect his beloved grandfather. I knew that Charley was, really, a decent man, but that decency had been sacrificed when he decided to keep his grandfather's memory clear, at all costs.

"Tyler? Earth to Tyler," Mary Sharon was bringing me back to the present time. "You left us hanging with Louisa demanding money to get away."

I sighed. "So, according to Charley, who heard this story from his grandfather, Joey and Old Man Chummy blew up at Louisa's attempt to blackmail them. They believed that their criminal activities were justified by the 'stupidity' of Prohibition, but they were incensed that Louisa thought she had the right to use their activities to finance her own dream. They were shouting—albeit somewhat quietly, it was the middle of the night, after all—when Old Man Chummy suddenly slapped Louisa across the face. She reeled backward from the force of the blow, lost her balance, and fell down the stairs to her death."

31

"Is that it then?" Ellie began picking up the dirty dishes and taking them out to the kitchen. She waved Celia away when she got up to help. Mary Sharon stirred the fire and added some logs. "Did anyone ever know—besides Chummy and the Johannsen fellow?"

"Oh yeah, they all knew. They had to—because the operations ended. That night."

"Why?" Mary Sharon interrupted. "I mean, they could've just gotten rid of the body somewhere and continued on, couldn't they have?"

"I got the impression, from Charley, that Louisa's death sort of traumatized them. They were, after all, just ordinary men who'd gotten involved in an illegal activity much like boys get into scrapes—almost accidentally. But the death shook them all up. I guess there was never any question but that they'd quit."

"But if this Chummy and Johannsen were the only ones there that night, how did everyone find out?" Celia asked.

"They just left that night, after making sure that Louisa was actually dead. There were still some bottles of whiskey down in the cave when they abandoned their activities. The sheriff found them when he checked it out. I suppose they're worth a lot of money now."

"It's yours, right, Tyler? It's your land," Sally inquired.

I shrugged and nodded. "Yeah, they're mine. Anyway, Old Man Chummy and Joey got all the guys together in the wee hours of the morning and told them what happened. They brainstormed and came up with this story about Louisa that Holger then put about to everyone—that she'd come to him in the middle of the night, acting completely out of her mind. He said he was scared of the way she was acting—that she might hurt herself or the baby—and he didn't want to involve anyone locally, so he drove her to Duluth to get some medical help. And then they—supposedly the doctors in Duluth—had her committed to the facility at Fergus Falls."

"And everyone just believed this story?" Ellie asked, a tinge of anger in her voice.

"Yeah. Her behavior was unconventional enough for most folks to think she did have a loose screw or something. And, then, of course, she just disappeared, so . . . it was easy to have a story that explained it all."

"What about the cave?" Hank asked.

"Under the cover of darkness, in the next few days, they cemented up the bay-side opening and piled rocks carefully in front of this concrete wall as well as behind and around the big bush that was already there—to hide it. The patio was created to cover the cliff entrance and a mammoth swing built and placed on top of that patio. The men swore one another to secrecy."

"Did your mother know all this?"

"I don't know, for sure, what she knew. Probably not much. Grandma, that is Alma, must have told her some of it— or left her a note or something—when she died. But I'm pretty certain Alma never knew most of it. Apparently, Holger started drinking a lot, the older he got. When drunk, he would ramble about all that had happened. Years before, Vera had warned Alma about Holger, but she had chosen not to believe Vera. So, Alma went back to Vera and got as much of the story from her as she could. This time, Alma believed her.

"I think she intended to start searching for Louisa, but she got so sick, she had to abandon the project. She did change her will, though. She and Holger lived in the house that Alma's parents had built back in the early part of the century. I can only guess at this, but apparently she didn't want it to go to anyone but her own true blood. Because she'd inherited from her parents, she owned it herself. So, she left it to my mother entirely and instructed Holger to leave everything else to Thalia.

"My guess is that Alma did tell my mom that she wasn't her biological mother; that it appeared that Holger had raped Louisa and then had her unfairly incarcerated; that she didn't know where Louisa might be, but it probably was in Minnesota. Maybe she didn't tell my mother even that much. I don't know. All I know, for sure, is that Mother knew there were secrets here that needed to be uncovered. And, for whatever reason, she didn't look for the truth herself. Maybe she was paralyzed by whatever information Alma had given her; Holger was, after all, her father. Whatever truth finding was to be done, she left for me to do."

"And you did," Hank said firmly.

I nodded, feeling a wave of sadness wash through me. "Yes, but at quite a cost." We were all silent for a few moments, staring at the flickering flames in the fireplace.

Celia finally broke the silence. "So, but . . . what was Jerome's part in all this?"

I sighed, feeling the sadness grow. "I asked Jerome endless questions, trying to piece the parts together. He knew about my grandmother—many of the second-generation men knew and carried the secret as well as the first generation had—but he decided that the silence should be broken, that I should be told the truth. So, he came to The Cedars to tell me. Only Charley and Lyle also came and were arguing with him, trying to dissuade Jerome, insisting that it was 'ancient history' and ought to be let alone."

"Why? Why didn't they all just let the truth finally come out?"

I sighed again. "In Charley's case, it was some warped notion of family honor. He hated the thought that anyone would ever know that his grandfather had killed someone. Even accidentally. And Lyle. Lyle was convinced that his brother would never be president of the United States if this story ever came out. So the two of them were trying to persuade Jerome not to tell me the truth. And Jerome was trying to make them see that the whole thing would never be over until the truth was told." I lapsed into a depressed silence.

Mary Sharon finally prodded me. "And?"

I looked at her with pain in my eyes, then shook myself a little. "In a way, history repeated itself. Jerome pushed past the two men to come tell me. I was sitting down by the water, eating my lunch, totally oblivious. Charley grabbed Jerome's arm and yanked him backward. Jerome stumbled on a root and fell and hit his head against a rock. It killed him."

I pulled the blanket tighter around my shoulders, staring into the fire. I thought about Charley, about how good he was to me, how kind and decent he was. And how, because of his misplaced family loyalty, Jerome was dead. Forever. Ineradicably. And Gertie was alone earlier than she needed to be.

Charley's goodness couldn't, didn't, make up for this moment of transgression.

"And Jerome's body in the lift?"

"Lyle's idea. He was convinced I had to be warned off. That I wasn't going to quit digging unless I was scared. Of course, it didn't work. When I borrowed the crowbar from Charley, he figured out what I must be doing with it. Lyle was already on edge, having found that the kids had discovered the bay-side opening to the cave, so he was sort of pacing the road when Charley came along with the idea that he could somehow talk me out of telling anyone what it was I was about to find. Lyle had different ideas, had already loaded his gun and was carrying it. When he closed the trapdoor on me and pushed the swing over, Charley says he realized it had gone too far. Aggie was agitated," I reached down and smoothed the hairs on Aggie's head. "She started growling, and Lyle shot her. She took off for the woods, and Charley tried to stop Lyle. Lyle turned the gun on Charley and shot him. Then, I guess he panicked and just took off, leaving Charley and me to die."

After a couple more minutes of silence, Sally asked, "Now what about Allen Granger, Tyler? You mentioned earlier this summer that you were a little suspicious of him."

I shrugged. "I was a *little* suspicious of everyone, Sally." Hank chuckled, and I shrugged. "I guess his grandfather was probably one of the smugglers, but it seems he didn't really know anything. I talked to him, once—he's very standoffish, you know—after . . ." I hesitated, ". . . after it was all done. He said he knew, from his father, that something 'bad' had happened up here and that's why his grandfather had moved the family to the Cities. But he never knew, and he didn't think his father knew either, any of the details."

Again, we were all silent for a few minutes. When Mary Sharon got up, once again, to stir the fire, Hank said, "What a story." I nodded, feeling exhaustion and sorrow and anger all whirling around together inside of me.

32

It was time for me to go back to San Francisco. I walked the point road each morning with Aggie, avoiding Chummy's—all closed up, a tragic reminder of good intentions gone awry. I couldn't imagine selling The Cedars, but—at least right now—I couldn't imagine staying there. It was haunted, the whole point was haunted for me. I thought of my Grandmother Louisa—so alive, so determined, so independent. All of that cut off and closed in a cold, damp crypt. The lies that grew up around her death had reached down through the years to affect others who didn't even know the details, finally resulting in more death, more tragedy.

I knew some of the locals felt it was my fault, for coming back and stirring up all those old ghosts. Sort of a "shoulda-let-them-dead-dogs-lie" attitude. Some days, I felt that it was my fault, too. Then Mary Sharon would do the good work of a loving friend and remind me that it all happened independently of me, that seeking the truth was never wrong or a crime, that good people could also be bad people, and that I may have been the catalyst, but it was not my fault, not my responsibility.

I knew she was right. It was still hard. I started going oftener to the AA meetings in one of the church basements in Grand Marais. I wanted a drink so badly that I got the shakes some days. I dreamt about drunken revels, blessed surcease of all feeling. Even after Mom died, I hadn't been this bad off. It scared me.

One evening, as Celia and Mary Sharon and I sat on the porch, watching the reflected sunset, Celia said, "Tyler, Mary Sharon and I have a proposal for you."

I turned my attention away from the horizon to look at the two of them. "A proposal?"

Celia nodded. "It seems obvious that you love this place and also that you can't possibly stay here. At least not now. Well, we wondered if you'd lease it to us, to Mary Sharon and me, and we'd run it as a B & B."

I looked from Celia to Mary Sharon and back to Celia. "You're serious?" They both nodded. "You'd move to Minnesota?"

"Naw," Mary Sharon said. "We thought we'd run it from San Francisco."

"Okay," I agreed, "dumb question."

Mary Sharon continued, "Tyler, you know my heart is in Minnesota, that I never really thought I could live in California forever."

"But you took the Bar there."

She shrugged, glancing at Celia. "I didn't want to leave Celia. But now that she's seen Minnesota, she wants to live here, too."

Celia smiled, dimples indenting her cheeks. "Tyler, I love the North Shore. And I love The Cedars. I've dreamed, for a long time, about running a B & B. I like to cook, and I like people. It would be a great antidote to the work I've done the past years." Celia was a social worker, dealing with some of the worst family situations.

"And you, Mary Sharon?"

"I could hang out a shingle in Grand Marais. Do some kind of family law: wills, and estates, whatever."

"You'd have to take the Bar again, wouldn't you?"

"Yeah, that's a pisser. But I think it'd be worth it. What do you think, Tyler?"

I looked back out at the fading colors on the horizon. I'd spent the last few days trying to decide what to do: sell The Cedars, rent it out, leave it empty and come back next summer, what? I hadn't made any decisions but recognized that the heavy rock I felt in my stomach every time I thought of selling probably meant I shouldn't.

"Well," I drew the word out, turning these new thoughts over in my head, gazing out at the rippling lake. "It sounds good." We smiled at one another.

We spent the next days working out the details to everyone's satisfaction. It seemed, to me, a brilliant solution. We agreed that they'd close The Cedars down each July so that Sonny and the kids and I could spend the month here. Both said they'd be glad to have a month off to go visit family and friends elsewhere. And I could have a room whenever I wanted and for as long as I wanted.

They intended to use the main bedroom on the first floor for themselves and the other bedroom as an office. The three upstairs bedrooms would be rented out to hikers, fishers, bikers, canoeists, North Shore diehards in the summer, downhill and cross country skiers in the winter, and all the others in between.

They were painting the outside of The Cedars when I left at the end of August. I stopped in the Cities to spend a couple of days with Sonny and the girls. Although I'd called and given them the bare facts, I now had to fill in all the details.

Then Aggie and I headed west. I realized it was time for me to write about my mother's death. I turned on the tape recorder I kept handy for just such moments and spoke. "Few deaths have the impact that losing a parent does."

"Amazing Grace . . ."

"Home, home on the range . . ."

"In the morning, in the evening, ain't we got fun?"

Other Titles Available From Spinsters Ink

All the Muscle You Need, Diana McRae	$8.95
Amazon Story Bones, Ellen Frye	$10.95
As You Desire, Madeline Moore	$9.95
Being Someone, Ann MacLeod	$9.95
Cancer in Two Voices, 2nd Ed., Butler & Rosenblum	$12.95
Child of Her People, Anne Cameron	$10.95
Common Murder, Val McDermid	$9.95
Considering Parenthood, Cheri Pies	$12.95
Desert Years, Cynthia Rich	$7.95
Elise, Claire Kensington	$7.95
Fat Girl Dances with Rocks, Susan Stinson	$10.95
Final Rest, Mary Morell	$9.95
Final Session, Mary Morell	$9.95
Give Me Your Good Ear, 2nd Ed., Maureen Brady	$9.95
Goodness, Martha Roth	$10.95
The Hangdog Hustle, Elizabeth Pincus	$9.95
High and Outside, Linnea A. Due	$8.95
The Journey, Anne Cameron	$9.95
The Lesbian Erotic Dance, JoAnn Loulan	$12.95
Lesbian Passion, JoAnn Loulan	$12.95
Lesbian Sex, JoAnn Loulan	$12.95
Lesbians at Midlife, ed. by Sang, Warshow & Smith	$12.95
The Lessons, Melanie McAllester	$9.95
Life Savings, Linnea Due	$10.95
Look Me in the Eye, 2nd Ed., Macdonald & Rich	$8.95
Love and Memory, Amy Oleson	$9.95
Martha Moody, Susan Stinson	$10.95
Modern Daughters and the Outlaw West, Melissa Kwasny	$9.95
Mother Journeys: Feminists Write About Mothering, Sheldon, Reddy, Roth	$15.95
No Matter What, Mary Saracino	$9.95
Ransacking the Closet, Yvonne Zipter	$9.95
Roberts' Rules of Lesbian Living, Shelly Roberts	$5.95
Silent Words, Joan M. Drury	$10.95
The Other Side of Silence, Joan M. Drury	$9.95
The Solitary Twist, Elizabeth Pincus	$9.95
The Well-Heeled Murders, Cherry Hartman	$10.95
Thirteen Steps, Bonita L. Swan	$8.95
Trees Call for What They Need, Melissa Kwasny	$9.95
The Two-Bit Tango, Elizabeth Pincus	$9.95
Vital Ties, Karen Kringle	$10.95
Why Can't Sharon Kowalski Come Home? Thompson & Andrzejewski	$10.95

Spinsters titles are available at your local booksellers or by mail order through Spinsters Ink. A free catalog is available upon request. Please include $2.00 for the first title ordered and 50¢ for every title thereafter. Visa and Mastercard accepted.

Spinsters Ink
32 E. First St., #330
Duluth, MN 55802-2002

218-727-3222 (phone)   (fax) 218-727-3119

Spinsters Ink was founded in 1978 to produce vital books for diverse women's communities. In 1986 we merged with Aunt Lute Books to become Spinsters/Aunt Lute. In 1990, the Aunt Lute Foundation became an independent nonprofit publishing program. In 1992, Spinsters moved to Minnesota.

Spinsters Ink publishes novels and nonfiction that deal with significant issues in women's lives from a feminist perspective: books that not only name these crucial issues, but—more important—encourage change and growth. We are committed to publishing works by women writing from the periphery: fat women, Jewish women, lesbians, old women, poor women, rural women, women examining classism, women of color, women with disabilities, women who are writing books that help make the best in our lives more possible.

Joan M. Drury

For part of the year, I live in a house on a sand spit that protrudes some six miles into Lake Superior—creating the harbor in Duluth, Minnesota that is the fourth largest international port in the United States. My house is nestled in a grove of mature red and jack pines, maples, fruit trees, and mountain ash on the edge of undulating sand dunes that stretch the entire length of this island. Although right in the city, it feels like it is in the north woods on the edge of an ocean.

I cross the aerial lift bridge connecting this plot of land to the mainland of Duluth and go to work every day at the Building for Women—a building owned by and populated by women's organizations. My offices, also, overlook this most astonishing of lakes and the shipping traffic—an incredible view of which I never tire. These enormous ships, some of them bound to the Great Lakes while some are oceangoing (called salties), are sometimes a city block or two long and never fail to delight me.

I oversee the operations of Spinsters Ink, a feminist publishing company, and Harmony Women's Fund, a private foundation that funds women's activities resulting in feminist social change in the state of Minnesota. I'm also involved in many other feminist endeavors. I can only do what I do and as much as I do because I work with a group of women who are exceptionally talented and capable, dedicated and supportive.

The rest of the year I live on seven quiet acres in the deep north woods in Lutsen, Minnesota, some ninety miles northeast of Duluth. This is a small town, mostly rural, on the edge of a million acres of wilderness on one side and the largest fresh-water sea in the world, Lake Superior, on the other. The sand dunes of my city home are replaced by wild, rugged, rocky shores. I share this location with gulls, eagles, bears, wolves, deer, chipmunks, and many other wildlife creatures. The almost-claustrophobic closeness of the tight forest gives way abruptly to the limitless horizon of endless and ever-changing water—creating, for me, a metaphoric and exhilarating clash of cultures.

Next door to me is Norcroft: A Writing Retreat for Women —a special project of Harmony Women's Fund—where four women, at a time, come to its ten acres to write. This gives me a kind of built-in community along with the good-hearted people who live in this area and who have been welcoming me back all my life. My dear and beloved friends, my daughter and two sons, my daughter-by-marriage, and my grand-daughter all come to visit me and share my glorious existence.

Here, in the serenity of semi-isolation and unutterable beauty, I write—and read, talk, think, solve problems, dream, breathe.